AT THE
SIGN OF
THE
NAKED
WAITER

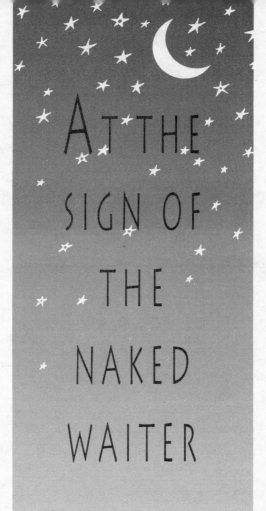

AT THE SIGN OF THE NAKED WAITER

A NOVEL BY

AMY HERRICK

HarperCollins*Publishers*

Some of the chapters in this novel first appeared as short stories in other publications, as follows: "Pinocchio's Nose" in *The Kenyon Review*; "House on Fire," in a different form and under another title, in *Schlaflos*; "In the Air, Over Our Heads," in somewhat different form, in *Triquarterly*; "At the Back of the World," in somewhat different form, in *Indiana Review*.

HarperCollins books may be purchased for educational, business, or sales promotional use. For information, please call or write: Special Markets Department, HarperCollins Publishers, Inc., 10 East 53rd Street, New York, NY 10022. Telephone: (212) 207-7528; Fax: (212) 207-7222.

FIRST EDITION

Designed by Cassandra J. Pappas

Library of Congress Cataloging-in-Publication Data

Herrick, Amy.
  At the sign of the naked waiter : a novel / Amy Herrick.—1st ed.
    p.   cm.
  ISBN 0-06-016534-0
  I. Title.
PS3558.E746A96   1992
813′.54—dc20   91-50448

92 93 94 95 96 MAC 10 9 8 7 6 5 4 3 2 1

For my parents,
Audrey and Harlan,
and for Sam

AT THE
SIGN OF
THE
NAKED
WAITER

1

PINOCCHIO'S NOSE

SARAH WAS SITTING on her bed watching the moon sail high above the treetops, when a cloud, blowing suddenly out of the sky, crossed its path and threw the night into blackness.

She was approaching thirteen and had been leaning on the windowsill in the oddest state of dumbness, feeling at once emptied and lit up, waiting maybe for some big thing. But when the moon went out, it was not at all what she was expecting. It's the end of the world, she thought, and shut her eyes tight and held her breath.

When she opened them, she saw that a little light had been switched on in the apartment on the top floor of the house across the way. She was surprised to see this light, for the apartment had been sitting vacant for some months now, and she had thought they didn't mean to rent it anymore. She crouched down and peered out from behind her curtains.

In a moment, a young man appeared and leaned way out of the curtainless window. Craning his neck, he searched the sky, then frowned and stepped back into the room and began to undress. He took his clothes off hurriedly, dropping them on the floor, and Sarah, who was not much used to judging and comparing the bodies of men, held her breath and watched with terrific concentration. This man was not really quite a man, but a boy, a few years older than her brother. He was of exquisite build, but rather on the small side, and when he took off his shirt he had what looked exactly like the beginnings of wings on his shoulder blades, little feathered nubs. This, she knew, ought to be the most distracting marvel, but she found that, after all, when he took off his shoes and then his pants and underpants, it was the male parts that got her. Her brother had grown modest in the last few years, and she realized that it had been some time since she had viewed these things. She stared furiously. How did you reconcile their foolish, dangling appearance with the tales you heard of pursuit and wild surrender, shameless pleasure and complete disaster? As soon as he had finished undressing, the young man strode from the room and disappeared.

The moon, silver and careless, a little fingernail of a boat, slipped out from behind its cloud and sailed away across the night, while, from her brother's room next door, there came several loud bangs, followed by a series of mysterious popping sounds, and then silence.

In the morning she found that spring had arrived overnight. The dogwood tree was in full bloom and held its earnest white blossoms up to the sky like little plates. As she walked to school squirrels raced up and down fences and birds shot through the air carrying twigs and string and bits of old mattress ticking. Insects fizzed and buzzed through the yellow veils of forsythia, and the air, as it warmed up unevenly, was gold in some places and in other places blue, and, in all places, smelled complicated and delicious. She did not notice the three little boys hiding behind the privet hedge at the corner. They jumped out at her, yelling and howling, and in her confusion she imagined that the ground had opened up and spit them out. She recognized them, though. They were little neighborhood boys, three or four years younger than herself, who had never paid the slightest attention to her before. They threw themselves upon her, yipping gleefully and pulled fiercely at her blouse, her skirt, her hair.

"Let go of me, you little creeps! Stop it!"

This only seemed to make them noisier and hungrier. She told herself not to panic, but they were pinching her in a peculiarly knowing way, then one grabbed her breast and squeezed it hard between sticky little fingers and another grabbed meanly at the inside of her thigh.

"Goose her! Goose her!" screamed the one who seemed to be the leader. He tipped his face towards her and grinned. She grabbed for one of his pointed ears, which stuck out malevolently, but it slipped through her fingers. Hands tugged excitedly at the buttons of her blouse, and hands scrabbled up her skirt and started determinedly to pull down her underpants. She screamed breathlessly and tried to run, but they clung to her like jellyfish, laughing horribly.

"Let go of me, you little creeps! Let go!" At this moment a girl she'd never seen before appeared down at the end of the block. This girl stood there staring for a few moments, then dropped her books and ran towards them yelling, "Hey!" She grabbed the nearest boy around the waist and pulled him off Sarah. She slapped his face once, hard, and let go of him. He scuttled back off into the privet hedge. Then she grabbed hold of the one with pointed ears and wrestled him to the ground.

Having only one to deal with now herself, Sarah was able to give him a good kick in the shins, and he went hobbling off to join the first. When Sarah turned around she saw the girl standing over the leader, waving a little pearl-handled pocketknife at him. He lay on the ground watching her in silent terror. "Just a little bit of nose for my nose collection," she said, bending towards him.

He put his hands over his nose and screamed, "No!" She laughed and gave him a little kick and said in a raspy voice, "Get outta here." He was gone in a second.

The girl snapped the blade of her knife shut and stood examining it fondly. Sarah stared at the girl. She appeared to be about her own age, and she was tall—almost as tall as Sarah. She had a wide and diabolical-looking mouth, and she wore ballet slippers and blue jeans. Her long, dark hair was loose. She had a mole on her left cheek, which looked distinctly fake. Sarah thought she looked stunning and highly untrustworthy. She felt the combined forces of gravity and fate pulling her helplessly towards some central mystery which she wanted nothing to do with.

"Thank you," Sarah said stiffly, as she pulled her skirt down and buttoned her blouse. "Do you always carry a knife?" she asked in a disapproving tone.

"Certainly," the girl said. "It was a gift from my French tutor." Sarah, examining the girl sharply, saw that she was lying and felt her own face turn red with embarrassment, as if it were she that had been caught out. The girl, however, looked back at her without flinching. She seemed to be trying to make up her mind about something.

"My French tutor is quite mad for me," she said. "I believe he may be my true soul mate. But I'm not sure." She paused. "Now the question is, is recognizing your soul mate something that happens only after terrible torment and ordeals, or do you recognize him instantly, the moment you see him?"

Sarah, who often pondered this question herself, but who

thought it a serious breach of etiquette to discuss such a thing publicly, answered stiffly that she had no idea and that she was going to be late for school. She gathered up her books, thanked the girl again, and hurried off without looking back.

Her first-period class was English, and, when she had seated herself and gathered her wits, she glanced to her left and noticed that Mitchell, the small, devious redhead who sat two seats down, had grown, overnight, a pair of huge and unmanageable feet. He was trying to keep them hidden under his desk while he solemnly studied the blackboard. When she looked to her right, she was astonished to see that Hazel, who had always been a vague and unsurprising kind of girl, had, somehow, come into possession of two large and buoyant breasts. She hunched over them protectively, shielding them inside her arms.

It's the end of the world, Sarah thought. Panicking, she checked herself over for any signs of unusual change but wasn't able to identify anything new. At that moment, the door to the classroom opened and the demon girl who had come to her rescue with the pearl-handled knife walked in and presented her pass and yellow card to the teacher. The teacher, Mrs. Dukofsky, an aged and dragon-faced woman, glared at these offerings as if they were the entrails of a chicken, while the class examined the new girl curiously. After a moment, she turned suddenly and raked the class with a long, defiant stare, so that the students all shuffled and murmured in their seats.

"All right, Robin," the teacher said. "Welcome. You may take the empty seat in the back, next to Sarah. Sarah will catch you up and give you the back assignments."

The girl marched down the aisle without looking right or left and slid in next to Sarah. "Call me Esmeralda," she whispered coolly, "and don't give me any back assignments."

Sarah, startled, looked directly into her eyes, which she

had not meant to do. The girl gazed back at her without smiling. It was, Sarah thought, an otherworldly gaze, cruel and electrically green. Sarah determined to have nothing further to do with this girl and, in fact, decided to lie low in general for the next seven years, read books and sleep maybe. However, when the bell rang at the end of the class, Robin leaned over and said, "God, this is some collection of boys you got here. Maybe it's something in the water."

Sarah looked around the room defensively but realized it was true—they were not an impressive lot.

"In fact, the only decent guy I've come across since I moved into this neighborhood is my French tutor. He's quite gorgeous, but then, being French, he's not from around here."

There was something about the smug and insinuating way that she said this that infuriated Sarah. "You should meet my brother," she said.

Robin looked at her sharply. "Your brother?"

Sarah had never done such a thing before. She stood riveted to the spot, waiting for some other message from outer space to issue from her mouth, but nothing came. At last, not knowing what else to do, she said, "Yeah, he's terrifically handsome."

She knew, as soon as the words were said, that her only hope was to get out of there as quickly as possible, but, before she could get her books together, the girl said, "Hey, I'm free this afternoon. How about I come over and meet him? You could help me with the math homework. You must be taking trig, right? They put me in trig, and I know I'm going to have a terrible time with it."

Sarah, who had recently won a citywide math competition, said, "I'm terrible at math. You'd better ask someone else," and fled from the room.

Her brother was sitting on the front steps when she arrived

home. He grabbed her ankle as she tried to pass and threw her into the grass. Then he went back to reading the newspaper and eating an apple. Next to him lay two bananas and several volumes of the encyclopedia. His plan was to know everything. She examined him from where she lay. He had a large, inquisitive nose in the middle of a long, mournful face, and, with his legs like a grasshopper's and his dark hair sticking up all over the place, he was the goofiest-looking boy she had ever seen.

I'm doomed, she thought.

"Listen to this," he said, tapping the newspaper. "Some scientists now think that if you could compress the atmosphere enough to create a black hole, you might be able to make a new world, a junior universe that would split off from the old one like a bubble. It would exist in the same space as the first world, but in a different dimension. Theoretically you could do this in your basement."

She tried to get up on her knees and gather her books together, but he reached over with his foot and gave her another shove.

"Why is everyone bothering me?" she yelled.

He looked at her, his eyebrows raised in surprise. "What do you mean? Who else is bothering you?"

She blushed guiltily but said nothing.

He examined her closely, then sighed. "Believe me, whatever it is, it's not a real problem. You want a real problem, look in the newspaper. Do you know how many people there are living on cat food in this city? Do you know that most of the rivers in this country are so choked with garbage and chemicals that the fish are all mostly dead or two-headed?"

Sarah managed to roll herself out of his reach and then stand up. "Let me pass, please."

"Eh? Eh? No te comprendo." He peeled a banana and ate it down in a couple of large bites.

"Let me pass, please," she said loudly, in case he was going to continue to pretend he was a foreigner.

"Sarah, you know I can't let you by unless you give me some token."

"Freddy, for God's sakes, let me by. I don't have anything to give you."

He smiled at that and finished the other banana. She wanted to scream but knew that would give him too much satisfaction.

"OK," he said. "Just look into my eyes for a sec. That will do."

She bent over and glared into his eyes furiously. God, how she hated him.

At last he sighed and looked away.

"Well," she said sarcastically, "did you see anything?"

"Sure I did, sure. I saw that you love me with all your heart."

"What?" She stamped her foot on the ground. "Be serious."

"Serious?" he said. "Serious? I am serious. Deadly serious." With that, Fred rolled over and pretended to be dead.

"Cut it out, Fred!" she screamed. But he just lay there, inert. "OK," she said. She stepped over him and went in the house and up the stairs to her bedroom and then walked over to the window and peered out cautiously. Her brother was lying on the sidewalk in exactly the same position. He lay there looking just like a dead grasshopper.

That night, the young man across the way was wearing green pants of some soft, velvety material and a white tunic. He walked to the window and stood there and peered out as if he were looking for something. Could it be me, she wondered. She held herself as still as possible and didn't breathe. He undressed slowly tonight, either as if he was very tired or as if he wanted to give her time to look. Because his movements were so languorous and so inviting, because she was so intent upon seeing her fill, it wasn't until he was all done and standing there stark naked, his legs slightly apart, his face tipped to the sky, that she saw his hair was on fire. He didn't seem to be bothered by this, or even to notice, and the flames appeared more playful than dangerous. Still, she was seized by an unholy desire to call out and give him warning, or maybe just to let him know she was there. Somehow, she understood this would be the worst possible thing she could do, and she grabbed the edge of the bedspread and stuffed it into her mouth. She sat like this for several minutes, resisting the urge to step out onto the soft and mud-sweetened air and walk over to him, then, suddenly, there was a loud crash and swearing from her brother's room. Her naked man frowned and slammed the window shut and disappeared from view.

Before English class began the next morning, Robin leaned over and asked in a husky voice if she could borrow Sarah's math homework. "I'm having trouble with a couple of the problems."

Sarah did not look at her but answered curtly that her math homework was in her locker. At this moment Mrs. Dukofsky entered the room. Robin put a piece of gum in her mouth and heaved a sigh.

"So," said Mrs. Dukofsky, who never wasted a minute, "where does Pandora get her name from?" They were studying Greek mythology this semester.

No one breathed. There was a general hope that before she could call on someone a fiery pit from hell would open at her feet and she'd fall in.

Robin leaned over and placed a small note in Sarah's lap.

Sarah didn't touch it, but it stared up at her interrogatively.

"Do you think it would be better to marry young and rashly, or old and wisely?"

Sarah shoved it in her desk.

"So?" said Mrs. Dukofsky. "Who can tell me the answer? Surely someone has done their homework?"

Sarah knew she had only herself to blame for what was about to happen, but she felt herself unjustly harassed and badgered from all sides.

"Sarah?" the teacher asked briskly.

Sarah blushed and looked around, but none of her classmates even glanced at her. She noted that Larry, who, as of yesterday, had always been a sober and plainly dressed sort of person, today was wearing a metal-studded leather band on his wrist and a thunderbolt-shaped earring in his ear. Robin cautiously unwrapped another piece of chewing gum under cover of her desk, popped it in her mouth, and blinked once like a crocodile.

Sarah faced the teacher unhappily. "It means 'all gifts' because the gods each gave her some special gift when she was born."

"Good." The teacher nodded and turned away.

Sarah took the little piece of paper out, wrote on the back of it "I shall never marry," and shoved it across to Robin without looking at her.

It was a good answer, Sarah thought, truthful and clear and to the point. She felt confident that, if she kept alert, it wouldn't be hard to avoid any demon influences.

A moment later Robin passed a new note over. "I know what you mean, but I plan to marry several times. Probably three."

Sarah eyed this with distaste for several moments. When she looked up, she found that Mrs. Dukofsky, who only a second before had been standing at the front of the room, was now, somehow, planted in front of Robin's desk like an aged and hungry viper.

"Do my eyes deceive me? Are you chewing gum in my classroom?"

Robin smiled at the teacher coolly, then shrugged her shoulders.

"Now, I will tell you," said the teacher, "that, when I was a girl, we weren't given a choice in such matters. However, this is a different time and place, so in this classroom I usually offer a couple of alternatives."

You are a fungus, Sarah thought.

"Either I will expect a paper tomorrow on—umm—let's say, Zeus and his taste for vengeance, or you may put that gum on your nose and wear it there for the rest of the period."

Now, no one had ever chosen the gum humiliation before, but Robin bit the inside of her cheek and seemed to consider. Then she took the gum out and, carefully rolling it into an indecent and Pinocchiolike shape, stuck it on the end of her nose. Mrs. Dukofsky stared at this coldly, then returned to her desk. The class sighed with delight.

Sarah couldn't imagine it—how anyone could willingly accept such an embarrassment—but Robin appeared well pleased with her bargain.

When the bell rang at the end of class, Robin took the gum off her nose and put it back in her mouth and leaned over and said, "You know what I discovered yesterday?"

Sarah tried to gather her books together quickly. "No, I don't," she said in as discouraging a voice as she could muster.

"I discovered that my French tutor is quite rich."

"Oh," said Sarah.

Outside a persistent spring wind was rattling the windows, which Mrs. Dukofsky liked to keep tightly shut because she had a horror of pigeons getting in the room and flying around.

Sarah was having the most amazingly difficult time lifting her math book off the desk. Suddenly it seemed heavier than any earthly object ought to be.

"He's going to take me to Paris this summer."

"Why?"

"Why what?"

"Why's he taking you to Paris this summer?"

"Because Paris, my dear, is the city of love."

Sarah tried to grasp the book again, but this time it seemed to wiggle in her fingers like a cold fish, and she dropped it, startled. What had happened to the steadiness of the world? She saw, in a flash, how difficult it was going to be to be certain of anything.

At this moment, Mrs. Dukofsky sailed by them. As she went through the door, Sarah saw that someone had taped to her back a rough sketch of a fabulously proportioned naked woman. Sarah blushed deeply, but Robin merely squinted a little and smiled. "My grandfather is quite rich, actually," Sarah said.

Robin turned to her, delighted. "You're kidding! Do you think he'll leave you any money?"

Sarah's book stayed stuck. She could not imagine what terrible thing afflicted her. "He's leaving it all to me and my brother. But it's not money exactly."

"What do you mean?"

"I mean it's diamonds and emeralds. He keeps them hidden in the house."

Robin's eyes opened wide. "Where?" she whispered.

Sarah thought for a moment. "In his saltshaker, on the kitchen table. It's one of those big ones. He keeps a little salt in it to fool people, and the rest is diamonds and emeralds. I'm the only one who knows."

"Wow," said Robin.

Now, at this moment, something or someone pushed the window open several inches, and Sarah knew it was probably her grandfather, who had died three years ago and left her his bird-watching binoculars. The spring wind rushed in and softened the chalky air and filled the room with the smell of the distant and central tree of the world about to break into bloom.

"What will you do with them?"

"With what?"

"All the diamonds and emeralds and stuff."

"Oh. I'll give them away. To poor people. To people who don't have enough to eat, people who can only afford to buy cat food for dinner."

"Ah," said Robin, exhaling slowly, staring at Sarah. "You see. I knew I was right. From the moment I looked at you I knew you were a person of substance, someone who understood what was important. I'm an air head, a cream puff. You can help me look the sorrows of the world in the eye. How about I come over after school today? We can do the math homework together and talk. You can introduce me to your brother."

Sarah could have sworn that the mole on her cheek had moved up several inches since yesterday. "My brother has basketball practice today," Sarah said, although her brother viewed all organized sports with suspicion and disdain and had never touched a basketball in his life. At this moment her math book came free from the desk. She grabbed it up and, not looking at Robin, fled from the room.

She went into her brother's room that night just to check and see if there might not have been some slight improvement which could give her cause for hope. She saw, with dismay, that he looked more preposterous than ever. Over his usual careless attire he was wearing one of their mother's flowered aprons, and, as he bent solemnly over some little jars on his windowsill, his nostrils were fully and horsily dilated to sniff some scent. He was a great sniffer.

"Are you gardening?" she asked.

He eyed her broodily without answering. His room, as always, looked like a hurricane had just passed through, first gaily picking up all the shoes and dirty dishes, mysterious toys and books and volumes of the encyclopedia, then flinging them carelessly down.

"What's that stuff on the windowsill?" she tried again.

"I can't tell you."

"Tell me."

"Wild strawberries couldn't drag it out of me."

She shrugged and turned to leave.

"All right, all right. I'll tell you. But you gotta cross your little tooth fairy's heart and hope to die if you ever tell a soul."

"OK," she said, feigning immense disinterest.

He rubbed his nose and considered for a moment. "Well, what it is, is I'm searching for the origins of life."

"What?"

"I'm starting from scratch, and so I got several different mediums going here. I got sand, I got seawater. I got clay, and I got my favorite—dust balls. Now you think about all the cruelty and madness and sorrow in the world. You think about all the wars and the famines and the baby seals being clubbed to death for their pelts and then tell me you think it wouldn't be a good idea to start over fresh."

It's true, she said to herself. It's time I knew about these things. But she had no sooner tried to picture one of them in her mind than it got jumbled up with the next, and, furthermore, when she thought about the jars on the windowsill, she knew it was perfectly possible he was pulling her leg. She tried to step closer to the windowsill to get a better look, but he blocked her way.

"My God," he said. "What's happened to you?"

"What?" she said nervously and tried to back up, but he was much too fast for her. He reached for her arm and, pulling her closer, scrutinized her face craftily. "You look different."

"I do not."

"Yes you do." He dragged her over to his dresser mirror and pointed. "Look. You got a funny shine on you or something— like you stuck your nose in a light socket. What is it?"

"Cut it out. I look exactly the same as always," she said, but, seeing the two of them together in the mirror, she was outraged to observe how clear it was that they were brother and sister. "Let go of me."

"Is it a boy?" he asked incredulously, as if a boy were something he was not, as if boys were not seen much around these parts. "It's a boy, isn't it? Oh, the rush and pickle of time. Why just yesterday you were a little girl hanging upside down on the monkey bars with your dress floating around your head."

"Let go," she said and slapped at him furiously, but hit only air.

She could think of a hundred other people she'd met in books or movies who would have made perfect siblings, but the stars had gathered them up from the crackling void and thrown them down from the sky shackled together. He danced at the other end of the room like a tremendous Rumpelstiltskin, grinning and waving his garden trowel, and, unless she could find some way to dissolve him back into the fire and dust from whence he'd come, she was doomed.

In the night she was awakened by the sound of singing. It was difficult to tell if it was coming from far away or near, as it was very dark and the singing was so unlike anything she'd ever heard before. For a while she was afraid to move, so she just lay there listening, as if maybe these were the last sounds she was going to hear. She would have thought the singing was quite sad if it didn't also seem so very unhuman as to probably not understand about sadness.

When she finally got up, she looked out the window and knew right away that the singing was coming from the dogwood tree in the back of the yard. It was hard to tell if it was just one voice or many, but she rather thought it was many, that each blossom was singing of a terrible and true sorrow of the world. In spite of the fact that the singing was mostly sad, it was the most spellbinding music she'd ever heard. She was just trying to figure out why this might be so when a light went on across the way and the window was thrown open and her naked man leaned out.

"Give it a rest, for God's sakes," he yelled.

For a moment, the tree, as if offended, fell silent. Then it gathered itself together and continued on. Sarah was filled with the most mysterious feeling of confidence and elation, as if it were not a done thing yet, but any minute now she was going to solve a big riddle which would give her the power she needed.

The man bent down to the floor and picked up a shoe. He leaned way out and, with all his strength, threw the shoe. It hit the tree with a soft *chonk* and dropped to the ground. This time the tree fell silent and, maintaining an injured and innocent air, stayed silent. The man eyed it suspiciously, but it didn't make a peep.

Sarah, knowing full well that she shouldn't, that she mustn't, her heart pounding with fear, leaned out the window and said, "Hello."

He jumped as if stuck from behind with some little, sharp object and then stared at her, outraged. "How dare you?" he said. "Have you no shame?"

She thought this was odd since it was he that was naked and not herself. But before she could say anything further, he leaped onto the windowsill and, gathering himself for a big jump, flew, his wingspread alarming now, up into the ailanthus tree. He seemed to sit there for a moment getting his bearings, hissing like a swan. Then he took off into the night.

In the morning she looked out the window and searched the trees for a glimpse of him. The sun shone brightly, and the air was still and warm, but he was nowhere to be seen. She looked down and saw Robin sitting on the fence across the street watching her house. Spotting Sarah in the window, she waved excitedly. Any minute now, her brother would go bounding out the front door, and there it would be, the final disaster. Sarah saw that she would have to go down and tell Robin the truth. She dressed more quickly than she ever had before, grabbed her books, and raced down the stairs, out the front door, and across the street. She came to an awkward halt in front of Robin and grabbed her by the arm. "Come on, I've got something to tell you, but not here."

It was the kind of morning on which anything might be true. A mockingbird, delirious with spring, sang giddily from some hidden spot, and the air felt like the kind of silk Sarah would want for her wedding pajamas if, after all, she decided to get married. Unidentifiable green shoots opened themselves up into daffodils, tulips, and hyacinths (the same tender blue as the sky) as they walked by them. Sarah tried to keep her eyes on the tops of the trees, especially the white-blooming pears, where it would be easy to camouflage a pair of wings.

At the end of the block, they spotted, huddled inside a forsythia bush, the same little thugs who had ambushed Sarah the other day. Robin opened her knife, and Sarah grabbed a big stick. They strode forward brandishing their weapons, and the forsythia bush trembled and shook and the little boys stayed right where they were.

When they were safely past them, Robin said, "Which do you think is the more powerful force—sex? or friendship?—I mean, in the long run?"

Sarah frowned. "I've heard of stories where a person betrays a friend for a lover, but never the other way around."

Robin made a face of impatience. "But I'm talking about the long run—not just one moment of weakness."

Sarah shrugged.

"Well, what was it you wanted to tell me?" Robin asked.

Sarah cleared her throat. A robin flew so close by she could have reached out and taken the worm from its beak. "It's about my brother . . ."

"Yes?"

"He's dead."

"What?"

"It's true. He was hit by a car on his way home from school yesterday."

"Oh my God, I'm so sorry." Robin, however, did not look at all sorry. She was studying Sarah hard, as if taking her measure for the first time. They were passing, at this moment, a bed of flame-colored tulips. Robin stopped and embraced her and said, "Let's sit down here." She pulled Sarah down into the tulips, then covered her own face with her hands. She seemed to be working herself up to something, and, in a moment, she began to sob.

Sarah was distressed. "Oh, please, don't cry. He wasn't a very nice person anyway. I wasn't at all fond of him."

"No, no," Robin sobbed. "It's not your brother I'm crying about, it's my French tutor."

"What's wrong with him?" Sarah asked suspiciously.

"He's gone."

Confused for a moment, Sarah turned and stared up at the trees again. "Who's gone?"

"My French tutor. I told you. I found a note this morning saying he'd been called away on a special assignment. Very hush-hush. He's a spy, I think. He could be gone for years. He could get killed."

Now Sarah gazed around at the tulips, which seemed to flank them protectively, holding themselves slender and erect as young soldiers.

"I'll search for him everywhere. I'll go to the ends of the earth."

At this moment Sarah saw her brother turn the corner down at the end of the block.

"Let's go," she said to Robin urgently. But Robin didn't move. Sarah looked at her imploringly and then down at her brother heading towards them. My God, what was he wearing today? He had on the strangest hat she'd ever seen. It looked like a beanie with an antenna on top. And what was even more inexplicable was that he was bouncing a basketball down the sidewalk.

She held her breath and waited for the darkness to come and the stars to rain down on their heads. But, of course, they didn't. Her brother threw the ball into the air, and it flew up through the forsythia and up through the pear blossoms as high as it could into the steady spring light, then it fell back to the sidewalk with a nice *plonk.*

Robin, hearing the basketball, turned and squinted in his direction. "Oh, my God. What is that?"

Sarah wanted to sink into the sidewalk and disappear, but there was no avenue of escape that she could see, and Fred came bouncing towards them. When he reached them he stopped. He stopped and stared as if they were the ones from outer space and not he. Sarah closed her eyes hopelessly and waited to hear what mortifying thing he would have to say.

But Fred didn't say anything. After studying them for a minute as if he were making botanical observations, he merely said, "Morning, ladies," and tipped his hat. Then he threw the ball into the air again, caught it, and continued on.

Sarah, drunk with relief, watched his back as he bounded away down the block, tall and extremely disheveled, his shirt half in and half out, his jeans unrolling around his ankles, his hair mashed down by his absurd hat. He was, no doubt, trying to electrify his brain with moon rays.

"Do you know him?" Robin asked in a whisper.

"No." Sarah swallowed.

"I thought he acted like he knew you."

"Yeah, well, I know him a little. He lives on my block."

"My God. What's his name?"

"His name? His name is Ralph."

"Ralph?"

"Yeah."

"Is he brilliant or something?"

Sarah eyed her uneasily and realized now that Robin's mole had disappeared. "That's what *he* says."

"He's gorgeous."

Sarah stared at her. She made a face around the word as if it were a pebble that had appeared quite by magic in her mouth. "Gorgeous?" she whispered.

Whether Robin, a girl about her own age and height, from the same planet and historical epoch, was seeing Fred with completely different eyes than her own, or whether this was a stupendous act of kindness, delivered up to ease her humiliation because she knew perfectly well this was Sarah's brother, there was no way of knowing. Fred was gone.

"You'll introduce me," said Robin.

Sarah stared at her impassively. "Show me the math problems you're having trouble with," she said.

Robin took her math homework out and showed it to Sarah. It had been done with stunning incompetence. Sarah took a deep breath and was about to begin at the beginning when a window flew open behind them.

"You girls! What are you doing in that tulip bed? Get out of there at once!"

They rose hastily, grabbing their books, and tumbled onto the sidewalk.

"What were you looking for when I saw you standing in the window?" Robin asked.

Sarah sighed, seeing that they were going to be friends till the end of the world and that the end of the world was nowhere in sight. A little wind blew the pear trees, which seemed, for one moment, full of winged men and the next moment stood empty.

2

OUTER SPACE

ONE DAY IN THE WINTER of their junior year, Robin announced that she was going to get married.

Sarah squinted. "Oh, for God's sakes, who would marry you?"

"My tarot cards have predicted it."

"You don't even have a boyfriend."

"I'm not expecting a boyfriend. I'm expecting love, which is a little over your head as you haven't been there yet."

"What do you know about it? Of course I have. Certainly I have."

Robin glanced disparagingly over at William.

Sarah looked at him too. She had been going around with him for several months for no decisive reason. He was sitting a little ways down from them at the lunch table playing table hockey with another boy. At that moment, the nickel they had been using for a puck overshot the edge of the table and landed in Sarah's lap. She covered it quickly with her palm and kept it hidden there. The boys immediately got down on the floor and started laughing and punching at people's feet while they looked for the nickel.

"I'm not talking about him," Sarah said.

Robin tugged on her lower lip. "Oh yeah? Well then, who *are* you talking about?"

"You shouldn't pull on your lip like that. You're ugly enough as it is."

The two boys had now reached the spot where the girls were sitting. Sarah felt a hand snaking its way up her thigh.

"Cut it out, William," she said.

"Get out from under there," Robin commanded, "before I break your teeth."

Sarah heard them laugh and move on. "You want to go to the library with me this afternoon?" she asked quickly.

"Sure. It's my dearest wish to spend Friday afternoon in the library. My second dearest wish is to do what my mother wants me to do, which is to go to the nursing home and visit my senile grandmother."

"Are you going to do that?"

Robin sighed. "Oh God, it's so depressing there, it's so end-of-the-line—all these old people sitting around, waiting to die. My grandmother never has the slightest idea who I am, she thinks I'm her little sister, Yetta, or somebody, and the stench of the place is unreal. I always think I'm going to pass out."

Sarah was not paying much attention. She was thinking with a terrible pang of shame that it was true—she had never been in love and her prospects of accomplishing such a thing looked fairly grim.

Robin sighed. "I don't know, maybe I'll wait and go next week. Can I borrow a pencil and the math homework?"

Sarah clicked the rings of her notebook open and handed Robin a sheaf of papers and a pencil. "Don't suck on the eraser."

Robin nodded and examined the papers. A look of hopeless wonder came over her face. "Your answers are completely different than mine," she said.

Sarah knew that this was because Robin's answers were all wrong and ignored her. She began dreaming a daydream in which she was so beautiful no man could look at her without weeping until a certain jealous and evil queen had her turned into a nightingale, the drabbest looking of birds. What could she do but clutch onto the highest branch and sing? Her song was so lovely that all the cats in the emperor's garden gathered below her hungrily, and the emperor's youngest son, wearing only the pants half of a pair of gold pajamas, had just opened his window sleepily to hear her song better when she realized she was being watched. She looked up and found Fiona—plain as mud and dressed, as usual, in an old potato sack or something—eyeing her sympathetically. Sarah imagined that she had seen everything, the nightingale, and the emperor's son, and, most certainly, the nickel. My God, Sarah thought, have I sunk to such depths that I'm worrying about what old Fiona thinks of me?

"Here," Sarah said loftily, "a lucky nickel." She shoved the hockey puck across the table to her. Fiona held it in her palm and looked at it in confusion, then nodded and dropped it in her blouse pocket.

The two boys had noticed nothing, as they were now busy lobbing peas from somebody's lunch tray at the backs of passersby. Robin, the delicate bride-to-be, paid no attention either but, with a furious frown of incomprehension, studied the page of math problems and sucked on Sarah's pencil eraser.

That night Sarah was playing Candy Land with Marcus Logan, for whom she was baby-sitting, when the yellow wall phone in the kitchen went off like an alarm clock. The teacups on the shelf nearby tinkled in warning, and Marcus, who was losing the game, threw all the pieces and the cards into the air. Sarah glared at him through this blizzard, but he refused to look at her and smiled secretly to himself. She rose and went into the kitchen, Marcus following slowly behind. She stared at the phone for a while, then, on the seventh ring, picked it up and said hello.

"Hello? Hello! Sarah, is that you?"

"Yes. Hello."

"Hi. You sound funny. You all right? I thought I'd come over for a while."

"Who is this?"

"It's the Pope, for God's sakes. Who do you think it is?"

Marcus sat down on the white linoleum and pulled the cupboard door beneath the sink open and shut. It rattled and banged.

"Oh, it's you. What do you want?"

"I just told you, Sarah. I'm going to come over for a while. Is that little kid in bed yet?"

"No," she said. "He isn't. Stop that, Marcus!"

"Well, put him to bed. I'll be over in a few minutes."

"Why?"

"Why? Why am I coming over? I'm coming over to explain two or three mysteries of the universe to you."

The mysteries of the universe glimmered faintly behind the veil of confusion that seemed to toss and tremble over everything. William had a tendency to wiggle his ears at serious moments and plant rubber spiders in the teachers' desk drawers. He wore high-topped basketball sneakers and foolish hats, and Sarah was fairly sure he knew nothing about the mysteries of the universe.

Marcus banged the cabinet door loudly, and it swung back and slammed Sarah in the leg. "Ow!"

"I'll be over in fifteen minutes," William said.

Marcus climbed up on a chair and, reaching the telephone, disconnected it. Then he jumped down and fled from the room.

William arrived a few minutes after she'd put Marcus to bed. As soon as he walked in, he grabbed her around the waist and began to kiss her. She pushed him away. "What are you doing?" she asked in irritable surprise.

He stuck his hands in his pockets and looked exasperated. "Nothing," he said. "I wasn't doing anything. Come on, let's study."

But they'd only been studying a few minutes when she felt him staring at her. She looked up.

"You're the most beautiful girl in this room," he said.

"What? What are you talking about?"

"You've got those crooked glasses and those knobby knees and those big feet and that long neck and that greeny yellow hair like seaweed, and, I don't know how it is, but you're the most beautiful girl I've ever seen. I know what you're thinking about and I'm thinking about it, too."

"I haven't got the faintest idea what you're referring to."

"I want to sleep with you."

Here it was. She looked at him coldly. "Don't be ridiculous. We wouldn't, either of us, have the slightest idea what we were doing."

"Sure we would, sure we would. We'd be great. We'd figure it out. We'd be terrific."

"I'm not going to bed my first time with a totally inexperienced person like you."

He looked at her searchingly, then leaned over and took off her glasses and kissed her. As the kiss lasted a very long time,

after a while she opened her eyes and looked around the room
and found Marcus standing there with narrowed eyes, watching
them. She jumped up, pushing William away.

"Hey, you're supposed to be asleep."

Marcus glared at her furiously. "Who's that?" he demanded.

"That's my friend William. He's visiting me."

"No."

"It's a fact."

William laughed.

"No!" Marcus screamed.

"Why are you out of bed?" Sarah asked again.

"There's an alligator in my room." He was absolutely definite.

"What?"

"There's an alligator in my room."

"Now, how would an alligator have gotten into your room?"

"It came through the window and jumped on my bed."

"I don't think alligators can jump."

"Yes."

"Yes, what?"

"Yes, they can jump."

"Baloney." As she reached out to cup his head in her palm,
she felt a shock, as if it were her own childhood rising back up
to meet her in the nick of time.

William watched them narrowly, trying to understand what
kind of team they made. "You know, he's very right, Sarah.
They do sometimes jump. Maybe I'd better go check it out."

Now Marcus looked at him. "What are you going to do to
him?" he asked.

"I'll shoot him," William offered. With his arms spread out
along the top of the sofa, he looked like he might fool a small
boy.

"No," Marcus said.

"I'll use my tranquilizer gun. It will just put him to sleep. Then I'll put him back outside where he belongs."

"And then, of course, it will be time for you to go," Sarah said.

"It will?"

"Yes," said Marcus.

"Certainly," said Sarah.

William shrugged, then trudged off down the hall to shoot the alligator. Marcus watched him go silently, then his little head tilted backwards under her hand to meet Sarah's eyes. She leaned towards him.

"Don't kiss me!" he screamed.

Later that evening she was sitting at her window watching the quiet street below when she heard Fred, who was home from college for the weekend, come whistling down the hallway. When he reached the doorway of her room, she felt him standing there, watching her, but she did not turn around. After a while he sighed and came in and sat down on her bed. "So what do *you* think about the notion of life on other planets?" he asked.

Fred had recently come into possession of a small but powerful telescope and had become nearly insufferable on this subject. She turned to look at him. "The idea is about as believable as Robin saying she's going to get married."

"Who would marry Robin?"

"Exactly. Now listen, Fred, this is probably beyond the scope of your imagination, but try to imagine that it actually gets on my nerves when people just waltz into my room without knocking."

The bed gave a little sigh as he lay down.

"Fred, I'd like to be alone. I've got a big history exam on Monday and I'm studying."

"Well, I'm convinced of it. It's not reasonable to suppose that in the vastness of space we are the only planet with the right conditions to support life. Of course there's life on other planets. The big question is, what kind of life and how do we make contact with it? I doubt that any race intelligent enough to devise a means to travel to other planets would go out of its way to stop here on *this* little ball of atrocities."

She turned around to yell at him to get out, and then stopped short. She was astounded, once again, by how beautiful he had become. One day he had been a frog, and the next day he was a prince. A strange and foreign-looking prince, it was true, with wild, stiff hair, and a mouth too mobile and big, and eyes that seemed to stare too intently at whatever he was staring at—but a prince nevertheless. There still seemed no reasonable explanation for this. "Would you kindly get your cruddy feet off my bed? Jeez." They were enormous feet and shod in old basketball sneakers.

He grabbed her pillow and threw it up in the air. After what seemed a long while, it came down and landed on his face.

"Help, I've been kidnapped," he said in a muffled voice.

"Yeah, I read about it in the flypaper."

"How tough you've become," he said sadly through the pillow. "I remember when you used to make pictures of you and me doing stuff and our arms would always be coming right out of our heads, without any necks or bodies or anything. I always loved that. You gave hundreds of pictures like that to me as presents."

"You're breaking my heart."

"You were always trying to take my pulse or get my clothes

off to check for measles. The soul of eroticism is curiosity, I think."

"What? What do you mean? I can't hear you. Take that pillow off your face."

"I can't," he said. "It seems to be glued to my nose."

She reached over and took the pillow off his face.

"Listen, Fred, have you ever been in love?"

He blinked at the light and frowned. "Certainly."

"Well, what's it like?"

He got up restlessly and came and stood at her back. "What's it to you? You can't ask questions like that. Each case is too individual. Sometimes it's like a bad sunburn, sometimes it's like falling off a roof. It varies."

She looked at him doubtfully.

"How about we go out in the backyard and eat snow with maple syrup like we did when we were kids?" he said. "I could show you some constellations."

She knew that if she went out in the backyard and stood under the stars she would feel more tiny and confused than before, that if she tried to eat snow like when they were kids she would be baffled by the recognition that she had already had a past and mystified by the idea of time passing, of how treacherous and imprecise a process it is, how it could turn somebody like Fred into a handsome swan and leave her quacking helplessly at him from the shore. "No," she said. "Please get out of here."

Down at the end of the block, under a great shower of stars, she saw Fiona turn the corner. She was wearing her awful green-and-blue-checked coat and carrying a paper sack with a carton of milk sticking out of the top of it. It was funny because Fiona usually walked fast and with her head half down and her shoulders half up, but tonight, perhaps because it was very late and there was no one else around, she was going very slowly and she stood so you could see that she was actually a rather tall and slender girl. She hadn't even bothered to button up her awful coat, and she came sailing dreamily down the block just as if she thought it was a summer night. She looked around at the clear sky and the naked trees, and, it seemed to Sarah, she was pleased with what she saw. At one point she even stopped to crouch down and call to something under a car. Probably a cat. She held out her hand, but the cat didn't come out, so after a while she got up and went on.

"Who's that girl?" Fred asked. "You know her?"

Sarah shrugged. "Sure. That's old Fiona. She's in my math class."

"How's her math?"

Sarah looked at him. "Fiona isn't what I'd call 'too with it,' but her math is great. Why?"

"Just curious."

Sarah stared at him. "Listen, I gotta study now."

"All right," he said and headed for the door. "I think I'm gonna take a walk. You positive you don't want to join me?"

"Positive. Please remove yourself."

He bowed and went out.

The next day, which was Saturday, Robin called and said she was at a phone booth. She claimed that she'd closed all the windows and left her parents in the house with the gas on and hopefully they were dead by now. She asked Sarah to come over and meet her on the front steps.

Sarah bicycled down the middle of the street between heaps of plowed snow. The sun shone, but the afternoon was bitingly cold. The air was the color of gold. The trip should have been ordinary; she'd made it hundreds of times, but here she was, whizzing through the air, held aloft on a little heart-shaped seat by two spinning wheels, while dogs walked past sporting hilarious coats. The street was filled with light and reflections of light running wild down to the vanishing point.

At Robin's house, Robin's mother, Selma, opened the door and guided and poked her into the kitchen.

"Sit down," Selma said.

Sarah sat down. Selma seated herself across the table and eyed Sarah speculatively. She tugged on her lower lip, so that for a moment she looked just like Robin. "It's murder," she said to Sarah and looked up through the ceiling into Robin's room. "You want to know what it is now? She says I should get ready. She says she's going to get married."

Sarah shoved her hands into her jacket pockets and smiled.

"Have an apple," Selma said, holding out the fruit bowl.

"No, thank you."

"Well, have a banana."

"No, no thanks."

Selma sorrowed over the fruit in her hands, then looked again at Sarah. "Some salted almonds maybe? What's going to happen to you? You're so skinny. You'll vanish. Maybe you'd like some mother's tears. I have a whole pitcher in the refrigerator from all the grief that kid gave me this morning."

"Selma, you're a real card. Where is she? Is she upstairs?"

"Listen, you're going to go up and see her? Do me a favor. Ask her to go and visit her grandmother in the home. That's all I ask. It's not a big thing."

In Robin's room, Robin was asleep, with her long, dark hair fanned out across the pink bedspread. Sarah, feeling safe from observation, regarded Robin tenderly. She knew that Robin loved her above all other things and would make great sacrifices and commit the most terrible acts to protect their friendship.

"Stop looking at me like that," Robin said. She opened

her eyes and frowned at Sarah. The room was hot and still.

"Your parents aren't dead."

Robin smiled. "It doesn't matter. I've decided that by the time summer comes I'll be married. So that gives me roughly six months."

"Good God, get real, would you, Robin? Nobody's gonna marry you. You're about as mature as an egg yolk and totally unreliable. Let's do some work," she said. "It'll make your mother feel better."

"What's going to make my mother feel better is when she gets to drink some of my blood."

"Oh, come on, Robin, she's not so bad."

"Make no mistake. It's going to be her or it's going to be me."

"She's your mother. She's helpless in the face of it. She's training you for the big time."

"She's from outer space. Wanna bet she's listening at the door right now?"

"Stop exaggerating."

Robin shrugged.

Sarah got up and opened the door, and Selma was standing there, innocently holding a pile of folded towels. "Laundry," she said. Sarah smiled at her pleasantly and closed the door.

"She washes the fruit with soap. I came downstairs the other day and there she was at the sink washing the fruit with a bar of soap."

Sarah laughed. "Listen, I forgot to tell you. She wants you to go to the nursing home and visit your grandmother."

Robin groaned. "It's such a downer, I mean knowing that someday that's where I'll be sitting—old and peeing on myself." She sighed and pulled on her lip.

"I wouldn't do that if I were you; it does peculiar things to your appearance."

Robin let go of her mouth and made a face. "All right, listen, I'll go try to find some pencils and we'll do some math."

After Robin had left the room, Sarah took off her shoes and socks. It was very warm. She went over to the window and opened it up and the room got very quiet. Suddenly, first one and then another flash of white light shot past her left ear. A very wild, unfamiliar smell filled the room, something like licorice. Nervously she turned around to see what was behind her. Obviously something from outer space. Two pale blue, ball-shaped things were sitting on the carpet, one slightly larger than the other. They seemed to be soft and porous like sponges. When they began to roll around, Sarah jumped up on the bed. They smelled sweet and excited, actually very lovely. The smell got stronger and stronger, wilder and wilder. They were about the size of basketballs. They rolled up and down the length of the room, then one hopped onto the chair and then onto the desk. It rolled over to a wedge of lemon which was sitting beside an empty cup and saucer. In a second the other one was beside it. They poised there attentively. The bigger one rocked slowly back and forth in meditation while the smaller one sat perfectly still. Suddenly the room began to fill with something approximating the smell of lemons. Sarah's eyes smarted and watered although the smell was actually lighter than the odor of lemons, more complicated and sharper. After a while this storm of lemons passed, and the two blue balls rolled over to the edge of the desk and dropped onto the floor. They bounced a couple of times and came to rest. Sarah felt that they were disappointed. The wild licorice smell was almost gone. Sarah tried to think what to do, but just then the smaller one gathered itself up for a big roll and bounced onto the foot of the bed. Sarah scurried up towards the pillow, her heart pounding in her ears. The ball followed her jauntily and came to rest on one of her bare feet.

Dear God, she thought.

The thing was surprisingly light, as if it were mostly air. The texture of it was silky. It didn't feel bad on her foot. She stood extremely still, hoping that it would not notice that she was alive. Almost immediately it began to give off its weird, agitated, licorice smell again. The large ball took a big roll, bounced onto the bed, and came up and sat on her other foot. It, too, was excited. In a little while Sarah began to detect subtle variations in the odor of each one. The smell of one got stronger or higher or lower or a peculiar herbal fragrance came and went. Then the smell of the other got weaker or lower or tinged with oregano. The courses of the two smells were running in a kind of counterpoint to each other. And then suddenly, how embarrassing, Sarah began to smell her socks. The odor got stronger and stronger, and she just stood there feeling mortified until she realized what was happening. It wasn't her, it was them. They were imitating and amplifying the odor of her socks in an attempt to speak to her.

"Hey!" she said in protest, and at the sound of her voice the spell of her socks was broken. For a moment the air was clear as a bell. Then two very distinct whiffs of terror poured from the aliens and they rolled madly towards the window.

She jumped down from the bed and walked over towards them. A terrible smell of desperation and fear filled the room, but, when she tried to speak to them, the sound of her voice must have frightened them even more, for they jumped up onto the windowsill and leaped out onto a gust of wind. The two light, light balls revolved quickly upwards, obviously making for the sky.

It seemed to Sarah as she watched them go that the problem she was having was one of perspective, that she was no more astonished to find a pair of sponges from outer space flying about the room than to see snow come pouring out of the sky, or red apples hanging from a tree, or herself, standing in front of a mirror, nearly seventeen. How had she gotten there? What she needed was an ordinary fact or two, a recognizable beginning or ending, a point of departure and maybe a solid piece of ground to swim towards. She wanted nothing so grandiose as love or sex, or anything as extreme as creatures from outer space, just a couple of true and immutable things she could say out loud, things that wouldn't keep changing into something else even as she tried to grasp them in her hands.

On Monday morning she left her house for school and had the feeling someone was following her. It was beginning to snow. She hurried to the end of the block, whipped around the corner, and banged, with terrific force, into Anthony Torelli, a boy she did not know personally but by reputation. She closed her eyes and hoped that things would improve and that he wasn't carrying a knife. After a while, when she heard no sound but the wind whistling by, she decided to take a peek to see what was going on. He was still standing there staring at her. Anthony was a tough boy, and, as such, he wore no hat or gloves, and his red hair and freckles stood out fiercely in the icy cold. He was staring at her strangely, as if she had two heads or a bird's nest in her hair. He sniffed.

"What's that smell?" he asked.

She had no idea what he was talking about, and she thought that maybe, if she pretended she hadn't heard this question and just quietly walked around him, he wouldn't notice, but when she tried to move she found that her feet seemed to have taken root in the pavement. Not knowing how else to handle the situation, she tipped her face to the sky and pretended that she had absolutely nothing better to do than stand there and freeze to death. He didn't seem inclined to move either. He studied her, frowning. "I've seen you around the hallways," he said at last. "That's some perfume you got on."

"I'm not wearing perfume," she said in a high, nervous voice.

He laughed. "Well, it's easy to see what's on your mind," and, before she could do anything to protect herself, he grabbed her around the waist and, there in the boiling snow, gave her a long kiss. She knew that William would not look kindly upon this. She pushed him away, gasping for air, and he stepped back, grinning at her. Then he shoved his hands in his pockets and, with the silver chains around his boots jingling faintly, disappeared down the block.

She found her feet had loosened up. She sniffed at herself suspiciously but, smelling nothing, clutched her books to her chest and headed into the rising wind.

William was waiting for her in front of the school. He looked like he had been waiting there for some time. He wore a black fedora that was a little too big in the crown, and it was covered with snow. When she stopped in front of him wordlessly, he took the hat off and smacked it against his thigh and put it back on.

"Listen, Sarah, I have something to tell you," he said nervously.

"Yes?"

"Listen, Sarah, I'm not as inexperienced as you think."

"What? What exactly does that mean?"

He shifted from one foot to the other. "It means that, actually, I've been to bed with someone else."

She tried to picture an afternoon in which everything came together just as it should—love, from out of the blue, along with sex and desire. She saw a dim room where gold light came in long shafts through the half-open shutters, and that was as far as she could get. Who it was that lay next to her and how his hand would feel resting on her leg, it was impossible to imagine. It infuriated her to think of William crashing and bumbling his way into this mystery and then to come bragging to her about it. She turned away from him and reached for the great iron handle of the front door.

"Wait," he cried. "Wait! I told you because I love you."

She shoved past him, out of the whirling snow, into the warm din of the front hallway and almost banged into Fiona. Fiona stood there, stock-still, in the middle of the traffic, looking dimly about her.

"What is it, Fiona? Have you lost something?" Sarah asked her.

Fiona was startled at this intrusion into her dreamy world.

What a noodlehead, Sarah thought. Though she looks nearly pretty with that pink flush from the cold. Maybe I should ask her if she'd like to run off with me and become a nun.

"Sarah," Fiona said with a smile.

"Fiona."

"I've lost my mitten. It looks like this." She held up a red, furry mitten.

Sarah scanned the hallway, then spotted the mitten sticking out of the side pocket of Fiona's book bag. She yanked it out and handed it to her. Fiona just stood there and stared at it as if she couldn't believe her eyes.

"I've gotta go," Sarah said impatiently. "See you later in math class."

It was the very next day that there was one of those miraculous thaws that sometimes comes in February. She and Robin went out for a walk in the park. A little green mist hung over the trees like a foretelling of leaves soon to come. When they lay down on the damp grass, their backs were cold against the earth, but the front part of them was warm beneath the sun.

Sarah closed her eyes, and, when she opened them again a few minutes later, she saw a big purple ball disentangle itself from the branches of the trees and swim into the clear blue arena of sky. For a moment she thought it was one of her acquaintances from outer space, but then she saw it was a hot-air balloon carrying a basket. There was a man in the basket watching them through binoculars. Robin stared back at him, then raked her hand tragically through her dark hair and said, "God, I'm bored. Nothing exciting ever happens around here." She pulled out her lower lip and brooded.

Sarah looked at her, dumbfounded. How could anyone with their hair all tangled up like that and their lip pulled out four inches still look so beautiful?

"Oh, I don't know," Sarah said. "Before you know it, it'll be summer. We can read books. We can go swimming."

Robin looked at her disbelievingly. "Swimming? Read *books*?"

Sarah fell silent in embarrassment. She looked around her sadly. Nearby was an old elm tree whose bare branches almost touched the ground. For no reason that she could think of, she was filled with a desire to climb it.

"Hey," Robin yelled. "Where are you going?"

It wasn't a difficult feat to perform. Even a baby could have climbed it, so thick and evenly spaced were its branches. But Sarah, once she had started up, was excited, as if she were going to outwit at last whatever it was that was shadowing her. After a while she stopped and seated herself on a particularly smooth, wide branch. It wasn't more than a few minutes before Robin was up there, too, sitting across from her.

"Why are you such an idiot?" Robin wanted to know.

They were inside the tree, and the whole afternoon seemed to rest in the air between them like an elephant magically held aloft.

Sarah couldn't see the balloon anywhere, but, when she looked down, she was startled to see a man—young, but considerably older than themselves—staring nosily up at them.

"Ignore him," Sarah whispered, but Robin pulled a stick of chewing gum out of her pocket and dropped it on the ground at the man's feet.

"Hey," Sarah protested, but in a moment he had one foot on a low branch and he was looking about for a place to grab hold. Before they knew it he was crouched on the branch below them with sinister, doll-blue eyes.

Sarah definitely didn't like his looks. "Get out of this tree. This is our tree. Good-bye."

"Did one of you drop this?" he asked, displaying the chewing gum. He had a tiny, blond mustache.

"A gift, not an invitation. Get down, buddy," Sarah said.

He looked at Robin, and Sarah looked at her too. Robin's face had taken on new planes of thought and sneakiness, though it was radiant with the afternoon light pouring through the branches.

"You've got a lot of nerve coming up here like this," Robin said. His smile was immediate, melancholy. She was warming him up somehow. "This is a private tree. You've got to go. It's nothing personal." She opened up her palms apologetically, as if they were full of tiny, ripe, just-picked bombs.

"Would either of you like a foot rub?" he offered.

"*Get the hell out of this tree,*" Sarah commanded.

The young man looked at Robin, and she shrugged her shoulders. He climbed down and dropped to the ground and walked away.

"You wanted him to stay," Sarah said accusingly.

"So?"

"You can't just go striking up conversations with any Tom, Dick, or Harry who passes you in the park."

"Oh God, you sound just like my mother."

"Your mother loves you."

"Believe me, my mother would eat me for breakfast, boiled, with ketchup, if she could."

Sarah marched home from the park righteously. You would think that there was only one thing that mattered in this world, that there was no such thing as beauty or mathematics or flowers, as poetry or spring or music.

She had sometimes thought of Robin as the other half of her heart, the one who most perfectly understood her and completed her, but, certainly, you would think that a true friend would not welcome strange men who barged in on your private conversations.

As she neared home, the sun disappeared and the sky grew low and ominous again. She came to the end of the block and turned the corner and saw a couple half hidden behind an evergreen tree. The young man and woman held each other tenderly about the waist, studied each other's faces, and then kissed. Sarah drew as close as she could without appearing obvious and slowed her pace. She certainly didn't want to be caught staring, but she peeked at the couple with great curiosity, trying to gather as much information as possible. As she drew level with them, she realized she was staring at Fred and Fiona.

She stopped in her tracks.

Fiona pulled her face back from the kiss and smiled at Fred. Sarah was astonished to see that Fiona looked, if not beautiful, absolutely sure of what she was doing and where she was.

Perhaps he's just kissing her out of kindness, Sarah thought.

But, at that moment, Fred looked around and saw her. The face he turned upon her was not a face of kindness. He looked flushed and shining and stern, and he frowned and drew Fiona around to the other side of the tree, where they could not be seen.

Sarah shook herself and hurried home, under the lowering sky.

Sunday evening, when she had finished playing Candy Land with Marcus Logan, she told him it was his bedtime.

He stared at her, dumbfounded at this betrayal. "No it's not!" he screamed.

"Yes."

"My bedtime is eight o'clock."

"It's past eight o'clock." She held out the watch for him to see. There was absolutely nothing he could do. He was as powerless as she, and he knew nothing about watches.

He refused to speak another word to her. Mutely, he allowed her to help him undress and put on his pajamas. Then he got into bed and pulled the covers over his head. She asked him which book he would like to read, but he made no answer, so she read him a story about a frog that taught itself to fly while the little mound his body made under the blankets lay stonily unmoving.

When she was done, she whipped the covers off his back and demanded a good-night kiss.

"I don't kiss," he said coldly.

"Oh dear," she said, "I'm sorry to hear that," and she began to tickle him.

"Stop!" he shouted, giggling furiously, but she wouldn't. She tried to imagine him ten years older. It was impossible. He was squirming, fishlike, but very warm, unable to express himself decently in any language. She stared down at him carefully, trying to figure out how time, using no visible machinery, with no apparent effort, got you so irreversibly from one place to another. When he was very pink and out of breath, she let go of him. He immediately pulled the covers back over his head and lay there breathing heavily.

"Good night," she said.

"Dumbhead!" he said through the blankets.

She called William and told him that this was his big chance if he could get himself over there in twenty minutes. She waited for him to say something, but he seemed to be utterly beside himself. She understood very well what this was like, but this did not stop her from feeling irritated with him. "Twenty minutes, William. Then the deal is off. Bring precautions."

He started then, in a choked voice, to say something, but she hung up the phone.

At lunchtime the next day, the room was filled with a pearly gray light as if the moon had risen up through the floor. The din was terrible. Chairs scraped and voices shouted and everywhere, like gunfire, were the sounds of paper bags being blown up and exploded. Across the table a girl pursed up her mouth like a rosebud and, using a small mirror, examined herself critically. "Fire!" yelled a voice that slipped away behind them, and Sarah jumped up with a scream, then screamed again as she found that her hair had been tied to the back of her chair.

"Who was that? Did you see who that was?" she demanded of Robin, who patiently untied her.

"Nope."

"Was it William?"

"No. I don't think so."

"It's just the kind of idiot thing he would do."

"You're right."

Sarah peered around guiltily, then lowered her voice and

said, "Listen, I wasn't going to tell you this, but maybe I better. Just to get it off my chest—me and William . . . we did it last night." Even as she said this, she felt exhausted, as if she could sleep now for a hundred years.

Robin looked at her suspiciously. "Did what?"

Sarah blushed. "You know . . . *it*."

"You're kidding me."

"No."

"I wouldn't have believed this of you, Sarah."

Sarah closed her eyes.

"Well, tell me about it. C'mon. What happened? What was it like?"

Sarah didn't open her eyes. "It was dark. I couldn't see much."

Robin frowned. "What do you mean, it was dark? That's all you have to say?"

She looked at Robin. "I mean it was dark," she said tiredly. "He turned out all the lights and pulled down the shades. It was the darkest room I've ever been in."

"Sarah," Robin said in a loud voice, "this is life and I must know what happened and if you're all right."

"Shhh . . . I'm all right," Sarah lied. "I'm perfectly all right. It wasn't a big deal."

"Did he hurt you?" Robin asked angrily. "I'll kill the little snotnose."

"No, no. Not really. He kept jabbing me with his elbow and saying 'oops, excuse me' like the amateur he is, and I kept sliding off the sofa."

"Well, I hope he was gentle. I hope he didn't think only of himself. The first time is hard enough as it is," she said indignantly.

Sarah looked at Robin fondly. "You know what it was like? It was like somebody sticking their finger up your nose. Like that. Not terrible, but not something I'd want to do real often."

Robin laughed. "You have to give it a chance. It will improve."

At this moment the five-minute warning bell went off. Robin put her hand on Sarah's arm. "Listen, I hate to change the subject, but I have to ask you to do me a big favor."

"Oh-oh."

"You're my best friend."

"Don't say that. What a terrible thing to say."

Robin laughed, then lowered her voice to a whisper again. "You have to cover for me this afternoon. I'm counting on you. Don't ask me to explain."

Sarah said nothing. She felt weightless, as if she were made of sponge and perfume, as if the littlest breath of air might blow her right up and out the window.

"If my mother asks, I want you to tell her that, as far as you know, I went to the nursing home this afternoon."

"But it's a lie. I can't do it. You know how I feel about stuff like that."

"You'll do it out of loyalty to me. This is a life-and-death issue."

"Is he very handsome?"

"No, no. Very ugly." She opened her arms up wide so that they could both easily imagine how rare it was in the vast heavens around them to find a really magnificent and true ugliness.

Across the table Fiona stared at the ceiling. Her face shone out like a lighthouse at midnight. Sarah wondered if she had been listening to them.

"I'm going to the girls' room," she said to Robin and rose and crossed out into the hallway. She stood and looked around. In a minute, to her surprise, she saw what she was waiting for. Anthony Torelli, as unreliable and hungry as a highway robber, came striding towards her. His hair flamed red and his chains jingled loudly and his tight black jeans made her eyes water. He was followed by a band of thuggish young men who cursed and laughed and threw various objects across the air to one another. Anthony paid no attention to them or anything else. He sauntered indifferently onwards.

She stood there reading the lunch menu posted on the wall, her heart pounding in her chest, and, when he drew near, she pretended to trip and banged, smack, into him. Their books went flying every which way. She waited impatiently, as he looked her over. She waited for him to recognize her. He started with her toes and went slowly and appraisingly upwards. When he got to her face, he said, "Why don't you watch where you're going?"

She saw that he had no idea who she was. The sensation was nothing so simple as that of a sunburn or falling off a roof. It was complicated and confusing and embarrassing, just as she had always known it would be. If she had had to describe it, she would have said it was like suddenly finding oneself on the streets of a crowded and barbaric foreign city with neither compass, nor money, nor a stitch of clothing on.

Anthony seemed to notice nothing of her discomfort. Or perhaps he saw it and took it for granted. In any case, he bent down and gathered up his books and, without another word, sauntered on.

That afternoon she went to visit Robin's grandmother in the nursing home. Sarah noted that the smell was just as Robin had said. It was a terrible, pungent stench of disinfectant and decay and cabbage. She held her breath for as long as she could and then took a little gasp of air and then held her breath again.

An attendant pointed out an old lady sitting with a tangle of purple yarn in her lap. She was trying to wind it up but was only making it worse. Sarah sat down next to her quietly and introduced herself. "Hello, Mrs. Binder, I'm Robin's friend, Sarah."

"This is murder," the old woman said without looking up.

"I brought you some flowers, Mrs. Binder."

"Don't exaggerate." She eyed the flowers from the side of her head like a bird.

Sarah brought the flowers back to herself uncertainly. "I'm a friend of your granddaughter's, Mrs. Binder. A friend of Robin's."

The old woman turned to her at last but was unable to find her and looked instead at something farther away, something long ago and suspended in the air. "Hello," she said and smiled. The smile was a big success, drawing attention to her ears and a papery white light behind her skin. Oldness, Sarah thought. The ball of yarn lay still in the old lady's lap. "My friend Eleanor?" she asked.

"No, Mrs. Binder, my name is Sarah."

"Come here," she said.

Sarah got right up out of the chair and knelt down in front of the old lady.

"Why did you come?"

"Your granddaughter Robin wanted to come, but she had a very pressing errand, so I came in her place."

"Liar."

The flowers whispered in Sarah's lap. She looked around the room boldly. It was not a pleasant sight, all the crumpled bodies in wheelchairs, the vacant stares, the little moans and murmurings. Yet she had the curious impression of some undefined and maybe dangerous energy poised and building itself up for a leap or a pounce. She looked back at Robin's grandmother.

"How are ya?" Mrs. Binder said.

Well, she thought, here would be a good place to test it out on the air. Who will judge or give a hoot? She took another deep breath (she was getting used to the smell). "I'm in love," she declared.

Mrs. Binder seemed to ponder this. "Ice. You wanna get gum out of a rug, you have to use ice." She held out her hand imperiously. Her hand was small, strong, bluish, and dirty. The little gold wedding band looked out of place to Sarah. She put the flowers in her arms. Robin's grandmother brought them up to her face so hard she knocked some petals off, and they fluttered into her lap with the yarn. She looked at Sarah coquettishly over her bouquet. "You're a sweet one. Always were." Her whole body trembled with laughter, and she strained downwards to kiss the kneeling Sarah. Sarah stretched up to help her. The kiss slipped uncertainly off her chin.

"Here, let me help you with this," Sarah said and took the yarn from the old lady's lap and sat down with it. "Maybe Robin will come on Sunday."

"Onions?"

"No. Sunday."

"Delicious."

An old man rose from his chair and floated over to them. He looked at Sarah, and his face broke up into a big smile, another big deal. "Hello! Hello! I haven't seen you in about a hundred years."

"Give him two dollars," Robin's grandmother whispered.

Sarah touched him timidly on the shoulder, and he floated away again easily.

Now Sarah tried one more time. She looked around the room bravely. A tiny lady in a wheelchair looked at her and said, "Please! Bring me my hat." When Sarah did not answer, she began to sing, in a frail, quavering voice, like a bird inside a hedge, "Do re mi fa sol la ti do!"

"Listen, Eleanor," Robin's grandmother whispered, "we've got to make a plan."

Sarah looked at her and gave a little cry of dismay. Mrs. Binder was pulling her lower lip out thoughtfully while she tried to come up with a plan. Sarah saw that if her motive in coming here had been to get a glimpse of the end of the line, to take a peek at the underlying mortal ordinariness of things, she was out of luck. There was going to be no getting hold of a trustworthy beginning or ending to the story. Wherever you were was always going to be the middle of things, and the middle of things was always going to take your breath away.

The old lady let go of her lip and took Sarah's hand. "You've always been my best friend, Eleanor." She looked into Sarah's eyes. "Let's meet in Asbury Park at three. And wear your blue coat. It's your best color."

Sarah smiled uneasily. Now, Mrs. Binder leaned forward and grabbed her wrist and brought it to her nose. "That's some perfume you got on."

Sarah sniffed at her wrist, but if there was some smell there, it was lost in the overpowering air of the nursing home. Not knowing what else to do, she returned the ball of wool to Mrs. Binder's lap and rose.

"Three o'clock," Mrs. Binder said.

"Three o'clock." Sarah nodded solemnly and headed for the door.

To the wedding she wore a yellow dress. It happened one clear, cold morning, late in the spring. Robin had gotten her parents to agree to the marriage by convincing them she was pregnant, which she was not.

Afterwards they all descended to a huge, windowless dining room to eat and dance. Sarah was seated at the bride's table and watched Robin cautiously. Robin was dressed in white and was horribly pale. She kept drinking the too-sweet wine and paid no attention when someone let doves go from a wicker cage. "Nice-looking boy," people whispered of the groom, and, when he asked her to dance, Sarah—witless, embarrassed, full of intimations of her own perpetual lack of poise—accepted. She tried to ignore his sinister, doll-blue eyes and tiny, gold mustache while they twirled clumsily around and around.

Once she saw Fred and Fiona go by. They were dancing too slowly, several steps behind the beat, but he was as handsome as the Fourth of July and Fiona wore a plain blue dress, which, for some reason, suited her perfectly. She waved at Sarah. "Relax," Martin said to her.

"What are you saying? How can you say such a thing?" Sarah replied.

"It's easy," he said. "Watch how I do it. I'll say it again. Watch." He mouthed the word slowly.

"Do you know what you've done? She's very, very difficult."

"The moment I saw her in that tree, I knew she was the one."

"In trees, well, yeah. But you have to see the thing in a broader perspective."

"She has only the nicest things to say about you."

She stared at him in disgust. Prig. Murderer.

"Take it easy. What you need is a good massage and your back cracked." He poked at her spine.

"Don't."

They continued to dance, looking over from time to time at Robin, who seemed a distant point traveling slowly and constantly away from them at one of those slow speeds of light into outer space.

When they sat down she was gone. Sarah ate another piece of white wedding cake slowly, swallowing the little silver balls whole. Suddenly Selma appeared from behind a great pink-and-white bowl of chrysanthemums and said, "Robin is asking for you. She wasn't feeling well and is across the hall lying down."

She was lying down on the floor with her face over a wastepaper basket, throwing up. Sarah fell on her knees beside her and held back her damp, dark hair. A little shaft of sunlight from a small, high window fell across them and onto the carpet. Robin groaned and asked for a tissue. When she had wiped her mouth, she asked Sarah if she would ever forgive her.

"For what?" Sarah asked stiffly, and Robin ignored her and said, "And will you always be my friend?"

"You know that I will."

Robin groaned and threw up again. Afterwards Sarah stretched out on the carpet beside her. They lay quietly for a while listening to the band playing from across the hall.

Sarah could not begin to imagine getting married. Lying there in the sun, she tried the idea on for size, and it hung hugely about her, white and, in its stiff folds, giving off a fragrance she had never smelled before. At last, because she could neither stop her amazement nor stifle the words, she said, "But how could you have done it? Really, Robin, I cannot believe your mother is so bad that you needed to go to these lengths."

Robin lifted her head and looked at her in surprise. "My mother? You think I did this because of my mother?"

"Well," Sarah said, embarrassed, "didn't you?"

Robin was silent for a long while. Then she groaned and said, "This had nothing to do with my mother." She lowered her face to the floor again.

When Robin's new husband entered the room, pleased with himself and full of concern, Sarah left quietly.

Fiona was out in the hallway. "Sarah," she said smiling. "I was looking for you."

"You were?"

"Yes, I have something I wanted to return to you."

Sarah watched her, mystified, as she fumbled through her purse.

"Here," she said, at last. "Your nickel."

Sarah took the coin and stared at it uncomprehendingly.

"Don't you remember?"

"No," she said, although she did.

Fiona smiled. "Well, put it in a safe place. That's my advice."

At around eight o'clock that evening, there they were again, the two sponges from outer space. She had been sitting at her desk, reading, when her room was suddenly permeated with the smell of blue cheese. She went to her window, sniffing, and looked out. They were perched in the dogwood tree like a pair of nightingales. Once they had her attention, they switched to another smell, a smell that seemed completely unfamiliar and cosmic, yet reminded her of something she could not quite place. It might have been the scent of grass on a summer morning, then, although she saw that it was not, that it was something even greener and more foolishly hopeful than that, she understood that they knew exactly who she was and were glad to see her. She was careful not to speak, not to make any noise that would frighten them. She studied them carefully for clues to what exactly their relationship might be. Now that she looked closely, she saw that they were not exactly the same color. The larger one was the color of the sky on a clear afternoon, and the other was more the color of a certain blue-gray marble she had kept in a shoe box under her bed when she was eight. Were they lovers, or maybe brother and sister, who had traveled together this great distance to see the sights? Were they parent and child, or just friends? Or maybe they represented some entirely new and extraplanetary form of partnership which people on earth knew nothing about yet.

They seemed to be waiting, maybe inviting her to come along, offering her an opportunity to unravel some of the mysteries of the universe. She wanted very much to give them a gift of some sort. She thought of the lucky nickel, then wondered if they would really appreciate such a thing, or even need it. So, instead, she rummaged around in her dresser until she found her old souvenir balsam pillow from Cape Cod. She held it out, and the smaller sponge hopped over to the window and tugged it gently from her hand with a tiny blue paw, which she hadn't spotted before. There was no need to say a word. The sponge took off into the air followed by the bigger one, and there Sarah sat, watching the sky, long after they were gone from sight.

3

HOUSE ON FIRE

BUT HOW HAD a mockingbird gotten into the room? It sailed easily from the window to the bed—the white bars under its wings flickering boldly—and perched upon the alarm clock. It was inconsiderate and ridiculously full of itself, like any mockingbird just after dawn. It danced upon the alarm clock and trilled and fluted and called. But, good God, give me a break, Sarah thought. What does it want? She was about to rise up and swat at it when she remembered, just in the nick of time, that it was her birthday, her twenty-first, and she lay there instead right on this side of sleep, behind the thin, sparked-up darkness of her eyelids, and attempted to foresee what was in store for her.

On your birthday it was still possible that someone who cared for you would undertake to know your heart's desire and bring it to you. For instance, when she was seven her parents had given her a bicycle. She had almost lost consciousness. They had to hold her up under the armpits and fan her with a newspaper. Even now she could see this bicycle perfectly clearly in her mind's eye. It was blue with silver trim and had a loud and clanging, cupcake-shaped bell. She had just mounted it and begun to ride it down the hill towards campus with the mockingbird on the front handlebars when the alarm clock went off and she opened her eyes to find the early spring light pouring into Jerome's room.

Sarah had fallen in love three times since she had been away at college, and each time had been worse than the last. This was how it was with love. It was a traveler from over the seas and out of the woods, and each time you welcomed it humbly and politely and gave what there was in the house and expected—it was true—everything. Its treachery was astounding, the way it fell on you with its terrible light and blinded you and filled the house with its gruesome smell of scorched flesh and hair.

She peered nearsightedly around Jerome's room. He was a theater major, but his room always put her in mind of a pirate ship come to grief upon the rocks. All the crew had certainly drowned in the storm, but, left behind and strewn about, were, first, the more ordinary things, like hundreds of pairs of underwear and single socks, and, then, the capes and cummerbunds, the pistols and wooden swords, the masks and hats with feathers, the shoes with buckles and a papier-mâché crown encrusted with glass emeralds.

She lifted the covers and stared at Jerome's body, which was pale and thin and highly strung, as if, even in sleep, he was ready to jump up and pretend to be somebody else. He opened his eyes and, for a moment, frowned at the ceiling, appearing to wonder what this was between him and the bright blue sky. Then he was standing up on the mattress in one quick jump, surveying his room cautiously. She stood up next to him and squinted and tried to see what it was he saw.

Jerome sniffed the air worriedly. "It smells like Tuesday. But that can't be right, can it? It's got to be Monday, right?"

All the hats and feathers and swords in the room held their breath. If he remembered her birthday, then she would be able to forgive him everything—that he was always late, that he promised to call her and then forgot, that he sometimes stared at her with a strangely cold and vegetable gaze, as if he'd never had a mother, as if he'd somehow gotten lost from his home planet and sailed through the stars until he'd landed here on earth, without the faintest idea where you could turn for comfort, or any expectation of comfort, and was now trying to make his way on the merest shoestring of invention and bravado. She examined him closely now, but he didn't appear to have the faintest idea it was her birthday. "What does Tuesday smell like?" she asked him at last.

"Well, you know . . . ," he said uncertainly, "like trouble. Like that little trickle of smoke that comes right before the whole house goes up in flames."

At this moment a strange golden face came into view over Jerome's shoulder. It was a large face with indistinct features, about the size of a dinner plate. It seemed to be eyeing her critically, as if it, too, questioned the prudence of her being here at this time, in this place. She took a step forward to get a better look at this intruder and realized it was only the sun, just now rising over the third-floor windowsill and shining into the room.

"What time is it, I wonder?" Jerome asked.

"It's eight forty."

"My God!" He leaped into the air. "Eight forty! I'm going to be late for my class!"

In three minutes he was dressed and racing out the door. "Meet me at one in the cafeteria!" he yelled back to her and vanished.

For a moment then, she stood alone in the room and imagined one o'clock in the cafeteria, because that was how it was with love, you skipped the rest of your life and just went right on to anticipating the next meeting with your beloved. Of course, she'd hardly be able to hear him when she got there because of her heart pounding in her ears, and she'd hardly be able to see him because of all that stuff that filled the air whenever she met him in a public place—gold dust, was it? or pollen? or maybe the smoke from leveled and burning villages.

It's my birthday, she thought self-pityingly. What would it take to feel at ease in the world? And then it came to her with unexpected force—as if a stranger had just stepped up to her and ripped her coat open, sending all her buttons skittering across the floor, as if a wind had come up from nowhere and blown her hat all the way down the street—it came to her that she didn't have to meet him in the cafeteria at one if she didn't want to. There was no law. She shivered and stepped off the mattress and dressed as quickly as she could and thought, with rising excitement, that she was still young—surely she might grow another inch or two, or find her old blue bike, or figure out just what it was she was doing here, who had sent her and what it was a person was expected to get done. She gathered her things together, and, holding her breath, she slipped out the door.

Out here in the rising light of the spring morning, she saw no sign of happiness yet, but surely the possibility of it lurked somewhere nearby. She decided she would walk home and make herself a birthday breakfast. There was, indeed, a small mischievous wind rising up from somewhere, looking to blow dust in her eyes, to send the last winter leaves dancing around her feet. She reached her block and turned the corner. She was searching the high branches of the trees—an old habit—when she noticed a a small, dark-haired boy coming towards her down the sidewalk. He was walking backwards.

When he reached her he seemed to realize, with some sixth sense, that she was there. He circled around her without a pause and continued on down the street. She turned to watch him and was intrigued to see that at the corner he had a mighty collision with another little boy, who was coming from the opposite direction, also traveling backwards. They seemed delighted by this encounter and shook hands in such wild and mutual congratulation that they almost pulled each other over.

She turned and walked on until she reached the front of the house where she shared an apartment with another student. She opened the gate and was startled to see a strange man going through the garbage. He was hunting so intently, and looked so odd, she saw immediately that he must be quite mad. He was young and wore, unbuttoned, over his bare chest, a red satin bowling jacket. Over his arm, as if he were imitating a waiter, was draped what appeared to be a white linen napkin. His blond hair was tied into several little pigtails. He did not, at first, notice her but went on intently digging through the garbage.

"Oh, oh, oh, what has my conniving mother done with her?" he muttered. She made as wide a berth around him as she could, but, as she passed, he looked up and fixed her with a perverse and glittering eye. "Ah, the birthday girl" she was sure she heard him say, and she broke into a terrified trot and hurried up the steps and into the house.

When she opened the door to her apartment, she heard splashing and low laughter. Her roommate was in the bathtub with her boyfriend. When they did this at night, they burned candles to make it more romantic, and the wax dripped all over the floor.

"I want to use the bathroom," she said, knocking loudly on the door. "When will you be finished?"

They consulted, giggling. "Well, we still haven't washed our hair. Come back in ten minutes."

"For God's sakes," she said.

She went into the kitchen and made herself a deluxe omelet with cream cheese and black olives and a bagel with raspberry jelly. She had just put her plate on the table when she heard a knock on the door.

She looked through the peephole and saw her brother, who was here in the graduate department working on a thesis in biology or physics or something—she could never quite figure it out.

"What do you want?" she said to him crossly as she opened the door.

He eyed her critically. "It's your birthday, isn't it? I've brought you your heart's desire." He handed her a shoe box with some holes punched in the top, then eased his way around her and made for the kitchen.

"Hey."

He sat down at the table and looked at her breakfast happily. He was so handsome it made her eyes water. Though handsome was not really the right word, she thought, since handsome conjured up the image of someone completed and a pleasure to look at. Fred's looks had the disturbing quality of an animal and a human traveling somewhere together, perhaps a man and a camel crossing the desert on some tremendous journey. He took a generous bite of her bagel.

"Well, aren't you going to open it?" he said with his mouth full, indicating the box in her hand.

She opened the box cautiously and found a small, disgruntled frog blinking up at her appraisingly. "You brought me a frog?"

He looked immensely pleased with himself. "Made him from scratch."

"What? What do you mean?"

Fred smiled and finished off the bagel before answering. "Well, you know that grant I got last spring? The one about exploring the origins of life? Yeah, well, the other night I set up a test tube with a tablespoon of sand and a pinch of dust from under my bed—sterilized, of course—and I poured some synthesized seawater over it. Then I chilled it to what I thought might be the typical earth temperature on a night about a hundred million years ago. Then I took this light condenser I invented—it works sort of like a magnifying glass, you know—and set it so the collecting end pointed at the Polestar and the condensing end pointed into the test tube. Then I forgot about it and went to eat my pesto salad and cranberry juice, which I'd taken out from the health food restaurant.

"The next thing I know, this weird bouncing vibration shakes the room, and I turn around and see that the test tube has exploded. All the stuff that was in it was shimmying and sliding and running off the edges of the table, and then the room went pitch black and when the electricity came back on there was this big mess of sand and glass and water and this little frog hopping around in the middle of it."

Sarah was certain that he had made this story up, just because it was her birthday, just because he wanted to annoy her. She glared at him silently.

"Look," he said and leaned forward as if he would kiss her, but then he pointed to his eyebrows. "Scorched, you see?" And it was true, right in the middle of each one there was a large bald spot. "You got any more of these bagels?"

"I don't believe a word of this."

He sighed. "Of course it doesn't prove a thing and it's impossible to repeat because this crazy woman who's in love with me, and thinks she's going to get me to fall in love with her by sneaking into my room and cleaning things up once a week, snuck in that very night while I was in the lab and not only vacuumed up all the dust under my bed but also threw out the vacuum cleaner bag."

"Listen, Fred, I've got some things to do. Maybe you'd better mosey along now."

"How's Jerome?" Fred asked brightly, and picked up her fork and began to eat her omelet.

"I'm through with him."

Fred stopped eating for a moment and looked at her with interest.

Sarah returned his stare coolly. "It's my birthday and on your birthday you can take your birthday energy condenser and blow up all the superfluous crap that's impeding your progress."

"Really?" He pursed his wide and mobile mouth and looked a little thoughtful. "You think maybe that's what Fiona did?"

The thought of Fiona made Sarah sad. "I don't know," she said. "At first I didn't, but then I thought you and Fiona were meant for each other."

He laughed. "You think there's a guarantee you get the one meant for you? Maybe some people are only destined to get the one meant for them for an afternoon. Or maybe some people have several people meant for them. Maybe that girl standing out there under the awning is only one of many, besides Fiona, destined to temporarily complete my soul."

"What girl?"

Fred didn't answer, and, at this moment, the frog made a loud sound somewhere between a croak and a belch. Fred lifted the lid and stroked him tenderly. "Anyway, I'm pretty sure that if we're here for anything it's not for love, although I believe Fiona did not agree with me on this."

Sarah frowned at him, distracted. "Oh? And what do you think we're here for?"

"Oh, you know—to search and understand, to stick our noses into the secrets of the universe, to figure out where time came from and where it goes, how we arrived here on this ball of dirt and why we can't stop ourselves from laying waste to all its treasures. Love, I think, is simply an engine to keep us going."

"Maybe you just don't like women."

"Whaddaya mean?" he said indignantly. "Of course I like women. Women are my favorites."

Sarah decided she did not want to delve into the implications of this right now. It was, after all, her birthday.

Fred replaced the lid on the box, walked over to the front window, and peered out onto the street from behind the curtain.

Sarah stood beside him and peered out also, looking for the man with the waiter's napkin in the red satin bowling jacket, but he was gone.

"There she is under that awning."

"Who?"

"The new girl. This new girl who's in love with me. She's sort of plain with brown hair."

Sarah looked where he pointed and saw a ravishing-looking redhead who did, indeed, seem to be staring heartbrokenly at Sarah's window, who gave the impression of being barefoot and hatless in the snow, who looked like she had never even heard of spring, like a pair of purple finches could nest in her hair and raise their young and teach them to fly around the top of her head singing "Hallelujah!" and she wouldn't notice a thing.

Sarah, who had stood so many times in just such an attitude, wanted to weep at the sight. "Don't be stupid, Fred. She's waiting for a bus. Go away. You're annoying me. It's my birthday."

Fred laughed and put on his jacket. "I'll bring over a tank for the frog tomorrow," he said, and then he was gone.

Sarah sighed and went back to try the bathroom. She knocked loudly. "Who is it?" they asked, giggling.

"Oh, for God's sakes, who do you think it is?"

"Listen, why don't you just come in?"

This was their challenge. She ripped the door open and was brought up short. They sat facing each other, bolt upright, sweet as babies. They had their knees drawn up in front of them and were so pudgy, and wedged so tightly, they could not move.

"Aren't you cold?" she asked, unable to stop herself, for the moment, from feeling concern. Only their lower halves were in the water.

But they simply smiled back at her, they were so happy with each other and so happy to have Sarah in the bathroom as living witness that they were wedged tightly in the bathtub together.

She closed the shower curtain and peed. Then she went over to the sink and washed her face irritably. They opened the shower curtain and looked out at her.

"Wouldn't it be a lot more efficient to bathe separately? You can hardly move in there."

She could have sworn they glanced at each other and suppressed a look of pity. "How's Jerome?" they asked.

"He's history," she said without a quiver. She dried her face and left, slamming the door behind her.

Fred had eaten all of her breakfast, so she made herself a bowl of cereal, and, as she sat down to eat it, the phone rang.

She sighed and went to pick it up, carrying her bowl with her. "Hello?"

"Happy birthday, my darling."

"Hello, Robin." Sarah could hear loud sounds of traffic and horns blowing in the background.

"I'm not going to be able to talk for long. I don't have much change."

"Where are you? What's all that noise?"

"I'm in a phone booth. I didn't want Martin to know I was calling you. Is it spring there? I think it's spring here. I see a bunch of twigs and ripped up newspaper sticking out of a hole in the streetlight up there. It looks like a nest. Oh-oh, there's a very strange person going through the garbage cans in the alley. He keeps looking at me like he knows me."

"What's wrong with old Martin?" Sarah asked hopefully. That nature not only allowed but encouraged your dearest friends to fall in love with people you couldn't stand had come as a terrible blow to Sarah.

"Nothing, nothing's *wrong* with him. It's just that he's decid-ed to take another wife."

"You mean he wants a divorce?" Sarah asked, delighted.

"No, no, he says he still loves me, but that my influence is so dark and tidal and brooding, we need to bring in a counter-balancing force, and he says I'm too hairy. He went up to the ashram this weekend and talked to the Master about it, and they decided he should take a second wife."

Sarah laughed. "But that's not legal."

"Oh, Sarah, what does Martin care for the law? The law is just another veil of illusion. He's looking for someone young and blonde and hairless. For all I know, he's found her already." Here Robin, who found crying difficult, began to cry in a strangely nasal, panting way. Then she broke off and said, "Oh-oh, here comes this weird guy. Hold on." She spoke to the side. "Yes," she said, "yes, I'll be off pretty soon, buddy. This is an important phone call." Then she spoke into the phone again.

"Listen, Sarah, I sent you something for your birthday. You're gonna love it. Did you get it yet? It's pretty big. I sent it to your campus postbox."

"Why don't you just leave him, Robin? I mean it. What do you have to lose?"

"Listen," Robin whispered. "I try to leave him. I do. But I get as far as this particular corner, and then something always happens. Once I tripped and broke my ankle, and once my wallet just flew up out of my purse and fell down into the sewer grating. Last time a manhole cover exploded and they roped off the sidewalk and wouldn't let anybody cross the street. Martin says we've been closely related to each other in each of our last eleven reincarnations and we still have big stuff to work through. Oh-oh, here comes this guy again. Listen, buddy, I told you I'd be off in a couple of minutes. Just hold your horses. You should see him," Robin whispered. "He's got on this red cardboard New Year's Eve hat and this red silk jacket."

"What? A red jacket?"

"Yeah. Hey, wow. There's a little tiny bird looking out of the hole in the lamppost! It's screeching at me. Maybe it thinks I'm its mother. I bet you'd know what kind of bird it was. God, I wish you were here. If I could have one wish in the world it would be to have you near me to tell me the names of birds and stuff. Did you get anything nice for your birthday?"

"Fred gave me a frog."

"Good old Fred. Is he still seeing that dip, Fiona?"

"No, she broke up with him. But he's got a couple of new girls following him around."

"Listen, tell him if he wants me to bump anybody off, I'll do it for him cheap. I'm getting very good at bumping people off, very subtle. I'll make it look like an accident."

"I wish you'd cut out that line of fantasy, Robin. It's not all that funny."

Robin laughed. "What about Jerome? Did he get you any-thing?"

"I ditched Jerome."

"Are you serious?"

"What's the point of such misery?"

"You said whenever he came in the room the furniture lifted off the floor. You said whenever you kissed him it was like sticking your mouth on an electric light socket."

"I'm through with him."

"What does he say about this?"

"He doesn't know yet. I'm supposed to meet him at one, but I'm not going to show up. Let him figure it out for himself. My God, he didn't even remember it was my birthday."

"Oh no, I don't believe it. This guy just pulled an old mop out of a garbage can and he's mopping the sidewalk. Here he comes. He's headed right this way. I guess I better go. Have a happy birthday. I'll call you next week." She hung up.

Sarah got her books and her jacket and, at the last minute, picked up the shoe box with the frog in it. As she closed the door behind her and stepped out into the sunlight, it went "gar-ruump" appreciatively and jumped hard against the lid of the box.

On her way to the English-Philosophy building, Sarah looked through the glass doors into the cafeteria. She imagined how it would be when Jerome showed up at one and found she wasn't there. How he would keep looking around absently as if he had lost something, and when he realized that it was not his umbrella but Sarah—Sarah, who had seen through all his most notable performances and evasions and forgiven him patiently and tried to teach him the way real, truehearted humans should behave—then he would go dashing around the campus grab-bing people by the collar and demanding to know if they'd seen her, and when he found her in the library she'd spit in his eye.

She went to her class and sat in the top row of the lecture room and looked soberly out the window into the spring. She was no longer in love. The spring opened up quickly, like one room into the next, and each room was wider than the last, but the last room was so big you could no longer see the walls in the distance. Flags flew, flowers unfolded, birds came and went, and the clouds, slow and stately as dirigibles dressed in white tea cozies, sailed across the sky. If there were laws governing all this, she was above them. She watched the spring with terrible calm. The professor could have been giving his recipe for meat loaf for all she heard.

On her way to the library she passed the cafeteria again, and it occurred to her that, perhaps, the courteous thing to do would be to go in there and tell him that it was all over. At this point what possible danger could there be? She lifted her chin and pulled up her shoulders. She made herself as tall as she could manage and opened the heavy glass doors.

Inside, she put her books on a table, then went and got herself a sandwich and salad and sat down. It was five to one. After a few minutes, two of Jerome's friends showed up and asked her deferentially if she was expecting him soon. Jerome had many admirers, and they treated her with grudging courtesy.

"I was expecting him at one."

Clearly the grim and threatening way she said this made them nervous. They glanced at each other and sat down, uninvited, with their salads.

Jerome did not show up at one o'clock.

As time passed, the air in the cafeteria gathered as if the members of an invisible orchestra were slowly straggling in. Sarah imagined the suspenseful pong and ping of instruments being removed from their cases, the disorderly breaking up of silence that precedes the music.

Jerome's friends were trying to discuss Chekhov, but there was something in the air, she could see, that disturbed them, too. They began and then began again, peering around the room uncertainly.

At one twenty she opened the textbook on the top of her pile and fiercely read through one hundred years of modern European history.

At a quarter to two, all the furniture in the room lifted several inches off the floor. She glared at it furiously until it dropped back down. Jerome was standing in front of the table. He had several more friends in tow.

"Hello!" he said heartily, singling out no one. She gave him an icy smile, but he didn't notice a thing. He was carrying his usual dog-eared pile of notebooks and scripts and, in addition, a large brown grocery bag. He put these down on the table and went to get some food. When he got back and sat down, she would give him the news. A few minutes later he came back with a bowl of rice pudding and a large root beer. In the past she would have focused all her mental powers on willing him to sit next to her, but now she was busy nerving herself to open her mouth and tell him it was all over. She was surprised when he sat down next to her and offered her a sip of root beer. She decided she had better wait. She squinted at him, trying to blur him into the background with the orange booths and the yellow wallpaper. He took a mouthful of rice pudding, then leaned over and toyed with her watchband, which was loose on her thin wrist. She shuddered gently.

Without letting go of her wrist, he turned to someone sitting next to him and asked, "How did the audition go? Did you use the breathing I suggested?"

They all adored him. He was generous and gifted, without

a trace of conceit. He could make himself cry at a moment's notice by concentrating on a tennis ball and pretending it was a dog that had just gotten run over by a truck.

Perhaps it would be better to take him out in the hallway and give him the news there to avoid a great public display of emotion. Yes, that would be the polite thing to do.

He let go of her watchband and seemed to forget about her. He leaned forward to talk to the girl across the table.

"Why are you so late?" Sarah yelled before she could stop herself. He turned to stare at her in surprise. So did everyone else. She blushed deeply.

"Am I late?"

She looked around at their audience and laughed.

"Didn't I say one o'clock?" he asked. He picked up a book of matches and toyed with it nervously.

"You did."

"Well, what time is it now?"

She didn't answer him. There was a large clock mounted on the wall facing him. He lit a match and stared at it distractedly, as if he wasn't sure what it was. When it burnt down to his fingers, he gave a yelp and dropped it.

"It's ten to two," she told him.

He looked at her in surprise. "But, Sarah, A, number one, my movement class ran late. Then, B, number two, I couldn't find the key to my locker. I went all over the gym looking for it, but in the end I had to get the janitor to break the lock open, and then the problem was I had all this valuable stuff in there that I couldn't just leave, so I had to find something to pack it up in. Then, C, number three"—he paused and looked around to make sure everybody was listening—"on my way over here it turned out that the physics building had been roped off because they had a big explosion in there. There was green smoke coming out of the chimney and I had to go the long way around and, as I was passing by the back entrance, your brother came running out, all covered with ashes and slime and grabbed me by the ears and kissed me. Then he ran back into the building. All of these things took a little time, so I knew I was going to be a bit late, but I didn't realize how late. Please forgive me, dear heart."

She could see that now that he had gotten to this point, he was enjoying himself immensely. He was enjoying the thought of how forces beyond your control could always be counted on for taking responsibility out of your hands. He enjoyed calling her "dear heart," and he enjoyed how happy it made everyone to have this opportunity to watch this performance. She wanted only to have the scales fall from her eyes, to have the seven veils of illusion ripped away so she could see past love into the daylight.

She squinted at him, again, and tried to turn him into wallpaper. She could tell he still didn't have the faintest idea it was her birthday.

"What's the matter with your eyes?" he asked curiously. "Why are you making that pruny face?"

The frog leaped against the lid of the box and croaked loudly. "Keep your pants on," she said to it. She picked up the box and her books and marched from the room.

She stopped at the gym and put her books in a locker, then headed up the stairs and out into the sunshine. She walked across the campus, past the dorms, through the swamp, and stopped for a moment at the edge of the woods. Then she entered among the trees. The light inside was wild and shifting. She found the path she was looking for and began to follow it. After a while it started up the mountain. There was a small breeze, and she watched all the movement it caused among the leaves. The woods seemed strangely silent. She did not have far to go before the path forked. She went to the right and soon came to a wooden log laid over a rushing brook.

She stopped and put the shoe box down on the ground and opened the lid. "Here we are," she said. "It's your lucky day."

The frog blinked up at her ungraciously. He was, she thought, a peculiarly unfroglike gold color—no doubt the result of the terrible experience he had been through.

She picked up a little stick and poked him gingerly. "Let's move it," she said. He bunched his muscles up, and, with one effortless leap, he was out of the box and in the brook. He sat for a moment, an inch deep in water, and turned and gave her a judicious stare. Then he took off, heading upstream.

Sarah went back to the fork in the path and decided she might as well hike for a while. She took the other path now and headed on up the little mountain. Near the top it began to get warmer, which didn't seem quite right to her. She took off her jacket and tied it around her waist, and when she lifted her arms she felt cool beads of sweat skid down her sides. She began the ascent again. The incline, to her surprise, suddenly became much steeper. The light, also, was behaving peculiarly. It seemed to take on a certain substance of its own, shooting above her and across the path in indiscernible shapes. She heard a sound a little above her and to the right, and, when she looked up, she thought she saw something white flash through the undergrowth.

She stopped for a moment, watching, but whatever it was did not reappear. Overhead, a blue jay began to call raucously. It called again and again, and, because it sounded so familiar, like someone reeling out a creaking laundry line, she was reassured. The smell of the mountain laurel, a sweet, crushed smell, rolled invitingly down from the top of the mountain. "There is nothing like a little exercise to clear the mind," she said to herself.

When she was almost at the top, when she could see the final dark ridge of evergreens above her, she noticed that her shoelace had come untied. She bent down and tied it, and, when she stood up again, there was a naked man standing on the path about thirty feet up ahead of her.

"Oh-oh," she said and began immediately to descend the mountain. She didn't look back and went slipping and sliding down the path, constantly having to break herself with her heels, her toes, in order to keep from falling.

She expected to hear him breathing heavily beside her at any moment, but when she finally looked around he was still standing motionless on the spot where she first saw him.

She turned hurriedly and dove into a thicket, which soon turned into heavy forest. Branches slashed her face, and thorns caught at her knee socks. She knew she was lost, but in her panic didn't give a hoot. At the end of what might have been minutes or what might have been hours, she came to the edge of a large clearing. The light stopped shifting, and the edges and outlines of all things became ominously sharp. Not just one bird sang, but hundreds of birds sang. The naked man stood in the middle of the clearing, looking a little impatient. She felt entirely betrayed. It was, after all, her birthday. She found she could not move. He was a large, golden-haired man, young, wearing silver spectacles, and whether evil looking or simply mad as a hatter it was impossible to tell. She tried to turn and leave, but the process seemed overwhelming, the way it sometimes does in dreams. He held up his hand irritably and indicated that he wanted her to stay where she was.

As he drew near her, he took his spectacles off and fiddled with them nervously. When he was right in front of her, he put them back on but then, immediately, made a face of annoyance and took them off again. A fingerprint perhaps. Seemingly from nowhere, he drew out a large, white linen napkin and wiped them off. Then he put them back on.

"You're entitled to a wish. Any wish," he said.

"What?"

"One wish. Payment for services rendered. For hospitality and kindness to gods disguised as beggars."

She stared at him.

"I'm perfectly serious."

She had no idea what to do; if she turned and ran, this might provoke him to go after her, but she also knew from fairy tales that you had to be a fool to take such an offer as he was offering, or at least to ask for anything very specific. She would end up with a pudding on her nose, or something much worse. He stared at her in a way she didn't like, as if he was not so much biding his time as restraining some enormous and treacherous energy. She thought quickly. "World peace, I wish for world peace."

He looked at her with a sort of grudging admiration and shook his head. "I'm sorry," he said, "it has to be something personal."

"Well then," she said, casting about wildly, "give me my heart's desire."

As soon as the words were out of her mouth, she thought, There, that's it, I'm done for. But he merely stood there frowning.

"All right. I'll do my best. Turn around please."

She certainly did not want to turn her back on this person, but neither did she in any way want to invite his anger. She turned around slowly and waited for him to pull an ax or something out of the bushes. After, perhaps, a minute, when nothing had happened, she sneaked a look behind her. He was gone.

* * *

She had no trouble finding her way down the mountain now, but all the time she kept looking behind her and around her anxiously. When she reached the bottom, the spring wind swept the last bits of the dead winter down the sidewalks, and tumbled little knots of students across the lawns, and seemed to blow wide the spaces between one thing and another.

The campus post office was here at the outskirts, and she paused uneasily outside it, then took a deep breath and went in. In her mailbox was a birthday card from her parents and a notice telling her to pick up a package at the front window. She approached the window slowly, then shoved the notice across the counter. The clerk disappeared for a minute, then returned with a long, narrow box, such as roses might have been transported in. Her heart jumped. Had Jerome remembered her birthday after all? She undid the brown wrapping and opened the box and found inside an ominous and inexplicable object. It seemed to be a gourd, bulbous at one end and, at the other end, tapered and curved like an umbrella handle. The handle part was painted bright red with orange and green dots, and on the rounded end was painted a vaguely familiar face, with horns and a green mustache, obviously meant to represent a devil of some sort. As Sarah picked it up gingerly to examine it, it made a pleasant swishing sound, as if it were filled with grains of rice. At the bottom of the box was a little card. Sarah lifted this up and read: "Dear Sweetie, Happy Birthday and felicitations of all sorts. I made this rattle expressly for you. It is meant to turn away the faces of most harmful spirits, so keep it near you at all times—love, Robin."

Sarah, looking at the devil face again, realized that it had exactly Martin's eyes and smug jaw. She was tickled at the thought of carrying this bulbous and noisy thing around with her wherever she went or at the notion that it could have anything to do with her heart's desire. She laughed, put it back in its box, and left the post office carrying it under her arm.

The spring made no comment but blew clear as a bell down the tree-lined pathways. She was on her own. As she walked past the gymnasium, she spotted her roommate up ahead, her hand clutched in her boyfriend's, her hair curling and bouncing like elflocks in the wind. When he touched her with his other hand and said something abusive, she looked up happily.

It wasn't until they had drawn close to Sarah that they noticed her. Then they smiled and waved wildly and bumped into each other as they tried to steer in her direction. Sarah expected to find them wrinkled and moist, but they were bundling across the sidewalk cheerfully, with smooth, similar baby faces. They stopped for a moment and said hello. Sarah was cold, suspecting that this was one more excuse to remind themselves that they were together, but they didn't notice. As they walked away, her roommate said something and her boyfriend replied, "Trained goldfish are smarter than you," and they laughed hysterically, rolling apart for a moment, then quickly pooling together again.

Sarah watched them turn the corner, then walked on. Suddenly, she stopped short. She was passing by one of the dorms, and there, in front of the trash cans, was a great heaped-up pile of miscellaneous items—clothes, records, books, a set of snare drums, a tape player. A sign propped against a pair of running shoes said, "NOTICE: Intending now to seek the path towards true inner peace, to reunite my soul with the light from which it has been sundered, I hereby divest myself of all worldly possessions and ask that you, the passerby, help me on my journey by taking some of this stuff and giving it a new and loving home. My deepest thanks." In the middle of the pile stood a blue bicycle exactly identical to the one she had received on her seventh birthday.

"My God." She giggled and wheeled it out gently. On the

front was the same wicker basket she remembered from years ago. She dropped the rattle and its box into the basket and slung her leg over the seat. The bike clicked and creaked but rolled along fairly serviceably. Could this be it, then, her heart's desire returned to her after all these years? She laughed again. From out of nowhere, two large, tail-waving dogs trotted towards her. One was golden and the other was black.

"Go away! Shoo!" she said, but they were not to be deterred. Affable yet highly dignified, they flanked her on either side and accompanied her to the Student Union building. Maybe they thought that she was a parade, or that she needed protection, or perhaps that, if left to her own devices, she would go astray. She did not argue with them anymore— they were, after all, large and unknown quantities—and as she rode along she felt herself growing light and optimistic, as if she and the bicycle, and maybe the dogs, too, were about to lift up without a bump from the pathway and set off over the trees. By the time she reached the bike rack, she was experiencing a most uncustomary general certainty that everything was going to be OK, that that which mattered would unveil itself at the right moment, that all the important things which had gotten themselves lost in the hind ends of time would get themselves found again and be none the worse for wear.

She was almost disappointed when a squirrel, thin and mangy from the long haul of winter, streaked past them, and the dogs seemed instantly to forget about her and raced off in hot pursuit. She had reached the gym.

She left the bike tilted rakishly against the bike rack and went down into the basement to retrieve her books.

She approached the corridor where the lockers were, humming "Happy Birthday to You" to herself, and found Jerome sitting on the bench with his back to her. She stood there and stared at him and saw how little she knew of herself or of how the world worked and remembered that your heart's desire is that which you go out looking for, and, if it is to do its job of lighting the way for all that may come, it is not meant to be found. For it was but the work of a moment to see that she was no longer in love, that while she had gone up the mountain love had somehow been lifted quite neatly and surgically from her grasp. There was nothing left. She examined him—weak-kneed with loss—and saw how skinny and round shouldered he was, how his thin, blond ponytail nestled limply against his collar. She stared, and she squinted (it seemed rather dark in here, as if a bulb had blown out overhead), and then she closed her eyes and sniffed as hard as could, and, no matter what she did, absolutely nothing happened. She did not feel a thing. The earth did not shift or shudder. The furniture did not lift from the ground. There he was, just another ordinary turnip of a human being.

In a moment, Jerome turned and discovered her standing there, and she blushed hotly. What possible motive could nature have for making you fall in love with a person whose ears stuck out like that? How could she have been such a dupe? Whatever could have possessed her?

She took a step backwards and, as she did, was distracted by the gentle swish of the rattle in its box. She lifted the box up uncertainly and stared at it. Who knows the names of all the gods and demons who crowd the air? She lifted the lid off, took the rattle out, and shook it hard in front of her, at arm's length.

Jerome gave a little start, as if someone had stuck him with a pin. He looked around the room suspiciously, and, as he did, the veil or cloud that had been thrown across the light vanished, and all that had been taken away was instantly returned to her. Jerome's face shone out distantly like a Roman candle high in the night sky. She took another step backwards in alarm and shoved the rattle back into its box.

"Hello," he said. It was a deep-voiced, slow question.

She shuddered.

"I have something for you," he said. He reached behind him and pulled, from out of nowhere, a white paper bag. He handed it to her very ceremoniously, as if it contained the moon and some stars, or perhaps a magical beauty cream brought back at great risk from foreign parts.

She looked at it uncertainly, then reached out and took it. She opened it with great care and found inside a bakery cupcake with a pink candle stuck in the top.

"Happy birthday," he said.

She peered at him in bewilderment and groaned. Each succeeding hour in this day seemed more difficult and inscrutable. How beautiful he was, but, as always, how far away he hung, a little ball of fire flowering out in space. Even if she started out now, this very minute, she didn't see how she could possibly cross the thousand dark and windy miles that lay between them, or reach home safe and in time to find out what the true words are that wait to be said.

"I thought you'd forgotten," she said grudgingly.

He lifted an eyebrow and looked at her with ostentatious horror. Then he got down on one knee. "Since the day I first spotted you in that tower and climbed up your hair and through your window and into your arms, I haven't been able to get a single particle of you out of my mind. Your birthday is a holy day on my calendar and will be engraved on my memory until the final trumpet calls."

"Oh, stop it."

He lifted her arm to kiss her wrist and, seeing her watch, saw he was late. "Oh, my God!" He grabbed his shopping bag full of books and mufflers and wigs and makeup, then leaned forward to kiss her so that several things fell out. She helped him pick them up and drop them back in. Then he was gone.

* * *

When she climbed the back stairs and swung open the heavy exit door, there was the spring moving along like a house on fire. She headed towards the bike rack, then stopped in her tracks and gave a sigh that came either from recognition or from the acute pain of an arrow going straight through the heart, for the bike—having been stolen or borrowed, or having ridden away on its next pressing and highly secret mission—was gone.

The sky was perfectly clear, and it hung over the university, blue and light with yearning. A mockingbird landed in the elm tree across the path and began to rigidly lift and lower its wings so that the white bars under its wings flickered and winked in mysterious urgent code. Nobody answered as far as Sarah could see, but it continued on, undaunted, signaling to the air.

4

BUTTON SOUP

SARAH MET MILO, whom she was later to marry (although that is another story), on the same night that she realized Robin had gone mad and her brother, Fred, had set off for a parallel universe in his parallel universe machine.

It was Friday, and she had a date with Phillip. She left work early and walked home through the park and saw it was the kind of evening when you might easily expect whatever you lifted in your hands to turn to gold.

She was in her second year of law school but had come back home for the summer to intern in a small city firm. She stayed with her parents for a while and then moved on to stay with her brother, who had an apartment near the university. She did not see much of him, as he was working on a research project which involved a lot of time staring through telescopes waiting for stars to explode. When he was not busy at the lab, he was in his bedroom working on a contraption which looked like a cross between a Cuisinart and the inside of a music box and was supposed to compress a small blob of matter to such a density as to cause it to split off into an entirely new world.

When Sarah walked in the door that evening, the phone was ringing and it was Marisa wanting to know where Fred was, as she was standing in front of the bookstore where he was supposed to meet her. Sarah, who was used to such phone calls, said she had no idea where her brother was, that he could be anywhere in the surrounding twenty-two million light-years, but she'd leave him a note.

After the call from Marisa, Sarah changed her clothes and went to sit by the window to wait for Phillip. She had met Phillip through Fred (he was one of the other research fellows who took turns manning the telescope every night). The moment they had met she had known at last what it was she had been searching for since opening day, since she had first hatched out into the wet grass. He wasn't gorgeous, but she had recognized him instantly in the way that you recognize that the sun has come up in the morning, even behind your closed lids. He appeared very self-contained, satisfied with all the black and empty space that he stared at night after night, and she saw that he knew nothing of his own flammable possibilities and that it was her duty, that she had been sent, that it would be an act of kindness, to give him a glimpse of the conflagration on which the universe burns. She was inching him forward to revelation, slowly but surely, and knew that, any moment now, she was going to get him there.

As she watched at the window, a pigeon with only one leg, the other maybe long ago having been bitten off by a cat, landed clumsily in the window box Fred had never gotten around to planting. It had a piece of dried grass in its beak. It flew off and came back a few minutes later with a white drinking straw. After that it came and went several times and brought three twigs, a chewing gum wrapper, and a spray of what looked like artificial forget-me-nots from an old lady's hat. It piled these things haphazardly on top of each other and then squatted and laid an egg. Sarah took this as a good omen.

A few minutes later the phone rang. It was Phillip.

"Sarah," he said. He sounded mildly surprised.

"Phillip? Hi. Where are you? I thought we were going to the seven o'clock show."

"Sarah," he said again.

She came to attention. "Phillip? What is it?"

He cleared his throat.

The phone was in the hallway. She stared at the little round whatnot table that Fred had stolen from their parents' basement. She stared at it as if she believed that the force of her gaze could keep it from rising up and spinning through the air.

"Listen, I'm not going to be able to make it to the movies."

She was silent.

"I think we should stop seeing each other," he said.

"Explain this."

"I've realized after a lot of consideration that this relationship is not good for my work."

"What are you talking about? What does this relationship have to do with your work?"

"I'm distracted, Sarah, by all that time we spend eating Chinese food and going to the movies and talking about our feelings. I find I'm very fatigued when I get to the telescope at the end of the day, and it is difficult to calculate things. I'm liable to miss something important."

"Feelings? You never mentioned any feelings," she said ominously.

"You're angry. I understand. But try to understand me. I need more silence and order. This isn't a personal thing. You're a little flighty, but an unusually intelligent woman, and I've enjoyed your company a great deal."

"What do you mean, 'flighty'? Just what do you mean by that? How dare you sum me up with piddling little words like that? I don't know what you mean by it and I refuse to accept it."

He sighed. "Well, this is exactly what I mean. You get excited by such trifles."

"Trifles! You call this a trifle! I offer you the most intimate portions of my soul. I loan you my heart. I exercise infinite patience in the face of your unremitting emotional puniness, and you call me flighty? I'm as steady as a rock. I'm as true as the magnetic north. Just what manner of dimwit are you?"

"I don't think this kind of name-calling will do us much good."

"Speak for yourself. I find name-calling deeply enjoyable at moments like this, you immature creep."

He was silent for several moments. "Let's have coffee together now and then," he said at last. "I wouldn't want to lose touch."

She took a deep purifying breath and lowered her voice to the calmest pitch she could muster. "Absolutely. Coffee."

He was silent again for a moment, as if he wasn't expecting her to back off so easily. "Listen, I want you to know that, in many respects, this has been a very pleasant phase of my life. I'm grateful."

"Oh, go stuff it up a black hole." She replaced the phone and stared at it despairingly. She had been staring at it for about half a minute when it began to ring again. She gave a gasp of relief, knowing that Phillip must have realized the magnitude of his error, and grabbed it up. A woman with a husky voice asked if Fred was there.

"No," Sarah said, weakly. "He's not. Can I take a message?"

The woman said her name was Eleanor and if he hadn't called by ten, his name was mud. Then she hung up.

Sarah replaced the phone again and went into the hallway and climbed the stairs and stepped out onto the roof. She was surprised to find that the sky was not filled with rain and stones, that the sun had not fallen out of the heavens leaving a sorrowing and unlit nighttime. In fact, it was still very early evening, and the air was gold and blue and peach colored and blew as glancingly against her skin as dandelion seeds. The clouds on the north side of the sky were piled up high and continually reshaping themselves into everything from dragons to teacups, while in the south and the east it was as clear as blue glass, and a wild and heady aroma came floating up the avenues from the park, but to Sarah, without Phillip, it all looked and smelled like so much coal dust.

It was before she could throw herself off the roof into the lines of laundry which crisscrossed so gaily and callously beneath her that Robin suddenly appeared at the corner in the exact spot where she had recently hoped to see Phillip.

Although she wore a huge and ridiculous straw hat and a tightly buttoned raincoat, and although she traveled unsteadily in a slow fog of silver evening light quite separate from the summer air around her, it was difficult for Sarah not to look upon her, at this moment, as a sign or a little lifeboat skimming across the water.

She raced down the stairs and waited for her at the front door. As she approached, Sarah realized with some uneasiness that she was carrying a little suitcase. She seemed to be staring at something halfway between the sidewalk and the sky, a gnat maybe, right in front of her nose. She didn't see Sarah at all until she was right upon her.

"Sarah," she screamed in delight. "You were waiting for me." Then in the next instant she threw her arms around Sarah, knocking her hat off, and whispered into her neck, "I killed him."

Sarah stepped back and looked at her irritably. It was amazing how in every instance Robin managed to grab the center of the stage before anyone else could get there. "Who? Who'd you kill now?"

She stooped and picked up the hat and waved it in the air. "Who do you think? Martin, of course. Martin, that hair ball. Aren't you glad?"

"Sure. I'm delighted."

"You don't believe me."

"Naturally I believe you, you being the soul of veracity. Come upstairs. Something terrible has happened to me as well."

They climbed the stairs, Robin humming a peculiar monotonous hum. In the hallway she hung her hat on a hook and carefully unbuttoned her raincoat.

"Where'd you get the hat?" Sarah asked uneasily.

Robin shrugged. "Found it somewhere."

They went into the kitchen together and sat down at the table. Sarah took Robin's hand and told her that Phillip had just called and broken off with her.

Robin withdrew her hand restlessly and batted at the air. Then she took a paper napkin off the table and blew her nose. "Did I know him?" she asked.

Sarah stared at her in exasperation. "I introduced you to him last Friday when we ran into you at the bagel store. Don't you remember?"

"You can't really expect me to keep track of all your boyfriends, Sarah. Was he the one with those close together eyes who looked sort of like an ape?"

Oh God, it was true. Phillip had a wonderful simian quality which was so in contrast to the abstracted, stargazing tilt of his mind. At the tender thought of it, of how terribly she was going to miss the absurdity of him, her eyes filled with tears.

At this moment the phone rang. Sarah picked it up and said hello. There was a startled silence at the other end.

"Hello?" Sarah said again. "Hello?"

"Uh, hi," a male voice said, at last. "Is Fred there? Do I have the wrong number? I was trying to reach Fred."

"This is Fred's sister. Fred isn't here right now."

"Oh. . . . He told me this would be a good time to call him, but I guess he got delayed somewhere."

"Fred is usually delayed somewhere. Can I take a message?"

"Well . . . just tell him Walter called, would you?"

"Sure, I'll tell him. Do you want to leave a number?"

Walter seemed to think this over nervously. "No, I'll call him back."

"OK, good-bye."

Sarah turned back to Robin and found her peering worried-ly at the saucepans hanging over the stove.

"So what happened with Martin?" Sarah asked unwillingly. She abhorred Martin, but clearly she would have to hear all about him before she could open up her own heart.

"He said he was going to kick me out because he thought I needed some time in the woods to fight my demons alone. He thought I was about to reach a turning point of light or dark."

Sarah looked around the kitchen. It was meagerly appoint-ed with old kitchen items salvaged from their mother's castoffs, some beat-up pots and pans and spatulas. A colander and a veg-etable steamer hung from nails. There were some glass jars filled with beans and rice, and there was one full bottle and sev-eral empty bottles that had contained spring water. The more interesting items were the radiant photographs a satellite had taken of the moon and the earth dancing in and out of each other's shadows. And on the windowsill there were several specimens of brightly colored molds and a profusion of burnt looking rocks which had supposedly bumbled into our atmo-sphere from outer space.

"Martin is a horse's ass. You don't kill a person just because they're a horse's ass."

Now Robin leaned closer to one of the little saucepans and tapped the bottom of it anxiously with her finger. "Did you see a little face in there?"

Sarah was seized with a strange, cold doubt. "Why, what do you mean?"

Robin removed the pan from its nail and slammed it down hard on the counter. "I'll make us some soup," Robin said.

"But what do you mean, did I see a face in there?"

Robin went over to the refrigerator and crouched down over the vegetable bin and said that Martin had come to her from out of the blue just when she had lost all hope of finding a way of escaping from her mother. He had arrived like an angel with his sword on fire and cut her loose from all that heavy furniture and all those draperies and all those little china dogs that kept staring down at you from all those little whatnot shelves.

Sarah went over to the saucepan and tried to pick it up, but Robin grabbed hold of it brusquely and dropped a carrot and two onions into it.

Sarah stared at her.

At this moment a key turned in the front lock, and Robin raised her eyebrows and said in a low voice, "Oh, poor Fred."

"Poor Fred?"

"He won't like to find me here."

"No, I don't suppose so."

"He's still crazy about me, and when he finds out I killed Martin, well . . . "

Sarah snorted.

Robin ignored this and took one of the onions out of the pot and turned to cut it up at the counter.

Fred stood in the doorway. He was wearing rumpled khaki walking shorts and a fluorescent pink T-shirt with a giraffe on the front purchased from the zoological society, and gave off a wild and saintlike impression. The two women stared at him admiringly. He sniffed at the air.

"What's that gunpowder smell?"

Sarah jumped up from the table and threw her arms around him and pressed her face against his neck.

"Hey, you're strangling me," he said and pulled her off. He looked around the kitchen inquiringly, sensing that something was out of place. He looked at his rocks and his molds and the cabbage Robin had taken out and left on the table, and then at Robin herself. "Good God, where'd she come from?" he demanded.

Sarah glared at him furiously. "Pay attention to me," she demanded. "Something terrible has happened."

He looked away from Robin. "Well, what is it, Little Broccoli Flower?"

Sarah's eyes filled with tears. "Phillip just called and broke up with me," she choked.

He stuck out his lower lip and raised his eyebrows. "Do I know him?"

"Oh, for God's sakes, Fred, stop it!"

He put his hands on her shoulders and leaned down and looked into her eyes seriously. "Don't be such a turkey. Phillip's got no vision at all. There are hopeless causes worth wasting your energies on. Phillip is not one of them. I've told you that before. Forget the old apeface."

"Don't you dare call him names!" Sarah shouted and then seemed to see herself evaporating, turning to mist here in the kitchen. "Fred," she croaked in despair, and he reached out a hand and pulled her to him and stroked her head.

"I want you to promise not to introduce me to any more men. If you bring anybody else home, I want you tell them I'm a deaf-mute. I mean it. I'm not kidding." She wept into his pink T-shirt.

"C'mon, let's eat something," he said. "People make a great mistake putting so much emphasis on erotic love, when it's really food that nature sent us for. The creation of life was simply one of the universe's ploys for capturing and organizing energy. It's up to us to make the most of a brief moment, to eat well, give form to what we can, and then gracefully fall back into the dust."

Robin, chopping vegetables at the counter, guffawed. Fred refused to look at her. "What's that gunpowder smell?" he asked again, sniffing.

Sarah took a deep breath but smelled nothing but onions.

"Hello, Fred," Robin said in her huskiest voice.

Fred looked at her briefly, then back at Sarah. "How did she get here in my kitchen?"

Sarah shrugged. "She's having a problem with Martin."

Robin smiled a very peculiar and private smile. Then she squinted again at something invisible in front of her nose and quickly clapped her hands together as if she were trying to catch something. "I killed him," she said.

Fred turned slowly and looked at her with raised eyebrows. "What a good idea."

"Martin's kicked her out," Sarah explained with a sigh.

"Well, he certainly took his time about it."

Robin, with a tragic air, scooped up a great handful of vegetables and carried them over to the pot. She did not seem to notice that many of them dropped on the floor as she went. The remainder she dropped into the boiling water. She began taking spices down from the shelf and sprinkling them wildly in with the vegetables.

"She may need to stay here for a while." Sarah sighed.

Fred looked at her sharply. "Now, here again is an example of how carelessly you dole out your acts of kindness."

"Ignore him," Robin advised her as she sprinkled. "He's mad

about me." Suddenly, she stopped and peered into the soup pot. "There he is again," she whispered to herself. She whipped around, grabbed up a fork from the table, then turned back and jabbed it furiously into the pot. "Get out of my soup!" she yelled.

Fred and Sarah looked at each other. Fred came over and examined the soup. "Something wrong?" he asked mildly.

At this moment the phone rang.

"Oh God," Sarah said to Fred, who straightened up and looked, with a stricken gaze, in the direction of the telephone. "I forgot to tell you—Marisa called, and Eleanor, and somebody named Walter."

For a while, caught between rings, the phone was silent. Sarah watched Fred pityingly as he stood there, hoping this silence would go on forever and he would be saved. But then the phone rang again, and then a third time more easily.

He groaned softly. "Answer it for me," he asked Sarah. "Say I'm not here."

"No, Fred, I can't. Really. You have to do this yourself."

He sighed and went into the hall and picked up the phone. "Spinoza's Plumbing Supplies," he said. "Marisa! Where are you? I waited for you for over half an hour. . . . But whaddaya mean, I waited in front of the shoe store. . . . The bookstore? What were you doing there? I never agree to meet people in front of bookstores. It's so phony. I thought we agreed to meet in front of the shoe store. . . . But of course I'm not making this up. Meeting you in front of the shoe store was going to be the big event of the day. It was what got me through. I even went in to try on a pair of basketball sneakers, but they didn't have my size. You can ask the salesman. I waited around and waited around. He probably thought I was going to hold him up. After a while I realized something must have happened to you and I went and had a falafel and then I came home. I just got here. I was just about to call you. . . . Well, actually I think I'm going to have to cancel tonight. My sister isn't feeling well and needs me to stay around. . . . Well, she got jilted by some jerk—"

"*Thanks a lot, Fred!*" Sarah screamed. "Just shout it out the window, why don't you?"

"Listen, Marisa, I gotta go now. How about I call you back in half an hour? OK? Speak to you then." He hung up and came back to the kitchen.

Sarah began to cry. "This is the worst day of my life."

Fred gave a beleaguered sigh. "You make too much of these matters, Sarah. There's nothing solid here to begin with. The world gets itself re-created every second. Try not to take things so to heart."

Sarah thought about how never again would she wake in the middle of the night to find Phillip's hairy and white legs visible in the moonlight, the rest of him half out of the window as he stared up at the sky, worrying about what might be going on up there that he couldn't see. There were, she was pretty sure, much greater agonies in store for her in the future, and far greater miseries at large in the world even now. But—and she was ashamed to find it—knowing this made no difference. Never again would she see him turn restlessly and throw off her blue silk kimono, which he had donned against the night air. Never again would she pretend to be asleep as he climbed into bed, muscled and palely gleaming, and, sighing, pulled her to him, his head full of stars.

"So how's the project going?" Robin asked Fred tauntingly.

Fred didn't bat an eye. "Fine."

"Still working on the origins of life?"

"In a manner of speaking."

"He's trying to create a parallel universe," Sarah said. "He's got this machine."

"Oh? You'll have to show it to me."

"I don't think so. It's very delicate. Why don't you tell us what happened with Martin."

Robin frowned and batted at the air again. "I killed him. What are all these moths doing in here?"

Fred and Sarah both recognized, at this same moment, that Robin had gone mad. They looked at each other.

"Come out in the hallway with me for a minute, wouldya?" Fred said to Sarah. Sarah did not want to go with him, not at all, but he gestured at her imperatively, and she followed him out.

In the hallway Fred said, "Well?"

"Well, what?" Sarah said angrily.

"She's lost her marbles."

"Listen, you're the one that's building a parallel universe in your bedroom."

"This is serious. This has been a long time coming and now here it is. I don't want it in my kitchen."

"Fred, I'm in no mood for this. In fact, I'm in no mood for any of this." She waved angrily at the little hallway they were standing in, not sure what she was waving at. Not only were they not going to give her an ounce of comfort, they were not even going to leave her a place to have a respectable sadness in. "She's perfectly harmless," she said defensively.

"You don't know that. How do you know that?"

"Look, this is probably just a little detour she's taken. I'd take a detour too, if I lived with Martin. What do we know about the fitness of all the places a mind might choose to go? We don't know peanuts. She's taking a short vacation, and she needs her friends nearby to watch over her. We probably all ought to take little vacations like that. It would make the world more open-minded and less inclined to war and genocide."

"But what about Martin? You think he's all right?"

"Of course he's all right. I'm telling you, she wouldn't hurt a fly. She's always fantasized about knocking people off and stuff like that. It's a hobby. Once she told Mom she'd accidentally pushed me off the deep end of the swimming pool and I'd hit my head and drowned."

"Well, let's call him and tell him to come and get her."

"Absolutely not. She needs some time away from him. That's what she needs."

"I think this is a big mistake."

"Just for a few days."

He shrugged and went back into the kitchen. Sarah followed him.

Robin looked from one to the other of them and smirked. "Listen, he's the one who's building a parallel universe machine," she said.

"This is true," Sarah replied.

"Tell us about Martin." Fred took a pear out of the fruit bowl. He felt the tip of it and sniffed it carefully, then sat down and bit into it.

Robin stared at the pear as if she had never seen such a thing before.

"Wanna bite?" Fred asked.

Robin reached out her hand, then jerked it back quickly. "I shot him," Robin said.

"Martin?" Fred asked.

"Martin. I couldn't stand it anymore. His face kept getting bigger and bigger and bigger."

"Oh, come on," said Sarah.

"Well, it wasn't just his face. It was his whole head. Every morning I would wake up and look over at him, and every morning his head on the pillow had gotten a little bigger. First it was the size of a honeydew, then it was like a pumpkin, and then, this morning, it was just as big as a watermelon."

"So then you shot him?" Fred prompted through a big mouthful of pear.

"Oh lay off, Fred," Sarah said.

"He kept a gun on the top shelf of the pantry behind the dried beans and the barley, but, of course since he always knows exactly what's going on in my mind, the problem was distracting him long enough to get the gun out and sneak up behind him and blow his brains out.

"So, what I did was, I set fire to the kitchen curtains and then I yelled, 'Fire!' and he came rushing in and started throwing pots of water out the window. He was so distracted I was able to grab the gun and sneak up behind him and shoot him through the back of the head. God, it was great. God, I never felt so uplifted."

"That's ridiculous, Robin, and you know it," Sarah said. "Martin wouldn't keep a gun."

Robin didn't say anything. She got up and stirred the soup and sat back down. For a while they all sat there silently in the light now turning blue and dusky, for, though the sun had not yet actually set, it had slipped down behind the roofs of the apartment buildings opposite.

"How about some soup?" Robin asked, apparently addressing the light fixture on the ceiling.

"Is it done?" Sarah asked.

"Sure," Fred said.

Robin ladled the soup out carefully, then she sat down and bent her head over the bowl and appeared to say a short, silent prayer. When she was done she looked up at Fred. "Don't think it isn't written all over your face."

"What's that?" he asked.

"That you've sold your soul."

"Good Lord, to who?"

"There's only one place to sell it, but the question is—for what? Just for the sake of knowing things it isn't given us to know?"

Fred very carefully balanced the bowl of a spoon on the handle of another spoon, then gave a deft flick and sent it flying gracefully through the summer air so that it landed, with a clink, in a teacup. "Why, I think that's the only thing that's given us—to know things, to figure stuff out."

"Martin says the only true task is to find the way back into the harmony we've lost. You can't do that by knowing things. That's a mistake."

"Martin says that because he's aware of how very little he knows and he doesn't want anybody else to discover it."

Robin frowned. "It worries me, you know, this idea of space going on forever."

Fred lowered his long and sensitive nose toward the soup and sniffed it appreciatively. He picked up his spoon and took a mouthful and nodded. "Well, actually, that's not what we think anymore, that space goes on forever. I know it's hard to picture, but it seems pretty clear that it must curve in upon itself."

Robin poked her spoon up into the still summer air as if she thought that maybe up there, coming right through the kitchen ceiling, was the underside of outer space. "Martin says that most of the things you hear about the universe aren't true anyway, that the scientists just make things up and then they cleverly bend the results of their experiments to fit their theories." She looked down suspiciously at the table and, using her spoon like a harpoon, jabbed at something on the tablecloth.

Fred, now that he had laid any responsibility for Robin's behavior onto Sarah, seemed to be thoroughly enjoying himself. He took a few more spoonfuls of soup. "Has Martin ever, to your knowledge, had a moment of self-doubt?" Fred asked her.

Robin slammed her spoon down. "Don't you understand?" She seemed to puff up with air like a large, ruffled blowfish. "Martin and I are not two things, we're one thing, just one soul that got accidentally snapped in two on that first morning when there were all those fool animals trampling around waiting to get named. We'll be trying to finish up our business till the end of time."

Sarah listened to this with interest and recognized with a pang of irrefutable sorrow that this was exactly the way she felt about Phillip. She glanced over at Fred to see his reaction and was surprised to find that he looked very angry. His face was red, and his eyes seemed to start from his head.

Now Fred stood up, knocking his chair over backwards. Sarah watched him wonderingly. Maybe he was going to hit Robin or something. But he just stood there making peculiar grunting noises, and his already prominent eyes got more prominent, and, in a few seconds, his mouth started turning blue.

"My God, he's choking," she yelled. She stood up, and, though it felt to her as if she was moving very slowly, perhaps it was really only a few seconds before she got to him.

He staggered towards her helplessly, and she grabbed him. He thrashed around wildly, perhaps not understanding what she was trying to do, but at last she got her arms around him from behind and, making a doubled-up fist, pulled in hard below his rib cage. Nothing happened.

He opened his eyes wide as if he saw something horrible appear in the air of the kitchen. "No," she screamed, and she pulled in again hard and now a small object, round and black, shot out of his mouth and he gasped and fell forward over the table.

Sarah picked up the little black thing and stared at it.

"It's a button," Robin said. "The recipe calls for a button from each person who shares in the meal."

"But, for God's sakes, you idiot, you don't put buttons in people's soup!"

Robin pulled out her lower lip.

Sarah bent over Fred. "Are you all right? You want some water?"

Fred was still trying to catch his breath, but, unquenchably curious, he looked towards Robin and asked, "Why does the recipe call for buttons?"

Robin looked sheepish, and for a moment it appeared that she might not answer, then she said, "This soup is supposed to bring the spirits of all who share in it more closely together and I suppose maybe the buttons stand for everything that has to be opened and undone before the inner light of anyone's spirit can reveal itself to anyone else. That button is from your pea coat in the front hallway. I took one from my raincoat and one from Sarah's sweater. I guess maybe you're not supposed to leave them in the soup. I don't really know. I never made this stuff before."

"For God's sakes, where'd you get this crazy recipe from?" Sarah asked.

"Why, Martin, of course," Robin said, looking surprised at such a foolish question.

At this moment the phone rang. Fred straightened up and looked towards the hallway. "Oh God, that's probably Marisa again. She's gonna cut off my nuts."

There wasn't a man worth spit anywhere in the universe, Sarah thought.

"Answer it for me, Sarah. Please. Just this once. I'll never ask you again. I swear."

Sarah looked at him.

He looked around wildly for inspiration. "Tell her . . . tell her . . ."

"You choked on a soup button," Sarah offered.

He looked at her hopefully for a moment, then changed his mind. "No, she won't believe that. Tell her the window dropped on my hand and I might have broken a couple of fingers and I'm in terrible pain. I'll call her in the morning."

"All right, but only this once." She sighed.

She went out into the hallway and answered the phone. While she was trying to convince Marisa that Fred couldn't talk to her, she examined her sweater where it hung on a coat hook. At the same moment that she saw it was, indeed, missing a button, she noticed a strangely smoky and acrid smell coming from Robin's raincoat. She lifted the hem to take a better sniff and felt something heavy in the pocket. She put her hand inside and lifted out a gun.

"Listen, Marisa, I gotta go. No, do not come over here now. No, do not come over here." She hung up the phone and stared at the thing in her hand. She heard them talking in the kitchen, but could not make out the words. "Fred," she called. "Would you come here a minute, please?"

Fred stuck his head out of the kitchen gingerly and, seeing that she had hung up the phone, came towards her. "What is it?"

She held up the gun.

"Where . . . ?"

"In Robin's pocket."

"Oh boy." He took a woolen muffler off a coat hook and, wrapping the gun up carefully, lifted it from Sarah's palm and examined it with curiosity. "Stinks," he said. "I don't think I've ever actually held a gun before. Poor old Martin."

"What'll we do?"

"Call the police, of course."

"Call the police? Oh, Fred, I can't call the police on her. How can I do that?"

He shrugged. "I don't think you have much choice, actually. They'll catch up with her anyway, I'm sure, but meanwhile you've got your fingerprints all over the thing. You'd be better off calling them, before they show up here on their own."

"But she's my friend!" Sarah wailed.

"And, I must say, you've got really impeccable taste. Phillip and Robin. Yecch."

"You introduced me to Phillip," she said.

"Yes, but I never dreamed you'd be such a jerk as to fall for him."

"I thought he was my soul mate. I thought he was the one I'd been looking for. I loved him."

Fred sighed impatiently. "Phillip has no soul. He doesn't have enough imagination to have a soul. He doesn't even have a enough imagination to be a good physicist. Believe me. Now you better figure out what you're going to do about Robin. I'm gonna work on the machine for a while. You call me, if you need me." He handed the gun back to her and turned and headed for his room.

Several large tears slid down Sarah's cheeks and splashed onto the gun. She went into the kitchen holding it carefully between two fingers as if it were a dead rat.

Robin was seated at the table, talking softly to a little pile of crumbs. When Sarah came in, she looked up and saw the gun. "Oh," she said.

"Is this yours?"

"No," Robin said.

"Did you shoot Martin with this?"

Robin smiled.

Sarah sat down heavily at the kitchen table. "But you loved him."

Robin closed her eyes and batted at the air. "Where's Fred?"

Sarah was silent for a moment. "Fred's in his room."

Robin opened her eyes. "I wonder if he'll notice that I improved some of the connections for him in his contraption," she said dreamily.

Sarah looked at her, startled. "Did you touch his whatchamacallit?"

"Sure. Well, I mean, just a little. When you guys were out in the hallway trying to decide what to do about me, I switched a couple of the polarities around."

At that moment there was a thunderous explosion from down at the end of the hallway.

What struck Sarah most forcibly, when the smoke had cleared and she was able to see in, was how tidy Fred's room looked. No socks or coffee cups littered the floor. The bed was made and the books neatly put away on the bookshelves. She asked Robin if she had done any cleaning up in there, but Robin didn't answer, only laughed nuttily. Fred, of course, was gone. The window onto the fire escape was wide open, and a breeze blew the curtain inward.

Sarah tried to imagine it, this world he had disappeared to, where the grass was peacock blue and the trees were pink, where walruses could fly and stones could talk and tell you just exactly how far you had to go to fathom the heart of another.

As they stood there looking into the room, the doorbell rang, and Sarah cursed, knowing it had to be Marisa, come to try once more to turn Fred into a presentable approximation of what a boyfriend is supposed to be. What could she possibly say to her?

When she opened the door, with Robin close at her heels, there was Martin. He was a tall man, with a wide jaw and blond hair and, as always, looked to Sarah like he was about to try to

sell you a stolen car. He was glowing with his usual self-posses-
sion and good health.

"You're supposed to be dead," Sarah said gloomily.

He raised his eyebrows in surprise and pondered this.
"Maybe I just died and came back. It's happened before. After
all, death is just a doorway." At this moment, he caught sight of
Robin, and the two of them stood there sizing each other up.

"Let me talk to you for a moment, Martin," Sarah said and
pushed him out into the hallway and closed the door behind
her.

Martin opened his baby blue eyes wide and gazed at her
with as much innocence as he could muster.

Sarah was not sure where to begin. "She says you suggested
she leave."

"Did she say that?" He laughed.

"I think you should let her stay here for a while. She's clearly not well."

He grew very sonorous and instructional. "It's easy to mis-
understand this process, Sarah. I know you care about her
and wish her well, but she's journeying right now and has
already gone far up the mountain. Without someone who really
understands the kind of work she's doing, as I do, she may get
permanently lost. I really must insist on bringing her back
home with me."

The door opened at this moment, and there was Robin
with her little suitcase in her hand. She had her raincoat over
her arm and was holding her big straw hat. "Good-bye, dear
heart," she said to Sarah. "You're gonna be fine. I'll call you
tomorrow." She put the hat on her head. "I'm ready," she said
brightly to Martin. Martin took her arm, and they went down
the stairs.

Sarah went back into the apartment and sat at the kitchen

table. The gun was gone. She wondered if she should call Martin and warn him. No, she thought. No more Mr. Nice Guy. These little acts of kindness changed nothing, did nobody any good. You were born alone and you went down your little path alone and it was an illusion to think you ever met up with anybody else or could change anything for anybody else. She'd finish law school and take a job in one of those big firms and make a lot of money and enjoy herself and that ought to do the trick as much as anything could do the trick. After a while she got up restlessly and grabbed her sweater off the hook and went down the stairs and out into the evening.

The sun had set now, and, though there was still light in the sky, she knew she would have to go quickly, for there was only a brief time left before all the muggers and rapists came out for their evening perambulations.

At the edge of the lake the world was transformed, for a wonderful moon, huge and pale orange and not quite full, had begun to lift itself up between the trees and the apartment buildings on the other side of the lake. She leaned against a willow which hung out, trailing its branches in the water, and watched the moon rise.

In a little while, around the bend, walking and pecking through the rich and cakelike dirt of the horse path, came a small family of ducks—a mother and three ducklings. When the mother duck saw the moon rising, she led them into the water, quacking softly and imperatively. They slid into the lake without argument and had started to paddle out towards the other shore, when suddenly one of the ducklings gave a terrible squawk and came to a halt. It flapped the tiny little down-covered limbs which would one day be wings and screamed again. It appeared to be sinking.

Sarah tried not to get upset. What business was it of hers? Nature or fate, or whatever it was, did what it wanted efficiently and matter-of-factly and was not obliged to make excuses or give explanations. It broke some hearts and drove some mad. It blew some out of the sky and in o parallel universes. Some it sank to the bottom of the lake.

"Are you caught on something?" Sarah called to the duckling, but it did not answer, and Sarah, seeing a small, leathery head suddenly appear above the surface of the water and then disappear again, realized that the problem was a turtle, a turtle with his mouth firmly clamped around the tiny leg of the duckling.

"Let go!" Sarah yelled. "Let go of that duck!"

The duckling's family and then other ducks, appearing suddenly from out of the dusk, gathered around the scene and honked and quacked and made a fearful uproar, to which the turtle, a cool and unblinking character risen up from the beginning of time, paid absolutely no attention.

"Oh, oh," Sarah wept and, casting about wildly, picked up a big stick and waded out into the muddy water. She reached them, scattering the other ducks, when she was up to her knees. She stabbed and stirred at the water frantically, until the turtle's head surfaced again, the duckling's foot still in his mouth. Sarah conked him hard between the eyes, once and then twice. The turtle, stunned, let go of the duck and, for a moment, floated at the surface of the water. Then, coolly, as if the loss of this little meal were of no consequence to him whatsoever, he looked Sarah in the eye to tell her that he would soon be back and then paddled himself slowly around and swam off in the opposite direction.

Sarah waded out of the murky water and sat on the ground up against the willow tree, panting. The moon had now risen higher and the tree leaned out over the water with foolish optimism, fishing for the moon's reflection, shining down there like a piece of pirate gold.

In the water the ducks were in an uproar. They ignored Sarah, since she was a force they could not begin to understand or contemplate, but milled all around, quacking and congratulating each other. The little ones peeped and flapped, then, slowly, they all headed off across the moon-filled water.

When she got back to the apartment, Fred was sitting at the kitchen table with someone she'd never seen before, a fellow about her own age, not exactly handsome, but tall, with a large and wide-awake kind of face. He was finishing off the button soup.

Fred was even muddier and dirtier than she was. His face looked like he'd come down a chimney, and his pink T-shirt had a great rent at the shoulder. His shoes were gone.

"Ah, it's my lovely sister returning from wherever she's been." He gestured towards her expansively, obviously feeling much pleased with himself. "She's a deaf-mute, so we have to talk to her by using sign language or writing her notes," he explained to the man.

Then he turned towards her, and, describing great curlicues in the air with his hands or drawing, with his pointer finger, what appeared to be little faces with triangular hats on the top, he pretended that he knew sign language. While he drew, he told her, exaggerating the movements of his mouth so that she could read his lips, that after he had set his machine for high compression and pushed the start button, he had been picked up by a blinding flash of light and whirled around and around in what seemed to be a supersonic, blenderlike motion. After what might have been a minute or several months, the whirling stopped abruptly, and he fell to the ground like a stone. It was fairly, though not completely dark, and he assumed he was in a parallel dimension, until he looked up and saw a streetlight and, off to the side, away from the streetlight, a lot of old junk, including an old bathtub with two teenagers in it, a boy and a girl, very inexpertly kissing and feeling around under each other's shirts. He was immediately certain, from the amateurishness of these proceedings, that he hadn't gotten any farther than the earth, and, indeed, he found himself, a few minutes later, to be in a vacant lot about three miles over on Blueberry Street. He hitched a ride home with this guy, whose name was Milo, and here he was. He considered the experiment to have been a great success, but where was Robin? Had the police taken her away?

Sarah could see that this Milo, whoever he was, though highly suspicious of the goings-on here, was completely enraptured. He kept peeking at her with a little crease in his brow, as if he thought that any minute now he was going to figure out where it was he recognized her from. She wanted to give him a warning, prevent the worst from happening, but, since she was now officially a deaf-mute, there was not a word she could say.

5

IN THE AIR,
OVER OUR HEADS

WHEN LAW SCHOOL WAS OVER and she had successfully passed
the bar, Sarah took an apartment at a rude and disreputable end
of the city—perhaps as an act of curiosity. In any case, she
couldn't afford much more. She took the job although it didn't
pay well, because she wanted to be on hand to deliver any possible blows of reason to this dark and ignorant age. (Milo had
helped her find it, just before they had had an argument about
the redeeming social value of a certain movie they had seen
and she had decided never to speak to him again.) She knew
she would witness much injustice, and she expected to see the
miserable and oppressed and mad thrown into dungeons
(where they could have time to grow even more miserable and
oppressed and mad). She recognized that *she* was as free as one
is granted to be—given the anarchy and disorder that roam the
universe like wolves—and she spent the winter training her

reflexes to stop on a dime. However, she didn't sleep well, perhaps because she was not sure how much actual power you got from being free in this great light world.

Early in the spring she was assigned her first murder case. Theresa Maldonado, after eight years of having her nose broken and her teeth knocked out, finally picked up a carving knife one night and marched Luis Maldonado around the kitchen table and stabbed him five times through the heart. Sarah thought she was ready for this. She, herself, sick of love, of arguing about movies, of raising hopes and watching them dashed, of jumping around deafened and myopic, kissing people on the mouth and later tripping over things in their darkened rooms searching for her glasses, threw herself with deadly seriousness into this case.

Theresa had a small, heart-shaped face with sadness as incurably stamped on it as a postmark. If Sarah could bring in a verdict of temporary insanity, then Theresa would walk away free. Sarah could not imagine who would not agree that stabbing Luis was as innocent and temporarily insane an act as you're likely to get on this whirling little planet with its rivers of blood.

Throughout the case the jurors sat up and listened to Sarah like daisies in three straight rows, alert and nervous and eager to please. But on the morning when they finished their deliberations, they shuffled back into the courtroom sheepish as a cloud of butchers. They declared Theresa guilty of murder in the second degree.

If they had won, they would have overturned a long-standing precedent, and there was a brief news report about the case on the eleven o'clock news. When the news was over, Sarah turned the television off and went and stood by the window and looked down at the street. The two plainclothesmen who had been staking out the storefront next door for drug traffic were standing there. She watched them for a while, then looked up at the little hunk of sky that showed over the roofs. After a few minutes the phone started to ring. It was Fred, asking if she was all right.

"I've been better."

"You want me to come over?"

She thought about it. If he came over he'd probably badger her with his cockamamie theories about outer space and the origins of life. This would be distracting, but, after all, she didn't think she wanted, or deserved, to be distracted.

"No thanks, Fred. I need to be alone for a while."

"I could come over and show you some photos. I have this great new one of a proton and an antiproton colliding and setting free a quark."

"That's OK. I think you showed me that one already."

"Listen, I'm sure you didn't put in more than the bare minimum of work on this case, that you could have cared less about this person, that the final decision had nothing to do with the sexist bias of the justice system, or the natural tendency for power to continue to empower itself. What happened happened because you, personally, blew it. It's entirely your fault that that woman is going to jail."

"All right, Fred, all right. But she *is* going to jail and I have to sleep with that and eat breakfast with that and walk through the park to the bus stop with that."

"OK, well have fun and call me if you need me."

"Sure." She went back to standing at the window, but she had only been there for a minute when the phone rang again.

"Hello, Sarah, it's me."

Robin's voice was still husky and recognizable, but there was a sleepiness in it now, a mutter of capitulation, that came either from the drugs they gave her or from the madness itself. It saddened Sarah deeply whenever she heard it.

"Where are you?" Sarah asked.

"Here. I'm here in the hospital. But, guess what. They're letting me out tomorrow."

Sarah's apartment, though small and shabby, was arranged with tender and hopeful care. She looked around it now unhappily.

There was a kitchen, a living room, a bedroom, and a tiny study, whose door now appeared, by some trick of the light, to throw itself open. Inside it she could see her desk with its stack of briefs and the futon sofa where she often lay strategizing. This sofa had pink camels marching across its upholstery and opened up into a bed.

"What are you going to do? Where are you going to go?"

"Well, I'm not sure. I could go to my darling father, though I can't stand him. Or I could call Martin Burnbauer, but Martin doesn't seem to remember me, even though he was my husband up until last year. Or maybe you . . ."

Sarah said nothing.

"Well, I'm not sure what I'll do. I'll toss a coin when I get out. My destiny will find me, I suppose. I saw you on television tonight, by the way."

"Yes."

"No offense, but you didn't look so hot. You looked tired and that suit wasn't great on you. Maybe you oughta get a blue one."

"I lost the case, too."

"Yes, I know. Oh-oh. Here comes Brunhilda, the night nurse. I gotta hang up. She's going to get me whipped into shape for tomorrow. You know, trim all my toenails with her little hacksaw and make sure my behind is wiped. That kinda stuff. I'll call you when I get out." She hung the phone up without waiting to hear Sarah say good-bye.

Sarah went back and stood at the window and watched the

blank face of the social club across the way. It had one window, curtained with blue burlap, and a door long ago painted red. Over the door was a sign, hand lettered on a large wooden board, that said: MIDNIGHT HOUR SOCIAL CLUB—EVERYONE WEL- COME. But tonight no one went in or went out, and Sarah thought she could hear the trillion tiny heartless voices of the stars singing in her ears.

The next day she waited across the street from the hospital in the shadow of a fruit stand, disguised in an old brown trench coat. While she waited, she watched a man with the brightest, drunkest blue eyes going methodically through the garbage cans. He wore two different shoes, and stacked on his head were five or six assorted hats. Who could be such a fool as to look for more hats in a world like this, she wondered.

When Sarah looked across the street again, there was Robin with a little suitcase in her hand, slipping quickly out of the arched and ominous doorway and down the shadowed side of the steps. But as soon as she came to the bottom and hit the sunlight, she stopped stock-still as if she were dazzled or stupe- fied by the sudden brightness. She put her suitcase down and stood there blinking patiently up at the sky. Her almost black hair frizzed out around her head as if the last nurse had combed it in a great rush and fury. Sarah couldn't blame this nurse a bit, and she stared unhappily from her hiding place at Robin and tried to make up her mind.

When at last she decided, she strode across the street with- out wasting any more time, almost hungrily. Robin cried out when she recognized her, and they embraced. Then Sarah pushed her away. "You have exactly two months with me," she said. "Use the time well. After that you're on your own."

"You're the same," Robin said, looking at her speculatively. "Though you look a little dried up. I talked about you a lot in there, but Carlisle, one of the twins, said you'd forgotten me, just like Martin Burnbauer has forgotten me. The doctor told him and his brother they couldn't have their street clothes back until they admitted that their mother doesn't really flap around their bedroom at night in the shape of a bat."

"And if you act or talk crazy, you're out like a shot. And I don't want to hear any of that stuff about bumping people off."

"I've reformed. I swear. You'll see."

"Good, because your special assignment is to get real and find a job." Grimly, she took Robin's pack and, shouldering it, set off without looking back to see if she was following.

They stopped on the way for some groceries, and, as they were toiling up the bread aisle, they passed a man in faded red sweatpants. His arms were loaded with yogurt.

"Too much dairy," Robin said to him as he passed. "It'll give you mucus."

"Mucus is good for you," the man answered. He had a deep, ponderous voice, which concealed at the bottom a not quite decipherable message. Sarah felt immediately that something had gone wrong. She could not bring herself to look at him. He wore a tiny gold earring in the shape of a cello in one ear. He had those kind of eyes that turned from green to gray to mud blue, according to what background he stood against. She knew she'd better leave. She rolled away up the aisle with her cart.

When he happened to get on line right in back of them at the checkout counter, Sarah was sure that he must have fallen for Robin already. This still happened all the time, even though she now slipped so regularly in and out of madness. The strangest people fell for her, the kind of people who telephoned in the middle of the night—gangsters and drug addicts and the guys who handed out advertisements on street corners, people she met in the loony bin and people she met in the grocery store. Sarah couldn't figure out how she did this.

When she turned to look at Robin now, she found her standing there sleepily, completely wrapped up in reading the headlines on the sensational newspapers: ALIENS RETURN ELVIS PRESLEY TO EARTH FIFTEEN YEARS AFTER HIS DEATH.

Sarah sighed and turned away to gaze with relief and boredom at the palatial, orderly press of the supermarket's treasures, so she was completely unprepared when a fat woman cut in line in front of them. She was tough and pasty looking but had balanced a disarmingly tiny pink hat on her head. Sarah did not say anything for a moment. Someone can always pull a knife, and, further, she was thinking about the fundamental social inequalities and miseries of which such rudeness is the natural consequence. On the other hand, Sarah thought, shouldn't a person define and make justice wherever they could? She took a breath and said in an unsteady voice to this lady, "Excuse me, but I believe we were next in line."

The lady turned and looked at her with one of those huge stone faces which are the result of a life of volcanic rage and said, "I'm in a hurry."

"Well, we're not," Sarah replied, "but the fair thing to do would be to ask if we minded if you went ahead."

"Life is tough," the lady snorted, and turned her huge back away.

Sarah heard her heart hammering hotly just inside the threshold of her ears. She tried to catch Robin's eye for some sign of fraternity, but Robin, it seemed, had noticed nothing. She was still reading the headlines. DOCTORS SAY HEAD TRANSPLANTS NOW POSSIBLE.

A few minutes later, when the time came for the fat lady to pay for her groceries, she found that her wallet had been stolen.

Sarah looked up, startled, at the squeal of rage. The transformation was wonderful. The stony flesh turned soft and tremulous. The tiny pink hat bobbed frantically as the woman waded through her purse again. The fourth or fifth time the woman was going through her purse, her attention was arrested by something. She stopped and slowly drew out a small, matted black feather, possibly an old pigeon feather that had been dipped in ink. "Where did this come from?" she demanded furiously. "Who put this here?"

No one, of course, answered.

Sarah was somewhat startled at the shiver of delight that darted straight across her pulse like a little fish and then disappeared. The fat woman threw the feather down on the counter and jolted and jounced out the automatic door.

Sarah prepared to turn and look at the man in red sweatpants accusingly. She set her face into a stern and unapproachable glare but was brought up short. He looked even better than he had a few minutes ago. She took a few steps backwards to keep her wits clear, but, seeing him gazing speculatively at Robin, she got a distinct whiff of some spice scent drifting down from the baking needs aisle. Nutmeg was it? Or More-Grief-to-Come?

That night Sarah watched the street below and listened for Robin in the study, where she had put her to sleep, but could hear nothing except the Midnight Hour Social Club, which had put a loudspeaker into its front window, maybe in the hope of drawing new customers. At around twelve this loudspeaker burst into music. Sarah pushed two chewing gum–like earplugs in her ears and watched the two plainclothesmen stir and stretch themselves in the shadows. In this ruined neighborhood it was a slow, cold spring, but still the grass and meadowsweet, the wild clover and dandelions steadily poked up into the vacant lot so that where the broken glass coldly sparkled like a field of stars through the winter, now there was a thin, creeping veil of green. She stood there with her earplugs in her ears and saw a figure in red sweatpants turn the corner and come jogging slowly down the street. She saw that it was the man from the supermarket. He was pensive and brooding, a little heavy on the feet. She stared helplessly at his running shoes, which, with their outsize, cushioning soles, looked like clown shoes to her. As he passed by their window, he seemed to slow down and look up. She felt a slight burning sensation on her face and the skin of her abdomen, a sweet, allergic kind of sensation, like she had eaten one too many strawberries. And she knew that it was nothing much, nothing that wouldn't pass digestively. Still, she was relieved to think that he must be looking for Robin. When he saw Sarah in the window, he faltered for just a moment, then raised one hand in greeting, like a traffic cop, perhaps perfectly serene in his faith that this one hand would be powerful enough to keep him from being smashed flat. She watched him as he jogged ponderously down the street and disappeared around the corner.

In the weeks that followed the spring blew itself out and rapidly turned to summer. In the morning she would leave Robin lying on the pink futon and find her in the same position when she came home at night.

Meanwhile, in court, for no reason that she could see, everything turned to gold in her hands. Muggers, car thieves, cat burglars exited gaily from the courthouse and melted away into the innocent crowd. She stood at her window each night with her earplugs in her ears and tried to figure this out, and all that came to mind was a picture of Theresa as she might be right then, lying pale and still in her dark cell, temporarily released from prison by sleep. Often she was up till dawn thinking it out—why the unjust, when the just would do as well? She would gaze through her bedroom window and strain to read in the movements of the clouds, the ravings of the city birds, the ups and downs of the sun, some secret message from nature, but none made itself clear.

Sarah was not surprised when she came home one night to find the jogger outside their door on the second-floor landing, playing the cello. She walked by him without a word and let herself into the apartment.

"Hey!" he called out to her indignantly as she shut the door behind her.

Robin was sitting dreamily on a chair in front of the open refrigerator. Every once in a while she leaned forward and pulled a little corner off of something and ate it. "Your friend is outside," she said in a muffled voice. "You know, the runner. He says his name is Max."

"Please don't pick like that," Sarah said. "It makes my skin crawl. Just take something out and eat it. A whole thing of something." Sarah knew that this request would not be honored. Robin needed to pick as a way of getting around her mother, who was now dead. But, in order to please Sarah, she tried. She slowly carried a whole cantaloupe on a blue-and-white plate over to the sofa and lay down and cut herself a tiny slice. She took a rest, and after that she ate another tiny slice.

In the hallway, Max stopped to tune his cello, then started up again. Sarah shifted her gaze and stared in fascination at the pattern of blue-and-white roses marching around the circumference of the chipped plate. She sensed that somewhere in there, somewhere in amongst those dancing roses lay the key—something that would give her the power to understand why she, Sarah, was free as a bird, while Theresa, who had finally found the courage to do what she needed to do, was in prison, and why Robin, who, after all, had committed only the most trifling of crimes, was pinned to the sofa.

"Fred called."

"Yes?" Sarah replied.

"He told me about WIMPs."

"What do you mean?"

"WIMPs. It's an astrophysics term. He says WIMPs are tiny little, very heavy particles that float around in space without attracting each other. You can't see them. Nobody can see them. You can only deduce them. Isn't that great? We probably bump into them all the time without knowing it. They're probably the source of most of our troubles."

"Did he say that?"

"No, not that last part. But I think that's what he meant. Anyway he said if I didn't get up off the sofa I was going to turn into one." Robin smiled.

"He's giving you good advice."

"That's what you think. But there's stuff neither of you understands."

"Such as?"

"Such as he's crazy about me, but he still doesn't know it."

Sarah snorted.

"He called to ask if you knew where your mother had put his old baseball glove, if maybe you had taken it."

"Oh, good grief, what a pin brain." She sighed. "I hope you looked for a job. Did you look for a job?" She was certain that Robin had barely moved all day, knowing how easily she was transfixed now by motes of light or little cracks in the wall.

"Actually, I've been very busy, but I can't take just any job, you know. I can't concentrate well, and, besides, I have to keep my feet up off the ground."

Sarah knew better than to ask why this was so. "Well, then

I hope you looked for a job where you can keep your feet off the floor."

"I suppose you mean a paying job. There's lots of ways to get paid, you know. I'd work for certain valuable sorts of information."

Sarah came and stood behind Robin's head and pulled gently on her long, almost black, hair. "What is it that you would consider valuable information?"

Robin looked up at Sarah and laughed. "Well, for one thing, I'd like to know if there really are accurate records kept of everybody's good and evil deeds and to what use these records are put and I'd also like to know what happens when you die. Though there's other ways to get paid. For instance, Martin Burnbauer, my ex-husband, used to often barter the jewelry he made for things he needed—vegetables or beans. Once he got a wisdom tooth extracted in exchange for a silver bracelet."

Sarah frowned in annoyance and let go of Robin's hair. "I don't want to hear about that creep Burnbauer. He's gone now, and good riddance. Why do you always want to be talking about him?"

A fat tear, blue against the light of the plate on her chest, slipped down Robin's face and dangled clownishly from her chin.

"Oh my God, how can you cry for that worm?" Sarah yelled.

"I'm not crying for him," Robin said in a low, unhappy voice. "He wasn't a worm. He rescued me from my mother in the nick of time and he was the moon and the stars to me, but I'm not crying for him anymore. I'm crying because something's been pinching my toes."

Sarah sighed. She checked the floor for any sign of demon

hands coming through the linoleum but couldn't see any. How had they become friends in the first place? She was irritated by the mystery of this, by what it implied about the limits of what you can know of your own desires and needs. She sat down at the bottom of the sofa by Robin's feet. "But the question is, did you look for a job today?"

Robin closely examined the air over Sarah's right shoulder. "You think I'm out of my mind, don't you?"

Sarah shrugged. "That's the general idea."

"But you can't imagine what I can see from this vantage point," Robin said.

Sarah, unable to stop herself, twisted her head to see what Robin was staring at. There was nothing there.

"Your friend is out in the hall, you know," Robin said.

"What do you mean, *my* friend?" Sarah said indignantly. "He's no friend of mine."

"I had a rather interesting conversation with him through the peephole. His name is Max, and he says he was born with a tail."

"Swell."

"But they operated on it when he was a baby and took it off."

"I hope he put it in a glass jar and preserved it."

"I don't know if he did. He didn't tell me that. But, as I say, we had quite an interesting conversation, and he warned me not to fall in love for a while because it might interfere with my convalescence. He said that people who are in love are very perishable and have very little resistance to colds and things because their pores are so open."

Sarah laughed. She cut herself a slice of cantaloupe from Robin's plate and lifted it to her mouth. The cantaloupe was very ripe and had that pungent, gluey taste, reminiscent of love. She thrust it away from herself. "One of the best things you could do for yourself is to stop talking to strange men."

"You don't need to worry. His Squatters were talking about food. You never need to worry when they're talking about food."

"What are you talking about? What Squatters?"

"You know what I mean, those invisible things that hang around people's heads. I call them Squatters."

"Maybe they're WIMPs," Sarah said sarcastically.

Robin shrugged. "In any case, they were talking about food, so he's perfectly safe."

"Oh yeah? Well, what about the tail? Never trust anybody with a tail is my motto."

"Don't worry about me," Robin said.

The last crab apple blossoms in the park gave up the ghost to a breeze, and Sarah and Robin sat quietly listening to the cello when the perfume reached them a few minutes later. Robin stirred restlessly as if she scented her mother's grave, but Sarah took it without flinching.

Later in the week the heat dropped down over the city like a net. Sarah stood in her bedroom window and watched the street. The Midnight Hour Social Club burst into music, and one of the plainclothesmen stretched and went off and came back in a little while with an ice cream cone. She wondered what propitious moment exactly they were waiting for to make their bust. Whether she felt sorry or not for the poor sniffling junkies she could not tell. Now there was a slow parade of movement down at the corner, and soon Max was galloping forlornly by in his red running shorts.

"Faster!" Sarah yelled out to him tauntingly, and the plainclothesman who was licking ice cream off his wrist looked up at her window suspiciously.

Sarah called the Midnight Hour Social Club and told them

that their loudspeaker was keeping the whole neighborhood awake and that they should turn it down. They asked if she was the person who had called last night. If she was, they said, she should be on the lookout for death. Then they hung up.

On Saturday Sarah cajoled Robin into getting up off the sofa and going with her to the laundromat. As soon as they got there, Robin promptly sat down and propped her feet up on a box of Cheer. She looked on calmly while Sarah loaded the clothes into the machines.

When Sarah was done, she came over and stood in front of Robin. "You could help me, you know. You really need to get up and move around and do more. Don't you understand how unhealthy this is?"

"Don't be an idiot, Sarah. I move around plenty. I have a whole other life you don't see."

Sarah rolled her eyes at the ceiling. "I'm talking about your body. I'm talking about getting your blood moving. You've got to get up and do things, help with the chores, exercise, look for a job."

Robin smiled. "I'm on top of that, Sarah. Really. I'm thinking about trying to get a job in a nursing home. I've wrestled with a lot of fat, greasy devils, and I think I might be able to help people prepare for the big time—dying, I mean."

Sarah pictured Robin going around propping everybody's feet up on boxes and stools. But now Robin was staring fixedly into the back recesses of the laundromat. Sarah turned to follow her gaze, expecting to see nothing, but there was Max. He was explaining to a little boy that he was from outer space and had grown from a benevolent pod. He told the boy to look inside his ear and see if he could see the blue lights. He said that, where he was from, people's heads were full of blue lights, not brains. He led the boy over to the doorway and pointed up to the sky where he lived in case the boy ever wanted to visit him. Then he sauntered over to Sarah's and Robin's bench and somehow managed to sandwich himself into the space between them.

"Hello, hello. How are you?" he asked, addressing either.

Sarah looked away.

"Sarah isn't sleeping well because of the loud music, and I've been plagued by something evil creeping around on the floor lately," Robin said.

"I know just what you're talking about."

Sarah whipped around and glared at him, but he seemed not to notice. He, too, stared at some invisible spot in the air overhead. His expression was lustful, but kind.

"I found it in my car."

Robin squinted at him, as if through a dense fog.

"I know this will sound incredible, but I was driving around late last night, and suddenly I had this feeling that there was someone or something inside the car with me."

"Where were you going?" Sarah asked suspiciously.

He looked at her coolly. "That doesn't come into the story. Assume I was joyriding. Assume I was out for a little air or something."

She flushed and dropped her gaze to his funny shoes.

"There I was and suddenly I had this feeling there was something in the car with me and I called out, 'Who's there?'— very loudly to put whatever it was on the defensive, but there wasn't any answer. I tried looking over into the backseat, but I couldn't see anything. Finally I panicked and pulled the car over to the curb and jumped out. I waited on the curb for something to happen, but nothing did. I waited a long time, but then finally I walked over to the car and looked inside. There, on the front seat, right next to where I had been sitting, was this watermelon."

Sarah looked up and was startled to find his eyes, half-closed, fixed on her. "It was inexplicable," he said sternly. "There was no way it could have gotten into the car. But there it was. What was I supposed to do? If it was a joke, it was the worst sort of joke. I opened the door and rolled it across the seat and let it drop onto the pavement. Then I drove away quickly, but I felt claustrophobic and had difficulty breathing, as if the car had filled up with smoke."

The way he was staring at her, she got the feeling he thought she was the one who had done it.

"I hear you're a lawyer," he said blandly. "It must make it hard to sleep at night seeing the wheels of justice turn so slowly. How do you feel about all those murderers and rapists getting off so lightly?"

She stared at him in disgust.

"Oh-oh," he said. "I've offended you."

"I'm a public defender."

"Don't tell me you're one of those guys who thinks everyone's innocent."

"It's probably more to the point to say that I think no one is innocent."

At this moment, one of Sarah's machines burst open, and everything—soapsuds, water, sheets, towels, underwear, and socks—came spilling out onto the dirty cement floor.

Sarah felt this indignity keenly, as if somehow it were her fault, as if this laundry all over the floor spelled out a secret and grave inadequacy, a lack of sexual poise or knowledge of how to talk smoothly at parties.

Max and Robin helped her to shove it all back in. Also the little boy helped eagerly, handing up dripping panties and socks, one by one.

Then the man who owned the laundromat came in, not a nice person, a densely fleshed man who obviously held all

these furtive humans with their sacks of dirty laundry in great
contempt. Sarah knew just what she must do. She marched
over to him and told him what had happened and that he
should make sure the catches on the doors were kept in better
repair. He looked at her as if she were a juvenile delinquent.

"You didn't shut the door. If you'd shut the door the way
you're supposed to shut it, it wouldn't open in the middle of the
cycle."

"I banged the door shut. I shut it as shut as you can shut it."

"You banged the door shut? You banged the door?" He
advanced on her menacingly. "That's why these machines are
always breaking down. People like you banging the doors."

"The door wouldn't shut. I had to bang it."

"This is what I mean. If you don't shut the door properly, it
will open in the middle of the cycle. This is not the laundromat's responsibility."

"You should get the doors fixed so that normal human
beings can shut them."

"Nothing wrong with the *doors*."

Sarah sat down on the bench trembling with rage. Robin
and Max, leaning up against a spinning washer, looked like
they'd noticed nothing.

When Sarah got up later to load her clothes into the drier,
she shut the door, and, before she even had a chance to put her
money in the slot, the drier began to turn all by itself.

Furthermore, she was not the only one this was happening
to. As she looked around the laundromat, she saw that people
everywhere were discovering that their driers had been liberat-
ed. Stuck in the round window of each one was a black feather.

Suspicious, she looked around for Max and found that he
was standing right next to her. "How is that done?" she asked
angrily.

He shrugged. "Oh, it's easy, I imagine. You just stick a little wire strip in the slot. A bobby pin might do it." He smiled at her lazily, first with just the corners of his wily eyes, then more slowly with his wide mouth. "I know a good place to go dancing," he says. "Would you and Robin like to come with me tonight?"

Sarah was not fooled by this. "You can have her all to yourself. I have a brief to write."

But Robin, of course, would not go either. She said she had plans to make, and, as soon as she got back to the apartment, she lay down on the sofa and began to make them.

For a week Sarah did not see Max, and she doubted that Robin could be seeing him either, for she appeared entirely disabled by her thoughts. When Sarah left in the morning, Robin lay on the sofa staring spellbound at what appeared to be ordinary, empty patches of air. When she arrived home in the evening, she was still there as if she hadn't moved all day.

During this week, as the northern half of the planet tipped closer to the sun, the streets and sidewalks appeared to shudder and shift with heat. But at night, as Sarah stood at her window and looked at the soft black sky speared on the towers and antennas of the buildings, she felt her other heart, the standing apart, direct as gravity one, the one which even in the midst of anxiety and indigestion and disappointment always remained cool and responsive, took note of beauty and memorized it, recognized justice when it came, she felt that one coming out more and more certainly, like a pale, far star.

She was on her way home from work on Monday night and just passing the Paris Movie Emporium where couples are welcome when Max turned the corner in her direction. She tried to go around him, but he grabbed her hand and stepped up very close as if he were going to steal her purse.

"Well, did you get him off?"

"What?" Sarah said, standing rigidly, ignoring her own hand in his. "What?"

"Don't be funny. You know what I'm talking about. The one you were writing the brief for the night I asked you guys to go dancing. Did you get him off?"

"Oh him. Yes, I got him off. Did you go dancing?" and, here, she managed to wrench her hand free. She was very relieved, like she had just safely pulled it out of a glass jar filled with bees.

He grabbed the other hand. "Don't you ever worry about some of these people getting off scot-free?"

"I've seen many people go to prison who needed something a lot different than several years in a tiny cell to heal them of what ails them. I worry about that a lot more. Did you go dancing or not?" She took the other hand back and looked at the evening sky. It was a clear, darkening green, and she had the impression that it was, somewhere, full of stars.

"No. I went to the movies. I saw this terrific film about this guy, this truck driver—very macho, you know—and he starts having these dreams he's a woman, a music hall dancer at the beginning of the century. After a while he starts realizing these aren't just dreams but memories of a past life, and this past life starts creeping into his present life and everything begins to unravel for him. It was terrifically funny."

This was the movie she and Milo had had the argument over. He thought it was a piece of soft-brained junk and mystical mumbo jumbo. She had thought it a very funny and sharp social satire and had loved it. She did not meet Max's gaze.

"How's Robin doing?" he asked.

"She leaves in a week. I gave her two months, and she has apparently spent that entire time lying on my futon sofa."

Here he stepped forward anxiously and stared into her

eyes. She tried to stare back at him without flinching but felt him poking around in there, searching for God knows what. Afraid that he would look into her heart and see Theresa there in her tiny cell lying on her cot and know how she herself had failed, she closed her eyes and took a step back.

"You're a real tooth fairy," he said sadly. "What did you want her to get done in such a short time?"

Sarah was furious but kept her composure. "She'll never have any idea of what's going on out there until someone pushes her out. Nothing will get through the fog she lives in as long as someone keeps giving her the opportunity to lie on their sofa."

"You don't really know that," he said worriedly. "Sometimes you can't see what friendship is doing for somebody. It works invisibly."

"Ha," she said. "Why, next thing I know you'll be telling me about hardened criminals who suddenly turn into balls of stardust after years of infamy and roll home to make soup for their mothers all because some friend stood by them."

"That wasn't what I meant."

The movie that week at the Paris Movie Emporium was *Schoolgirls' Recess.* As she turned away, she saw him staring unhappily at a large poster photograph of a young girl lifting her blue-and-green Catholic school uniform to expose her childish rump.

When Sarah got home she was surprised to find Robin lying on her back on the sofa grating a carrot over a plate on her stomach.

"What are you doing?" Sarah asked in a threatening voice.

Robin turned to her smiling. Her cheeks were pink with exertion. "I'm making carrot balls for dinner."

"Carrot balls!"

"Martin Burnbauer, my ex-husband, used to make them.

They were good, but I can't remember what all the ingredients were, so I'll have to improvise."

"Well, I'm not going to eat them, you know. You're just making them so you can wallow in your memories of that creep Burnbauer."

"Martin was a king."

"He was a creep and a hustler. He exploited and abused you."

"You're misinterpreting things. You didn't like him. I liked him. Besides which, you're not getting enough sleep, which clouds your judgment."

"Those are voodoo carrot balls, aren't they? You probably put some of Martin's leftover hair in there, didn't you?"

Robin laughed.

"I'd like to remind you that you don't have much time left to find some work."

"I've decided to take the test for the fire department."

"The fire department test is extremely difficult, and they're very selective. You have to be able to climb hand over hand to the top of a fifty-foot rope and then slide down, plus a lot of other difficult endurance tests."

"No problem," Robin said from where she lay on the sofa. "I'm feeling very strong."

Sarah, reflecting only idly on the injustice that gave Robin so much love and attention and left her with carrot balls, was surprised to find the thick stem of her own heart snap and flood. She turned away quickly so Robin would not see, but Robin, quick as a whip, grabbed up a pepper shaker from where it was sitting on the floor nearby and started flinging clouds of pepper into the air over Sarah. "Take off, you demons!" she shouted. "Don't worry, Sarah, this usually routs them!" Sarah stood meekly, sneezing and weeping, while Robin waged battle.

* * *

When Sarah passed by the Paris Movie Emporium the next evening, she noticed that the pictures on the billboards had been changed, and she looked at them curiously to see what the new movie was to be about. Stuck in the top of one of the billboards was a black feather, and she was taken aback to find that the new pictures were cutouts from women's magazines: banana cream pies, brides, babies in diapers.

She and Robin sat out on the stoop that night, and, to Sarah's disgust, she found that all up and down the street, everyone was talking about The Black Feather. On this stoop there was a mother and baby from the third floor and some old ladies who fanned themselves with tabloids. On the sidewalk in front of them, four men had just unfolded a folding table and were playing cards.

Sarah juggled for the baby with an orange, a tennis ball, and a small white leather shoe that had dropped off the baby's foot.

At first the conversation here ranged far and wide, as if they could look into a glass ball and see all those tiny, sinister Russians lining the streets of Moscow or as if they could zoom right into the living room of that family where the little boy pushed his sister out the fifth-floor window, but eventually it came round to The Black Feather.

"He makes Sarah want to spit," Robin said confidentially to the old ladies.

"Why's that?" asked the young mother, listening in.

Sarah let the objects she was juggling fall to the ground, and she glared furiously at everyone on the stoop. "Because these are just childish revenges. If you want to make people kinder and better behaved towards each other, you have to make them feel welcome in the world. Revenge just makes everybody dig themselves in deeper."

"Well, I don't know," said the young mother, "sometimes I think it cheers people up and lets them get on with things."

"Oh boy," said Sarah. "Don't you see this Black Feather guy is probably just making greedier people greedier and dangerous people more dangerous. And he's certainly not doing anything to further his own course of self-improvement."

"How do you know he's a he?" asked one of the old ladies scornfully.

Sarah shrugged, but the baby, reclining on the stoop in a paper diaper, stared up at her with that perspicaciousness of those who speak no language. Blushing, she picked up the orange, the tennis ball, and the baby shoe and began to juggle again. For a moment, the objects hung shining and suspended in the light of the streetlamp. She saw the plainclothesmen in the shadows staring suspiciously into the air at these flying items.

In the last week Sarah had given her, Robin lay on the sofa counting softly under her breath. Sarah won three more cases, and at night she stood at her window and saw that the city, at heart, was really only constructed out of little dots of light. Toy trains twinkled in the distance around the elevated tracks and disappeared. Would I cross that bridge when I came to it, she wondered. That little hammock of fireflies.

By Friday evening she had decided to tell Robin it was time to go. When she got home, Robin was sitting on the sofa with her feet stretched out in front of her on a stool. She was watching them narrowly, as if they were an enemy force. Sarah, in the ominous heat, moved around the house irritably, banging and sweeping and dusting.

"Do you remember my mother?" Robin asked. "All she did

all day long was squeeze cantaloupes and change toilet paper rolls and throw out spoiled food. Do you remember what she looked like? Like a big gray squid. That's what's happening to you."

"Oh, I don't think so," Sarah said, distracted by the thought. She insisted that Robin get up off the sofa and take a walk with her around the Ukrainian street fair, which was just opening its week of festivities tonight. Before she went out, Sarah put on a soft, lavender-colored skirt and a white blouse and went to look at herself in the mirror to see if she did look like a squid. She was taken aback to find that she had entered on one of those unaccountable phases of great beauty, and she turned away fast, as if she had seen a spook waving at her shyly from a cloud of light over her head.

Robin was in the kitchen, inspecting the inside of her sneaker.

"What are you doing?" Sarah asked.

"My shoes feel slippery."

"Well, put some talcum powder on your feet and hurry up about it."

In spite of the heat, there were hundreds of people jammed into the three-block street fair. Stalls lit by strings of colored lanterns lined the streets, and the summer dark lent to the scene a grim, fairylike purpose. The smoke from the sausages and deep-fried pastries thickened the air. Religious articles leaned over the counters and beckoned to them—red-daubed and thorny saints, the Virgin Mary posed as if for a graduation picture in her nimbus of light.

At the end of the street was a raised platform skirted with a cloth decorated in twining birds and flowers. The folk dancers twisted around in a speeding circle. Against her will, Sarah felt her hopes rise. If she could not have love, at least she had within her the power to stand up to the anarchy and disorder of the world, to name what was fair and bear it company.

Behind her she heard Robin cry out as if she saw something coming too. When Sarah turned she saw a little boy, perhaps four years old, standing in front of them, stock-still in terror. Obviously lost, he scanned the crowd desperately with dark, bright eyes. He seemed to feel instinctively, like a bird that had flipped prematurely out of its nest and crashed into the grass, that he had better not move. He whimpered and tried to look around without moving his head. He was dressed to kill with a plastic sword tucked into his black pirate sash and a red bandanna tied around his head.

Sarah was tempted by doubt as she stood there. It seemed to her that she saw the expanding and contracting universe replaying this scene, mercilessly, again and again. At last, however, she took a step towards him. Out of the corner of her eye, she saw Robin step forward too. Before they could reach him, his mother appeared.

They knew she was the mother because she was holding in her hand a plastic pirate ship. Her pink sundress was too tight, and the straps cut into the soft flesh over her breast. She was scanning the crowd desperately, and her eyes were strained with fear, but, when she saw the child at last, all emotion seemed to drain out of her face. It went dead and white. She rushed over to the boy and grabbed his arm and, with the back of her hand, slapped his face.

"Didn't I tell you to stay with me?" She slapped him again. "Didn't I?"

The little boy, at the sight of the white, blank face bending over him, closed his eyes. He whimpered each time she hit him but, other than that, stood quite still. The tiny sight of him standing there without resistance drove his mother into a fury, and she slapped the side of his head.

"Do you hear me? Do you hear me?"

He nodded yes but didn't say a word. He was concentrating on some far black sail on the blue horizon.

Sarah heard Robin give a long, low hiss, but, when all the breath was gone from her lungs, she seemed to slump and turn away. Although this scene was taking place right there, off the curb, the space surrounding the mother and child appeared theatrically bright and far away, and the great crowd on the street seemed to squint and lean forward as if they watched from a high balcony.

Someone has to explain this to me, Sarah thought. These terrible gaps in the world with no pity in them. How all around the earth tonight there are little rooms noisy with pain where torturers crush their victims' kneecaps, and how great a distance we bystanders have to travel before we can open our mouths to say a word.

Sarah sighed and stepped towards them. "Excuse me," she said to the woman. "I think maybe you're making a mistake. This little boy was lost and he was looking for you."

The woman stopped what she was doing and frowned at Sarah. She wrote her off with a glance. "You got any children of your own?" she asked and, without waiting for the answer, turned back to her son. She dug her fingers into his arm and shoved the pirate ship into his hands. His fingers curled around it automatically, and he was dragged away.

Sarah stood there furious and mortified. The woman seemed to be implying that she could read a secret truth about Sarah. Some hidden barrenness maybe, or inability to hold a man. She walked back through the crowd, her face burning.

She and Robin wandered slowly up and down the street, examining the things for sale on the tables. They were standing in front of a table overflowing with a jumble of stuff—spatulas and tablecloths, flea collars and key chains—when Max came up to them. "Very Ukrainian," he said, picking up a plastic cup filled with assorted screws and nails, six for a dollar.

Robin beamed at him, but Sarah tried to freeze him out with an icy stare. He tagged along with them happily. Sarah, in a fury, decided to leave them behind in the crowd. She wove her way in and out of the knots of people until at last she found herself alone, standing in front of a lemonade booth. She bought herself a cup. It was freshly squeezed, with honey and ice, and, as sometimes a food or drink can, for a moment it perfectly answered her thirst and loneliness. Recklessly, she bought herself a second cup and, of course, was suddenly struck with the thought of Theresa imprisoned in this heat without any possibility of such succor. She dropped the cup into a trash can and turned away.

Halfway down the block, she spotted her brother. He was talking and gesturing, and eating, with obvious relish, a large lump of deadly-looking fried dough. He loved street fairs and hardly ever missed one. She started towards him, thinking tonight she would not mind some of his extraterrestrial comforts, but then she stopped short, realizing he was not alone. On one side of him was a tall woman with short, black hair, slender and straight as a tree, perhaps ten years older than himself, who kept glancing at him with possessive tenderness. On the other side of him was a fierce-looking young man, who kept eyeing the older woman as if calculating how most easily to murder her. Sarah contemplated this delicate little family for a while unobserved. The young man kept pointing out sights in the crowd, and, whenever he did, he would step closer to Fred and rest his hand lightly on his shoulder. The woman watched these contacts closely, but Fred, who was busy describing rapidly whizzing elliptical shapes in the air, seemed to pay no attention to either of them. Sarah was filled with a scorching envy but vowed she would take religious orders before she came to such a sorry pass. A moment later, Fred looked up and spotted her. As he started towards her, waving happily, she turned and ducked into the crowd.

When she was pretty sure she must have lost him, she stopped, and there, in front of her, was the plump child abuser and her pirate son. The woman was examining a pot holder in the light of the streetlamp. The child stood next to her, perfectly still, his face swollen with crying, his eyes straining at some invisible spot up in the shadows.

Sarah turned her gaze away for a moment, so missed what happened in the next few seconds. When a whispering and tittering began in the crowd behind her, she thought at first that it must be for her, that everyone had noticed her immense sadness, but when she turned she saw that after all they were laughing at the pirate boy's mother, who was suddenly standing there in just her panties, her dress lying in a circle around her feet. She was looking in moonlike bewilderment at the laughing and gaping crowd. It was a difficult sight, and Sarah understood why everyone laughed. She thought how the human nude never lends much glory to the landscape, not like a tiger or a python would, or even an everyday horse, standing in a meadow; it's too soft and hairless a thing, too tipsily bipedal. And this human in particular was so pale and biscuitlike in appearance that the crowd could not help but be convulsed with hilarity.

But when the woman suddenly understood that she was naked, it became a different matter. Before their eyes she seemed to blow up into a supernaturally huge and furious figure, a crimson-faced banshee or vampire. She shrieked something foul at the crowd in a strange and hellish-sounding tongue, and they fell silent, waiting for her to burst into flames.

However, what happened after all was that her lower lip began to tremble and tears sprang into her eyes and she leaned over to pick up her dress. When she tried to arrange it back over her shoulders, she found that someone had neatly razored open the shoulder straps and neatly razored a long slit down the back.

Here, a man bent down and picked up the black feather where it had fallen and lain covered by the dress, and Sarah groaned in shame for everyone. When the man tried to hand it to the woman, she knocked it away, and it fell back to the ground. She held the dress around herself as best she could and hustled the little boy in front of her and out of the crowd.

Max, of course, was leaning against a car watching the scene calmly, and Robin was standing next to him. In a minute everyone was laughing and chattering again, as if the world was after all just an elephant standing on the back of a turtle, a finite and knowable place. The children, grossly innocent and particularly joyous, pretended to be the fat woman, sketching her breasts in the air and replaying, again and again, her discovery of her nakedness. The adults laughed at the children, and the folk dancers swung around very fast. Sarah watched Max closely from the corner of her eye. He looked sleek and content. His eyes were half closed.

She stormed over to him in a fury. "And what do you think will happen now?" She watched him carefully for some betraying sign, but he merely opened his eyes a little wider and stared at her in surprise. "Whaddaya mean?" he said.

As his gray eyes met hers, she felt her skin turn pink and then dissolve, no doubt leaving all her internal workings clearly revealed.

"To the child!" she shouted at him and tried to hold his gaze so that he would not look down and see her insides shining out eagerly. "What do you think will happen to that child now? Why, she'll probably just take him home and beat him up some more, out of pure spite and misery."

He frowned and seemed to think this over. "Well, that may be true," he said slowly, "but then, on the other hand, I know you agree that people have to tell each other things, that you can't be a witness to such things and not speak. If you don't, your heart dries up."

"I have blood in my shoes," Robin said suddenly. She had been shifting miserably from one foot to the other for several minutes now.

"What do you mean?" they both said to her sharply.

"Well, I don't know. I've been feeling something slippery in there all evening, and now I've realized it's blood."

"Show me," Sarah ordered.

Robin bent down obediently and took off one of her shoes. She held it up to the light to show them. "See," she said.

The shoe looked slightly sweaty, but there was not a trace of blood.

Sarah stared at Max as if this, too, were his fault. Then she looked at Robin. "Tomorrow your time with me is up, you know," she said gently. "You've got to go."

When they got back home, Robin went into the study and shut the door quietly behind her. Sarah stood at the window in the dark and watched the street. She knew what to expect. She was running it wide open and light, aboveboard. She was getting a grasp of the inner nature of things, and a street like this held no secrets from her. At ten thirty the plainclothesmen appeared to take their places in their doorways. At twelve, the Midnight Hour Social Club's loudspeaker came on. At twelve thirty, Max went by.

At twelve thirty-five, the moon appeared over the vacant lot, silent and critical, white and cool. Sarah greeted it sternly, without even blinking. At twelve forty, to her astonishment, Max came galloping back up the street with a bouquet of flowers in his arms. Without even thinking about it, she leaned way out to stare at him, unable to make head or tail out of the meaning of this.

He stopped at the bottom of her fire escape, smiled up at her, and grabbed hold of the ladder, which someone had foolishly left down. The plainclothesmen stared at him sleepily as he climbed up to her window.

"Well!" he said, as he jumped, with a thud, into her room.

She took a quick step backwards and found herself in the dark, out of the light of the streetlamp.

"Why aren't you sleeping?" he asked accusingly.

She was certainly angry at this intrusion, but she also felt caught in a curious tight spot—as if at the very brief space where the tide changes, both helpless and languorous, about to be thrown back up on the beach.

"Insomnia," she said briefly.

"Aaah," he said. "That would explain several things. I suppose the music from across the street doesn't help either, does it?"

She didn't answer him.

The streetlamp hovered at his back like a pink alien spaceship, so, while his outline glowed brightly, he was otherwise dark and faceless. She breathed very deliberately, wanting to keep her reflexes sharp, but this plan backfired. The air was filled with an overpowering scent of summer leaves and pollen, and her head swam. When, at last, she took a step forward, she saw that it was because of the big, feathery, plucked-looking, bouquet of flowers.

Well, he is surely in love, she thought wistfully. He was standing there looking smug yet defenseless, the way you look when you undertake to crawl up out of the sea onto land for the first time.

Sarah heard Robin open her bedroom door and step into

the hallway. "Well, go ahead." Sarah sighed. "There she is."

Sarah went over to the window and looked out. The moon was now riding high over the tenements, and the street was caught in its steady, penetrating light. Nothing would escape. It held everything transfixed with its baleful, white glance. It seemed to her she had been standing there looking out this window into the moonlight for a long, long time, when Max, whom she'd thought years gone, said sadly, "You've been misunderstanding me, I think. I brought these flowers for you."

At first these words only got to her in the way small matters do, like flies at a picnic or a shoelace coming undone or someone saying, "Please pass the pepper." And even as she realized, with a lurch, what they must mean, and even as she was wondering, with that curious thrill with which one wonders such matters, what his kisses would be like, she knew that this would come and this would go, and maybe it would be a sweet matter, but it wouldn't be of much importance.

Sarah was pleased to find herself so lightly snared, and she thought about how not only was the world no longer considered to be a finite place, lodged solidly in the heart of a bright-faced God, it was also no longer considered to be an infinite place, constructing itself endlessly out of an endless variety of chances and accidents. No, nowadays, it was supposedly the organization itself of the world which was so magical, which threw off stars and gases, which created its own energy and fell into dust and then rose up out of the dust even more terrible and complicated. She was eager to win as much power and influence as she could over the secret nature of these things.

Plainclothesman number one shook himself and walked off to get his nightly ice cream cone. Plainclothesman number two sauntered over to the vacant lot to take a pee. He waded into the tall grasses, and, the moment he disappeared, a dark figure detached itself from the shadows below and raced lightly across the street towards the Midnight Hour Social Club. This hooded figure, sure of itself and fast, had in its hand a long, pointed instrument, and, for a second, Sarah's heart stopped, for she thought she recognized Theresa's bloody knife, but then she saw it was a screwdriver.

Sarah wanted to yell out some warning but didn't dare for fear of adding any more dangers to the situation. And, indeed, in a moment a couple emerged from the club. The hooded figure hesitated only briefly, then stepped back into the shadows. The couple was not dancing now, but that they had been dancing recently was easy to tell, for their feet skipped a little and the man was snapping his fingers. The woman was dressed in a full, red skirt, which was only now beginning to deflate slowly. Sarah held her breath in terror lest they turn around, but their eyes and ears must still have been ringing, and they walked happily to the corner through the loud music and disappeared.

Instantly the hooded figure leaped from the shadows again and dashed towards the loudspeaker, which was propped high in the window just out of reach. It leaped up and stabbed the speaker once, twice, three times in the guts with the screwdriver, and suddenly the street was silent. The figure paused for a moment, hand in pocket, then dropped a black feather to the ground and turned and raced back across the street.

Sarah found herself urgently sleepy and yawned a big yawn. "Did you realize it was her all along?" she asked him irritably.

She could barely keep her eyes open.

"Sure," he whispered, then he leaned forward and touched her cheek with just the tips of his fingers. They felt cool and smelled sweet from the stolen roses and foul from the daisies plucked out of vacant lots. "I saw her take that lady's wallet in the supermarket. Besides, who else could it have been?"

Sarah just managed to reach out and brush his cheek lightly with her sleepy fingers.

In a minute they heard Robin reenter the apartment and close the door to the study.

"You're not really going to throw her out tomorrow, are you?" he asked.

Then, only mildly astounded to find that *this* was the place she got caught, she said, "No, of course not."

"I knew you wouldn't," he said.

She yawned right in his face and, smiling, urged him to come back tomorrow. Gently, she persuaded him out the window and onto the fire escape.

Even before he had reached the bottom, she had fallen into bed, knowing that this might be the last holy moment for a long time and that it was not given to her to know just where the next would come from.

She acknowledged grumblingly to whoever hovered in the air over her head that although she might have within her the power to stand up to the anarchy and disorder of the world, she actually had only the most limited authority over that power. It would choose its own times and would behave erratically in accordance with some impenetrable plan. All she could do was be as ready as possible to make good.

Then, turning her face against the cool pillow, she was swept out towards the far morning on a wide, untracked river of sleep.

6

AT THE BACK OF THE WORLD

AT THE END of that summer, Robin's father suggested Robin go out west to stay with her great aunt Ella, an eccentric and wildly demanding invalid who was looking for someone to help her with the housekeeping. To Sarah's surprise, Robin accepted. "I'm sorry," she said to Sarah. "Aunt Ella needs me now more than you do. But I'll come back to visit." She packed her little suitcase and was gone. Sarah was sure that Robin wouldn't last more than a week, but though Robin called all the time and described with outrage each of Ella's extravagant and tyrannical whims (she would wake Robin in the middle of the night and send her out to the garden with a flashlight to search for rhubarb, or make her wash the rice five times in cold water, and then twice in hot, before allowing her to put it on the stove to boil), it was clear that each was the perfect foil for the other.

Sarah and Max lasted about a year, then he was offered a job with a decent symphony orchestra in a distant city. With mild but not overpowering regret, Sarah watched him trundle his cello off down the road. He had no sooner disappeared in the distance than she ran into Milo at the dry cleaner, and he was so comically huffy at the sight of her, so prickly looking, like a large and offended porcupine, that she was unable to restrain herself from going straight up to him and kissing him between the eyebrows. Before it was fully possible to understand how such things happened, they found themselves living together.

The apartment they chose was not large, but it was pleasant, and filled, on most days, with an interesting gold light. For the first five months, if things were not unutterably perfect, there was, at least, no hint of ghosts.

Then, on one of those balmy May nights at the dead center of spring, when the real stories behind things can't wait to get themselves told, Sarah and Milo started out for dinner at the Mexican restaurant. They had just reached the bottom of the front steps when Sarah was struck with the thought that maybe she had left the gas on. She ran back upstairs and into the kitchen and received the distinct impression that there was a portly, transparent gentleman hovering over a pot of something on the stove. When she walked over to get a closer look, there was, after all, nothing there but the pot, which was filled with some darkish, gooey substance.

"Are you making pudding?" Sarah asked Milo, who was waiting impatiently for her on the front stoop.

He scowled at her, but at this moment they were interrupted, for Mrs. Solloway stepped out of the front door carrying her folding chair. She was wrapped in several overcoats and flannel scarves. Sarah smiled at her, but Mrs. Solloway, ignoring this and all other earthly traffic, merely unfolded her chair and sat down.

Milo took Sarah by the arm and steered her down the steps.

They walked down the avenue silently. It was a beautiful, sweet-scented night. The very dogs were so lighthearted that, like balloons tethered to lampposts, they appeared to hover and yelp several feet off the ground. All up and down the street, windows were being pushed open to receive the warm and thrumming air. Sarah had been a public defender long enough to know what a temptation an open window could be to some people. Even angels would break into people's houses on a night like this. They would drink half the wine in somebody's wineglass, then back drunkenly out the window again like a bee pulling out of a flower.

As they passed the fruit and vegetable stand, a little boy striding down the street in a silver cape and helmet stopped to point at two pigeons pecking in the gutter. "Eagles," he said coolly to a woman, perhaps his mother, who stood near him. Then he strode on. While Milo laughed, Sarah shivered, knowing a portent when she heard one.

Upstairs in the restaurant, while they were waiting for the waitress, Milo carefully studied the tiny bird-sized sombreros which decoratively lined the walls. Sarah watched him for a while. The sight of his long face, friendly and mildly conceited, so absorbed in his examination, filled her with alarm and restlessness. She looked away, down at the street through the big plate-glass window. Then she looked back at him and leaned over and rapped his knuckles.

"Well, now that we've been living together for five months, do you still like me?" she asked.

He squinted as if the room had suddenly gotten very bright and, reaching out for one of the tiny sombreros, took it off its hook and put it on his head. "Sure," he said. "In fact, I like you better than ever."

She wondered if it were true.

"What about you?" he asked. "How do you feel?"

She stared at the tiny hat thoughtfully. He complained about her all the time—that she disturbed the peace, invented monstrous difficulties, and always read much more into matters than was actually there.

"I like you about the same," she said.

If she married him, she'd be marrying a slob. His socks would dangle like party favors from the drawers. His pants slung over the shower rod would always seem to be regaling a wet towel on the floor with tales of their travels abroad. Pennies and gum wrappers would consort gaily in every dark corner.

And, worse, of course, if she married him, there would be no more of those wonderful trips where you rushed out towards the great rim of the world with the moon boiling and thundering in your ears and all the ordinary things—the lampposts and the dandelions and the park benches—singing to you as you went by. She would have to make her starry bed and lie in it.

The waitress arrived with the taco chips and the bowl of hot sauce but, instead of plunking them down and zooming away, she kept readjusting them carefully, as if they were some kind of elaborate flower arrangement. After she finally felt she'd gotten it right, she lingered to polish the saltshaker. At last, Sarah and Milo looked up into her face. It was an amazingly large face, and, although pale and round and not pretty, it was striking because of its very size. She was staring at Milo unhappily.

"Pleez," she said. "You are two lawyers?"

Milo sat up, instantly kind and interested, the little hat bobbing on his head. He looked as if he were about to invite the waitress to sit down, but then seemed to realize this wasn't a thing you did.

"I hear you talking in the restaurant before," she said in a whisper. "Maybe you help me. I can pay," she added quickly.

"What's the problem?" Sarah asked.

But she ignored Sarah and continued to address Milo. "My visa, it is finished, and I have no green card," she whispered.

"Well," said Milo, looking around quickly and lowering his voice, "my office is a government office and we are not supposed to help people without green cards, but I will give you my number, and if you give me a call, perhaps I will be able to advise you."

"You advise me on the *teléfono?*" the woman asked hopefully. "Thanks to you, sir. I am thanking you." She carefully folded and pocketed the piece of paper with the number on it and hurried away.

Milo ate three taco chips with great and rapid satisfaction before he bothered to look at Sarah. "Oops," he said. "You're mad."

It seemed odd, Sarah thought, that someone with such laughing blue eyes should have the interior life of a cabbage. She leaned over and took the little hat off and returned it to its hook. "Well, what are you going to do, Milo, marry her? What advice can you give her? I don't think there's anything else she can do except marry a citizen."

"Don't be ridiculous. You know I don't believe in marriage. I wouldn't marry her or anybody else for a million bucks."

She raised her eyebrows mockingly. "Not for a million bucks?"

"Nope."

"There's no inducement that could be used to persuade you to marry?"

"Well, actually, there is *one* thing."

"Yes?" she asked politely.

"I might be willing to make some kind of deal if, in

exchange, I could be the fastest baseball pitcher in the universe."

"You think they play baseball in other parts of the universe?"

"Oh sure. They already proved that. Some lab out at Stanford."

Sarah felt, uneasily, that the question of her destiny was sitting right here, between them, invisibly feasting on the taco chips. The window, which looked down at the street, also looked up at the sky. She saw a round moon rise and come to a rest first on the edge of one rooftop and then on another. It didn't look substantial, but rather, she thought, like a white hole in the sky, like maybe a traveling doorway into the world in back of the world. It paused here and paused there and waited brightly for some heedless roof walker, or even pigeon, to bumble through. But no bumblers appeared.

The next morning, she woke up with a bang. It had seemed to her that first someone spoke her name very softly but insistently, and then that a gun went off in the kitchen. She lay there listening, but then there wasn't a sound except for the cats, who were curled up by her ear, snorting sleepily.

If anyone was shooting guns off in the kitchen, wouldn't both cats be under the bed? She must have been dreaming. She settled back into the pillows sleepily and was overcome with the pleasantly confused sensation of being a young girl again, back in her parents' house.

When the alarm went off, she sat up with a bolt, and there was a large, rumpled man sleeping beside her. She stared at him in horror. He was lying innocently on his back, and he smelled of apple juice. As she leaned over for a closer look, she saw, with a start, that it was Milo. She shut off the alarm and leaped out of bed.

She showered and dressed and fed the cats, who bumped and hissed around her ankles like sharks.

She dumped some birdseed out onto the tray on the fire escape. "Vultures!" she yelled to the little brown sparrows who cheerfully sang and hopped from branch to branch of the ailanthus tree.

She called him at his office later.

"Why didn't you wake me this morning?" he demanded angrily.

"You're a slob, Milo. I've had it."

"That's why you didn't wake me?"

"Milo, I'm serious."

"Because you want some neat guy who irons his underpants before he puts them on?"

"Cut it out."

"Some guy who flosses his teeth and washes his feet with Listerine every night before he gets in bed? That's why you didn't wake me?"

She looked up from the paper clips she was arranging on her desk and down at the little park below. Several blossoming crab apple trees seemed to have floated loose from their assigned places like huge pink-and-white umbrellas.

She felt her heart unfolding in spite of itself.

"This isn't working out for us, Milo," she said quickly. "Either it's all over or we hire someone to clean the apartment once a week." She knew he would sooner jump into a snake pit than hire someone to come in and clean any apartment of his.

He was silent for a moment. "You know how I feel about this," he said at last.

"Just someone to do the basics for us—you know, the bathroom and the vacuuming. Then maybe I could deal with the finer points more patiently."

"Sarah, you know it is always the poor and disenfranchised people out there who have to take these kind of jobs. How could you look a person who was cleaning your apartment in the eye?"

"There are people out there *looking* for this kind of work, glad to get this kind of work."

"Sure, because they have no choice. Because they're desperate. You want to be partner to a business like that?"

"Sometimes people need jobs like housecleaning because they're on their way somewhere. They're going to school maybe. *I* cleaned houses when I was in college. And, who knows, maybe some people clean houses because they like it. Because they're talented at it."

"How could you live with knowing that this poor schmo who's cleaning up your little messes gets forty bucks a day, while your shrink gets seventy-five an hour?"

"Fine, Milo, fine. I accept what you're saying, although it means curtains for us. Although I know someone out there would be thrilled to clean our apartment for us."

"I'll think about it." He slammed down the phone.

When she got home that evening, he was crouched in the middle of the hallway playing with the cats, who rolled around him adoringly. He was in his running shorts and drenched in sweat. When Sarah stepped around them, he didn't even look up. "Time for your break-dancing lesson," he said tenderly to the big black cat and, grabbing him by the front paws, spun him around on his rump. Sarah heard the cat purring foolishly as she passed by them.

As she headed for the kitchen, Milo looked up from his labors and said, "Robin called a few minutes ago." He had met Robin only once or twice but did not approve of her.

"Yes?"

"She said Ella was driving her nuts because she kept complaining about finding long, dark hairs on the furniture and in the bathtub, and she ordered Robin to wear a hairnet, and Robin went out and got all her hair cut off and dyed orange. She's exceptionally pleased with herself, because now Ella is too mortified to go out in public with her."

Having related this message as coldly as he could, Milo twirled the cat around twice more, then blew in his face, so the cat went skittering down the hallway in annoyance. He looked up at Sarah again. "How was your day?"

Sarah knew that he was going to pretend that the conversation she had had on the phone with him that morning never took place. He was a slob and a con man, full of distractions and cunning strategies to outmaneuver love, heedless of the planets singing and of the truth behind ordinary things. "Fine," she said and went into the kitchen.

She was sweeping up some peanut shells from under the table and imagining Robin with orange hair when, a few minutes later, he came in and, taking off his sweatband, crossed to the windowsill and wrung it out over the begonia.

"Cut that out!" she yelled.

"By the way," he said, "I found someone to clean the apartment for us."

Sarah stared at him. "What?"

"Yeah. I met this guy when I was out running. He's a drummer and he was looking for odd jobs."

Sarah laughed. "Oh, you're kidding."

"No, I'm not kidding. His name is George."

"But, Milo, what makes you think he can clean?"

"He says he's very neat. Don't look at me like that. It's no big deal. I certainly never would have gone out of the way to look for someone to clean the apartment. But this was one of those blows of fate I couldn't ignore. Besides, it helps me that he's a man. It helps my conscience in this matter."

The begonia had never looked better. In the rapidly advancing twilight of the kitchen (for no one had bothered to turn the lights on yet), its small, pink flowers shone brightly like birthday candles.

"He'll be coming next Wednesday," Milo said.

The following night Sarah got home before Milo. She changed into her jeans and T-shirt and went into the kitchen to feed the cats and start dinner. She took the can of cat food out of the refrigerator, and when she turned around again there was an old gentleman, dressed in a blue-and-white-checked flannel bathrobe, standing by the stove holding a saucepan. He looked perfectly healthy, but the blood from the bullet through his heart had soaked through his bathrobe and was now beginning to drip onto the floor.

Sarah gave a hoarse cry and ran out of the kitchen.

When Milo got home, she was waiting for him on the front stoop. "There's an old guy bleeding to death in our kitchen," she told him, but, of course, by the time they had both climbed the stairs and gone back into the kitchen to take a look, he was gone. There was no sign of blood anywhere.

Milo grabbed a damp dishcloth off the handle of the refrigerator door and wapped Sarah on the legs with it.

Sarah struggled to grab it, but he danced in a circle around her, wapping at her calves. "I'm getting tired of this stuff, Sarah. I mean it." He wapped her again.

"It's true," Sarah cried. "It's true! There was an old guy standing by the stove. I swear. Give me that thing. You're hurting me!" She managed to grab one end of it, but Milo held firmly to his own end, whipping it up and down sharply, trying to loosen her grasp. Then he gripped his end tightly and pulled and somehow they ended up in an embrace. Sarah had tears in her eyes, and the dishcloth burned in her hands. They struggled dumbly for a while, and it seemed to Sarah that some satisfying bloodshed lay just out of reach, like the sparrows outside the window always affectionately flicking themselves just beyond the jaws of the cats.

At last Milo seemed to sigh and bent over to breathe upon her hair. "All right, then," he whispered. "Let's get married."

She held herself wildly still, like a giraffe hiding behind a potted fern. What did he mean? When she sneaked a glance at him, she saw that he was very pale.

The first fly of the season clownishly bumbled in through the open window and, singing to itself, flew tipsily past the cats. In an instant, the big black one wapped it out of the air and had it in his mouth. He made a face of disgust but dutifully finished chewing and swallowing, then washed his face very carefully with his paws.

"You can invite your mom and dad and fifteen people you like and I'll do the same," he said.

"Why?" asked Sarah.

"Why?" he said irritably. "I don't know why. People get married to give themselves a certain social status, I suppose, to give a public weight to their connection. They get married so other people will throw rice in their faces and make it as difficult as possible for them to undo the contract."

"You sound as if we had a choice. As if it weren't just the earth binding up two more of its creatures towards its own mysterious ends."

"What are you talking about? Of course we have a choice. That's the whole point, isn't it? That we choose each other?"

"Well, maybe," she said. "I don't know."

She wondered if Robin would come back for the wedding and, if she did, what unpardonable monkey wrenches she would throw into the works.

Milo stared at her aggrievedly. Except that she could still hear the fly singing round their heads like a happy lunatic, everything was silent.

The next morning, he was gone. The apartment, filled with a peculiarly buoyant mixture of air and light, seemed to tug and bob at its moorings, but no underwear dangled from his drawers and his duffel bag had disappeared.

Under the kitchen table the cats were arguing ferociously over a white slip of paper. Sarah picked it up, but it said only, "Cold feet. I'm sorry. Love, Milo." She crumpled it up and threw it back to them. They leaped upon it, snarling and hissing.

It was the apartment itself which seemed to have expanded with relief and sorrow. She sensed, with a tremor of guilt—for hadn't she kept it out for so long now?—that her true fate was fanning the air effortlessly, with papery wings, up near the overhead light. It smelled of hyacinths and felt perfectly famil-iar, like something that had been traveling in her direction since she was only a grain of light tumbling in the void.

She looked up at the ceiling nervously. She knew she had only to let her guard down for a moment and it was going to drag her out of the house and drum her down the street. It would throw her out past the edge of the world and rake her over the stars and, finally, leave her for dead in the snow where the wolves would rip her heart out and feast on it.

However, after a while, when nothing had happened, she sat down at the kitchen table with her bowl of cereal. As soon as she was seated, she saw that she had forgotten to bring a spoon. "Oh crud." She sighed and looked out the window.

When her gaze returned to the kitchen again, there was her portly ghost in his blue-and-white-checked flannel bathrobe, sitting across the table from her.

"What a morning I'm having," she said to him, but he ignored her. He was eating a dark-colored ectoplasmic substance from a saucepan, which was hovering slightly off the table in the air. The weightlessness of the pot seemed to disturb him, and he kept trying to swat it back down with his spoon. After a while, he looked up and glared at something over her shoulder. Another ghost, this one tall and thin, in an expensive white suit, had entered the kitchen. He was holding a gun.

Sarah eased herself out of her chair, grabbed her coat and her briefcase, and fled out the door and down the stairs.

She had just started down the stoop when she was yanked backwards with a terrific pull. Here we go, she thought, and held her breath. But, when she looked around, she was surprised to see only old Mrs. Solloway, who was holding on to her skirt and sniffing, for some odd reason, at her hem.

"Hello," Sarah said, not unkindly, although she was impatient, wanting to be off, let loose into this dangerous morning.

"Humpf," Mrs. Solloway said and dropped the skirt. She was wearing several heavy overcoats buttoned to her chin. Her only concession to this lovely spring weather was a little pink chiffon scarf tied tightly around her head. "So, they came to see you, those two old brothers?"

"You can tell from how my skirt smells?"

"Ghosts, they stink. But you gotta have a nose."

"I've got a nose."

"Maybe. Maybe not. Girls these days, they don't keep a house too clean. They don't pay attention to the odors."

"Well, Mrs. Solloway, girls nowadays have to work or they starve."

"Your young men, they're bums."

"True," Sarah said and laughed. She wondered what Milo would say about that. "All my young men have been bums in one way or another." She glanced eagerly at the street, which ran swift as a river down to the traffic light and disappeared.

"I don't mean personal. I mean the young men in general. Your young man is a good fella."

"And were the young men of your day good fellas?"

"No. They were bums. But at least when one of them fell in love, it was something. He fell like a star out of the sky. He dropped down at your feet and burned a hole in the sidewalk. Why, look at those two brothers. Look how they made such a hoopla. There was love for you."

Sarah sat down on the steps. "It was? What happened?"

Mrs. Solloway shrugged. "Who knows?" She sat silently on her folding chair for a moment, then leaned over and whispered at Sarah, "They left all their money to that woman. This is a fact."

"Which woman?" Sarah asked eagerly.

"Why that one that cleans their apartment. What did she know about cleaning? Nothing. She was on the stage. A magic act. At night she gets cut in half. During the day she moves the dust around in people's apartments. They really made big fools out of themselves. The younger one shoots the older one and then *his* heart goes off, pooff, like the Fourth of July, and he's dead too. Now there's falling in love for you."

Sarah looked up at the sky nervously for signs of any stars burning down out of the blue towards her, but all she saw were the little brown sparrows, whizzing around in the trees with twigs in their beaks. "But what are these guys doing, hanging around in my apartment? What do they want?"

"Don't look a gift horse in the mouth."

"Gift horse! They go parading around my kitchen at all hours, dripping blood on the linoleum and scaring my eyebrows off and you call that a gift horse?"

"Wait a little. When they give you whatever it is they got to give, you gotta give something in return. This is the way to finish the business off. Around in a circle."

"Great," Sarah said and shook out her skirt. She started down the steps but then stopped and asked Mrs. Solloway whatever happened to the housecleaning woman.

Mrs. Solloway sniffed and adjusted her little scarf fussily. "A flower shop. She took the money and started her own business. It's right around the corner there. I wouldn't be bringing any of her flowers into your apartment, though, if I were you."

Sarah laughed and turned away. That which meets the eye and that which doesn't, spread out in front of her, and she stepped down eagerly.

When she got home from work that night, her brother was sitting at the kitchen table eating something out of the saucepan. Next to him was a large shopping bag with a pair of Milo's running shoes sticking out of the top.

"How did you get in here?" she demanded.

"What is this great stuff?" he asked, smacking his lips like a little kid.

"How did you get in here, Fred?"

He sighed. "Milo gave me his keys. He asked me to pick up some things for him. I was supposed to whiz in and then out. He's staying with me, but he doesn't want you to know."

Sarah leaned up against the sink and folded her arms. "Well, that's nice of you—to put him up, I mean."

Fred shrugged. "I like Milo. He's one of the few tolerable people you've ever been involved with."

The little orange cat jumped up on the rim of the sink and rubbed itself against her elbow. Sarah scratched its chin absent-mindedly. "Milo is a slob and worse."

"You got any more of this stuff?" Fred asked hopefully, waving the pot at her.

"Don't ask me. Ask the ghosts, or whatever they are," she said.

Fred frowned. He got up and opened one of the kitchen cabinets and took out the jar of peanut butter and a box of crackers. "Milo claims that's why he left, because you've been making up ghost stories."

Sarah sighed. She sat down at the table and worked her shoes off her feet. "There you are. That's exactly what I mean. Milo is this very simple guy, with this very simple approach to life. During the day, you go to court and maim and slaughter as many landlords as possible, and at night you come home and put your baseball cap on your head, drop socks and newspapers and gum wrappers all over the house, and just generally yuck it up. Milo has allowed his imagination to develop to the size of a large Rice Krispie. He misses a lot."

"Well, but, Sarah, you can't just go waving ghosts around in people's faces like that. It's too intimate. It's too startling. It's like walking down the street wearing your underpants on your head. I can understand why a man would feel like he needed a little distance from that."

"Oh, phooey. He asked me to marry him. Then he got scared and split. That's what happened."

"What?" said Fred, astonished. He stopped spreading peanut butter on a cracker and stared at her.

"He asked me to marry him."

"Is that true? He didn't tell me that. Why on earth would he ask you to marry him?"

She glared at him irritably. "Just a momentary lapse, I suppose."

"Well, no wonder he took off." Fred looked at his cracker thoughtfully, then gulped it down in two large bites. "He's much too young to get married."

"He's thirty-three. Just like you."

"Well, there you are. He's an infant. You can't ask somebody to marry you when you're only thirty-three. You need to be mature before you can make an educated move on something like that. Tell him to come back in a coupla hundred years or so. You sure you haven't got any more of whatever was in that pot?"

"There wasn't anything in that pot."

"Whaddaya mean, of course there was something in that pot. I don't know what it was, but it was creamy and delicious."

Sarah picked the pot up and showed it to him. It was perfectly dry and clean. Fred gazed at it in bewilderment and scratched his nose. "That's a wonderful trick," he said.

Sarah shrugged.

"By the way," Fred said, "your lovely friend Robin called just before you came in."

"What did she want?"

"She said Ella wasn't sleeping well because of a noisy bullfrog who's been looking for love down at the end of the pond every night, and she sent Robin down to catch it and kill it, and Robin went down and caught it and put it in Ella's flannel nightgown drawer. I think they were definitely made for each other, don't you?" He picked up the shopping bag. "Now, don't mention to Milo that I told you where he was."

"Don't worry. I have no intention of speaking to Milo."

* * *

For the next few days she was all nerves, starting at the slightest sound. If someone stopped to ask her the time, she jumped several feet in the air. This is it, she thought, and, although it wasn't, although each time the inquirer walked away, glancing back uneasily at her, she wasn't the slightest bit discouraged. Never had she seen such high blue skies, and the strawberries were the sweetest she had ever tasted.

The cats, it was true, moped around. The little copper-colored one sat by the door waiting for him to come home. The big black cat, not one to be trifled with, peed angrily on his winter coat. Sarah just laughed at them.

All week, people stared at her on the street. She returned their glances nervously, searching for signs of what she was looking for. One night in the elevator, as she was leaving the office, she found herself alone with a gray-eyed woman wearing a perfume that smelled of woodsmoke. The soles of Sarah's feet and the palms of her hands burned hot as coals. A woman, she thought. I should have known. And, indeed, the woman seemed to be examining Sarah affectionately and curiously. Now, what would Milo say to *this*, she wondered. However, when the elevator arrived at the ground floor and Sarah followed her through the front doors and out into the evening, the woman immediately disappeared into the rushing crowd without a backward glance. Never mind, Sarah thought, undaunted. When it comes there will be no mistaking it. It will rip the ground open beneath your feet.

On Friday night, when she was coming home late from work, she was kissed by a cabdriver. Hearing that she wanted to go over the bridge, he had refused to move, saying that it was too far for the time of night. She, for her part, had refused to get out of the cab. Finally, he came and opened her door and, just at the moment when she was staring ahead stubbornly, steeling herself for his act of violence, he leaned over and kissed her.

She backed out of the cab quickly.

"Sorry about the bridge," he said to her. "No can do on a night like this."

Although she hadn't really looked at him, her impression, as he drove away, was that he was breathtakingly beautiful, a Greek god type, with a great mass of curly, gold hair and a mouth that seemed peculiarly alive, like something that had just recently been turned from stone to flesh.

Never mind, she told herself loudly over the noise of her beating heart. At the right moment, the whole course of history will be changed in the wink of an eye.

By Tuesday she was in a fever pitch of excitement and was not thinking about ghosts when she sat down at the kitchen table. The cats eyed her gloomily from the perches where they had been snoozing, the fat one on the stove, the little one from inside the mixing bowl on the shelf over the sink. They'd been very slow to accept Milo when she first brought him home, but now they pined for him to come back and make fools out of them again, to rub balloons on his pants and then stick them on their backs, where they clung with mysterious horribleness, or to give them spoonfuls of peanut butter, which made their tongues cleave to the roofs of their mouths.

Sarah was too excited to pay much attention to their looks of bitter reproach. She was keeping her eye on the phone, the windows, the door, nervously waiting for delivery. When she looked across the table again, there was her portly ghost, sitting down with a newspaper. The saucepan was there again. However, this time it did not float but instead sat innocently in front of him. He opened up the newspaper and began to read. Sarah studied him carefully and saw that he was not quite transparent, but more opaque, like rice paper. Tentatively, she rapped on the table with her knuckles, but either he didn't hear her or he was ignoring her.

A moment later the second ghost entered the kitchen. He was clearly younger than the first and clearly the dashing one. He wore the same spectacular white suit, and, at first, Sarah's sympathies went to the older, portly fellow. Surely he would be the underdog in any romantic duel. But, then, when he looked up from his newspaper and leveled a cool, rather humorous glance at his brother in the white suit, Sarah was not so sure. He returned to his paper.

The ghost in the white suit picked up the saucepan and banged it down hard on the kitchen table. The first one looked up annoyed and appeared to say something to him sharply. In a moment they were obviously both shouting, but the odd thing was that, although Sarah could hear the bang of the saucepan quite clearly, their voices were completely inaudible to her.

And, in a few minutes, when the ghost in the white suit removed a small revolver from his pocket and shot the other one through the heart, Sarah heard the report clearly, but the words the dying man spoke were beyond her ears.

At first, the white-suited ghost did not seem to understand what he had done, for he bent over his fallen brother and patted at his cheeks fearfully. When the life finally gushed from his dying brother's nose in a spurt of blood, he stepped up the cheek patting and, for one moment, even pulled on the dead man's ears as if he thought this might arouse him back to life. But, of course, it was to no avail, and, in a moment, just as Mrs. Solloway described, now *this* one grabbed at his chest in astonishment and toppled over backwards.

Sarah saw that it must have been a terrible and ridiculous unwillingness to compromise which had brought these men to such a pass. Yet this example of love determined to cut no deals served only to fuel her wild hopes. She went over to the window and threw it open and leaned out. Although no one spoke, she heard someone nearby heave a little sigh, and she knew that it was almost time and thought, with a gush of enthusiasm, how brief a reprieve we get from being nothing in the dark.

There was no sign of the ghosts in the morning. The cats accepted their food in accusing silence. Sarah laughed at them. But they paid no attention, and, when they were finished, they settled down into their squares of sunlight to wash themselves gloomily. They didn't bother to look up as she walked out the door into the dangerous spring morning.

She had to go to the courthouse first, and, as she was walking up the steps, almost reaching the top home free, a man coming down seemed to stop in astonishment. He grabbed her roughly by the shoulders. This is it, she thought, closing her eyes and holding her breath.

"Edna? My God. Is that you?"

Well, yes, of course, that's it, she thought. I must be Edna. And here's what love's for, to upend you entirely. Dizzily and with satisfaction, she opened her eyes, and all she saw for a second were the trees dancing tipsily on their heads. Then slowly everything swung around and righted itself, and she was standing near the top of the courthouse steps, staring into the eyes of a man she had never seen before.

He frowned and said, "Oh, I'm sorry. I've mistaken you for someone else." He looked puzzled and a little disappointed. She wanted to tell him not to worry, that, when it's time, true love will go straight to its mark like a baseball between the eyes. But, instead, she said only, "Never mind. That's quite all right" and climbed the last steps quickly and fled into the courthouse.

* * *

When she opened the door to her apartment that evening, there was a strange man wringing out a mop in the kitchen sink. Well, of course, she thought. What a dope I've been.

She examined him with disappointment. He was small and compact and neat as a fox.

Where are the cats, she wondered. And what kind of light is this? The lovely golden evening light of her kitchen had turned stagy and plum colored.

"Who are you?" she demanded, although she knew perfectly well who he was.

"Whaddaya mean?" he said and waved the mop at her. "I thought this was the arrangement." He looked at her inquiringly with his eyebrows raised. "You want me to come another day? I'm George, the guy your husband hired to clean the apartment. I could come another day if you want, although not Tuesday."

She put her briefcase down carefully and stood in the kitchen doorway.

She could see that he had done a wonderful job. Not a single crumb called to her from the toaster oven. Not a ball of cat fur came rolling out from under the sofa. She examined the apartment uneasily as it sparkled in the amazing evening light. She found she couldn't bring herself to look him in the eye. She stared at his sneakers.

"Why can't you come Tuesday?"

"Tuesday is my tai chi class. I'm a drummer, you know, and I take it to counteract my tendency to go for the big 'Boom, Boom.' It keeps my hands aligned with more mental forces." He held his hands out and glared at them suspiciously. "These are your basic rock-and-roll hands."

She shifted her gaze to his hands. They were small and compact, too, and did, somehow, give off an air of having a life of their own. She was seized with an urge to giggle, which she stifled immediately. She felt the ground rumbling far down below, as maybe a subway train passed, and knew there wasn't much time left. He was beginning to pack up his stuff.

He put the cleanser back under the sink, and, when he straightened up, he paused and stared at her thoughtfully, fingering a tiny gold earring in his left ear.

All week she had been stopping in her tracks, amazed to think that, while all the other planets were reputed to be covered in clouds of noxious gas and fire, somehow she had found her way to the only one known with certainty to roll its way around the stars sporting apple trees and air and slippery blue seas.

Perhaps too late now, she remembered what a dangerous sign it was, this feeling out of left field of being lucky.

She forced herself to look him right in the face. He had a sharp, devilish beard, and in his eye was a luminous, slightly off-world look.

"The place is haunted, you know," he said.

Oh no, she thought, and made her face as dumb and courteous and blank as possible. "Oh?"

"It's not easy working with two old guys glaring at you like that. They want something, but I don't know what it is. And what's wrong with you? You look like you just swallowed a spider. You better sit down and let me make you some tea."

Not knowing what else to do, she sat down obediently and waited.

In a couple of minutes he brought the tea over and sat down across from her, sighing. "You don't happen to know any single women, do you?" he asked. "I guess the time has come."

She stared into her teacup fixedly. It was a perfectly made cup of tea, fragrant and hot.

"It's not that I've ever had any desire to get married," he said. "I'm a drummer, you know, and if you're a drummer and

you get hooked up with one person, usually the Power Company right away cuts you off from a lot of your big sources."

"The Power Company?" she said, grunting a little this time
in her effort not to giggle.

"Sure," he said, frowning and making a round, wide gesture
probably meant to indicate the whole universe and whoever
runs it. "Anyway, I was never very interested in long-term
arrangements, but all of a sudden I'm getting this definite feeling it's about to come no matter what I do. It's a physical sensation, like I'm running down a very steep hill. You know how
your feet just go on automatic? It has the feel of fate to it. I figure I might as well ask around. Better not to fight with this kind
of thing. You just end up getting your bones crushed. You know
what I mean?"

Sarah, suddenly meeting the gaze of her own murky reflection in the bottom of the teacup, was unable to help herself and
laughed wildly.

When she was finally able to look up, ready to apologize,
she found that he was paying no attention to her. He was glaring threateningly at his hands, which, seemingly with a will of
their own, were rapping out an excited bridal riff against the
edge of the table. When they were finished, he sighed and
looked up at Sarah. "I'll recognize her when I see her, I think."

It was difficult to know later if among the things that happened next was the thing that should be counted as a gift or if
it was all just a series of unfortunate accidents.

In any case, it happened very quickly. The door buzzer
sounded, and Sarah, jumping up with alacrity to answer it,
found the large-faced waitress from the Mexican restaurant
standing there in the doorway, but, before either of them could
say a word, the big black cat appeared from nowhere and
zipped between Sarah's feet, out into the hallway, and up the
stairs to the roof.

"Go on in and sit down," said Sarah to the woman. "I'll be

right with you. That's George there, in the kitchen." And she ran up the steps after the cat and out onto the roof, where she found the cat crouched at the edge, staring interestedly at something down in the backyard. Sarah, following his gaze, saw her portly ghost sitting stark naked astride a branch of a tree outside her window. He sighted along his index finger as if it were a gun, peering intently with one eye into her kitchen. She couldn't hear him but saw him lower his thumb and say the word *bang*. What would Milo say to that, she wondered.

When she got back down into the kitchen, lugging the sullen black cat under her arm like a trussed turkey, she saw that it was already a done thing. George was leaning across the table towards the strange woman. He could not take his eyes off her. He was pale, much paler than when she had left him, and breathing shallowly. The woman sat stiffly erect, not meeting his gaze. Her shyness was formidable. Her dark hair was pinned up in a braided crown, and she wore a pink blouse embroidered with dragons.

"This lady will not be able to help you," he was arguing hurriedly. He nodded in Sarah's direction. "No offense," he said to Sarah, then looked back at the other woman. "The only thing you can do to get your citizenship is to marry."

Sarah wondered how much of this speech the woman understood.

The woman addressed Sarah. "Your husband advised me to visit your house on this night. He spoke to me about the problem to become a citizen. This man, he is a lawyer, too? What is it he wants?"

Sarah shrugged. "This is George. He comes to clean the apartment once a week."

The woman looked around the kitchen critically. "He does a good job, no?"

"Yes, very good."

"It's a rare gift in a man," George said patiently. "Look, let me be frank. Maybe we could have dinner together or something?"

Again, the woman looked at Sarah for guidance, but Sarah could only hold her palms up in the air helplessly. "My friend doesn't live here anymore, and, I think, even if he were here, there's not much he could say to you. If the authorities find you working without your green card, you will be forced to return to your own country."

"How about Chinese?" George asked. "You like Chinese?"

The woman looked at him bewilderedly. Her large, still moon of a face blushed pink in the great warmth of his attention. "Yes, I like. I like him pretty much," she said uncertainly.

He leaped to his feet. "Well, let's go," he said. "Let's go." He helped her up and ushered her into the hallway and grabbed what was, perhaps, his green umbrella off one of the hooks there. In his rush he clumsily brushed the catch on the umbrella, and it opened up fully with a magical *pop*.

The woman stared at this with wide eyes. "Is great good luck, no?" she asked nervously.

"Yes," he said, "yes," and, holding the umbrella over her head protectively, bundled her through the door and down the stairs into the perfect spring evening.

Sarah watched them disappear, then turned and went back into the kitchen. She had the odd thought that a heavy weight was lifting from her head, a crown maybe, that she had been toting around with her since she was quite a young girl, a dumb gold thing, trimmed with fruit and white veils, little cakes and silver babies. Just as the unseen hands were about to pick it up kindly and lay it aside somewhere, she heard a faint rustle behind her. And, of course, when she turned, there was Milo standing in the doorway with a huge bunch of daffodils.

The cats threw themselves at his feet, purring and wiggling.

He picked the little copper-colored one up in his free hand, and she licked at his nostrils, purring wildly.

"Oh, for God's sakes," Sarah said disgustedly.

"You know," he said, "the first thing I want to tell you is that I started over here feeling calm and ready, resolved to ignore your wild fantasy life and basically looking forward to being with you again, but then I stopped to buy you these flowers, and the woman behind the counter told me a crazy story about this apartment which got me annoyed with you all over again."

Sarah didn't say a word. She was having a moment of doubt. Supposing he was right? That what lies in front of you is simply the never-ending task of learning to choose wisely and that there was nothing at the back of the world to help take you where you were going except a ridiculous assortment of chances.

"Nevertheless," he said, "here I am." He stood there confidently, as if he thought he were a large birthday present. When she didn't move, he walked across the room and put his arms around her.

"You're a slob," she argued into his shirt.

"I've reformed," he said. "You'll see. In a minute I'll give you a demonstration, but first I want to hold you for a little while."

She let him do this, and, with her nose in his chest, breathed in surreptitiously. He smelled of apple juice, but they were deceptive, she knew, these fruit juice smells that made you think you were, at last, in the arms of someone safe and sweet.

"So I assume you talked to this florist?" He waved the daffodils at her. "That that's what inspired you to make up this story about the ghosts?" he said.

She pushed him away in exasperation. Across the room the two of them appeared suddenly, standing side by side in the kitchen doorway.

They waited expectantly, watching, one in his white silk

suit, the other, dressed now, in his blue-and-white-checked bathrobe.

She sighed. "No. I never talked to her. But I can make a good guess at what she told you."

"Yeah, what?"

"She told you she worked for them and that they both fell in love with her and one day they had a big fight and the younger one shot the older one and then he was so upset at what he'd done, he had a heart attack."

He looked at her intrigued, as if he couldn't quite figure out what she was up to now. "Well, no," he said, "not quite. She did say she worked for them, but nothing about love. She said they fought a lot over domestic chores and stuff and that they killed each other over some dishes in the sink or something." He blushed faintly. "Well, don't look so stricken, Sarah. I told you, I understand this now. If you must know, I've been staying with someone who is surely one of the messiest and most disorganized of living beings and it's taught me a lesson. I've turned over a new leaf. Really." He grabbed hold of her awkwardly and stroked her hair, but she ignored him.

She stared bewilderedly over his shoulder at the two shadowy figures in the doorway.

"Look, see, I'll show you," he said and, letting go, turned to look for something to clean up.

Sarah saw the two ghosts come to attention, and she scanned the kitchen quickly, on the alert. But it was too late. Before she could stop him, Milo had picked up the little saucepan from the kitchen table, where it had appeared from out of nowhere. He carried it swiftly over to the sink.

The night air was soft and warm. Out back, in the tiny, postage-stamp gardens, the birds, getting ready for bed, swooped and scolded and carried on. Milo turned the water on, plunged the pot into the sink, and began to scrub.

"Wait!" yelled Sarah, but it was too late.

In the final moment, the two ghosts seemed to fill with light. They shimmered and floated upwards, and when they hit the ceiling they popped like soap bubbles and were gone. Sarah stared after them sadly.

Milo, however, triumphant, waved the shiny pot in the spring air.

The big black cat, who had been sitting nearby, watching Milo with devotion, reached his paw under the stove, where he had been storing a green toy mouse for just such an occasion. He pulled the mouse out and, bringing it over to Milo, dropped it at his feet. Milo picked it up and flung it into the air.

"Quick," said Milo. "We need a little privacy."

While the cats went racing the other way down the hall, he grabbed her hands and pulled her into the living room and dragged her down behind the armchair, where he kissed her nose, her eyelids, and her hair. But then he paused and looked into her eyes so searchingly that she understood he was looking for all the invisible things she claimed to see. After a while he sighed, and she knew that, of course, he had found nothing. She was curious to hear what he would say, but he didn't say anything for a while, just opened the top buttons of her blouse rather humbly and laid his ear down somewhere near her heart. "Did you know there are no two identical breasts in the world?" he said at last. "They're just like snowflakes."

In a moment, the cats came tumbling around the side of the armchair arguing over the green mouse, but when they got a look at Sarah's and Milo's faces they stopped suddenly at a respectful distance.

"Why what's the matter with you, you old fur balls?" Milo asked them.

Sarah knew. It was the worst of disasters. The linoleum trembled and opened at their feet, and the birds, getting ready for bed, stopped what they were doing and sang like bells.

7

THE JEALOUS GODS

PART I

THEY HAD BEEN married a year when they decided it might be a good time to start working on a baby. However, when the actual moment arrived, she found herself overcome with panic. She could have yelled out to him to stop, but, of course, when it gets to that point, it's not a moment you can stop.

She thought of the millions of possible babies spreading out, racing, blind as little comets, towards her ovaries. Her position of responsibility in all this, to be the vast and milky night sky in which it would all begin, felt like more than she could bear. Furthermore, it shook her terribly to think that a tip of her hips to the right could bring forth to the world one person, and a tip of her hips to the left might bring forth another, and that, no matter which way she decided to lean, a million other babies would be left behind. Unless, of course, the baby was already a done thing, long ago chosen, its name written down in the book that everything got written down in at the very beginning. Which was certainly another disturbing possibility.

Milo kissed her nose and rolled off to the side. The two cats, who did not approve of sex, now came out from under the bed and made their way up over the blankets with careful distaste. As they went, they stopped here and there and circled around fussily, testing different spots for warmth. At last they settled down, wedging themselves tightly into the space between Sarah and Milo.

"So whaddaya you think? You think we did it?"

It was Christmastime, and this very evening she had lugged a pine tree home from the corner vegetable store, then sweated tenderly over the baking of three dozen gingerbread men. Now the air of the season waltzed loudly through the house, like children clanging saucepan lids together, festooned with popcorn and little bells, and Milo, who claimed to feel nothing different about this time of year except the coldness and the heightened misery of the lonely and homeless, who laughed at her notion that December was more round with the expectancy of light about to break through than other months, who hooted rudely at the notion of holiness or miracles in any form, now had the nerve to ask her if she thought that the ridiculous and awkward thing they had just done was likely to throw off the spark that would set into motion an entirely new and never-before-thought-of human being.

"You fall for that old story?" she said spitefully. "You actually think that *sex* makes babies?"

He closed his eyes. "Don't start with me, Sarah."

"Milo, c'mon, for God's sakes, that's just one of those modern science theories that'll be passé before you turn around. Everybody knows that the pixies make all the babies.

They recycle them out of the peaceful electricity that dances in the void and they use sex as a front. They do it because they like to make trouble, because they don't like to see things in a state of rest or harmony. They think it's a waste of energy. They sit around up there watching for some likely couple to have sex, and then, when the female is sleeping, they whip up a baby out of quarks and neutrinos and stick the baby in through her ear and blow it down into her inner recesses and they lead the couple into thinking that sex is what did it because they know sex, being, on the one hand, so slimy and ridiculous and, on the other hand, so redemptively satisfying, confuses people. And they want people to be as confused as possible, right from the beginning."

She had been trying to lie perfectly still as she spoke, but now an awful cramp gripped her left calf, and she was forced to point and flex her foot. When the cramp finally subsided, she turned on her left side with a sigh and looked at Milo and found that he was fast asleep. The smell of pine and gingerbread did not seem to bother him at all as it made its way innocently through the apartment.

Christmas came and passed, and she was perfectly fine, her attention absorbed at work by the small- and big-time criminals who sullenly submitted themselves to her for legal counsel. At home she was distracted by the leftover turkey and the final celebrations of the old year. Then, quite abruptly, it was January, and she counted up and found her period was several days late.

On the seventh morning, when she had just finished pouring the pee into the little home pregnancy test tube, Robin called. "I dreamt you accidentally swallowed a penny," Robin said.

Now you never knew how it was going to be with Robin anymore, whether her mind would be in or out to lunch, here in this world or visiting one of those spaces which lie between stations on the radio, where the darkness is filled with static and many singing voices come and go. However, that she was calling at seven o'clock on a weekday morning was not a good sign.

The last time Sarah had seen her had been at the wedding, where she had sat through the ceremony quite sedately but during the reception had jumped up on the table and announced, "I will now do a magic trick in honor of Milo, the groom, who, just this afternoon, has had the unearned good fortune to marry one of the truest and most intelligent of human beings, my best friend, Sarah."

She bent down and snatched up a white linen table napkin and a bread roll, and she told everybody that if they kept their eyes on the bread roll she would make it disappear, and, in its place, she would produce a three-headed frog. She covered the bread roll with the napkin, then pulled it off with a flourish, and there sat the same bread roll.

"Voilà!" she proclaimed. "I will now saw this frog in half." She bent down and picked up a knife and began sawing at the roll so that crumbs went flying every which way, spraying into the hair and eyes of all the nearby guests. At this point Milo told Sarah to get her crazy friend off the table or the marriage was off.

Sarah coaxed her down with a piece of wedding cake, and after that Robin appeared to sit quietly at the table, resting on her laurels. Milo claimed that she never took her murderous eyes off of him for the rest of the dinner and clearly looked like she was plotting something. But Sarah dismissed this with a laugh.

The next day, Robin went back out west but continued to

call Sarah regularly to keep her updated on how it went between her and Ella. Now, however, if Milo answered the phone, she hung up. This was fine with him, as he had no more desire to talk with her than she did with him.

"You're calling to tell me you had a dream last night that I swallowed a penny?" Sarah said, irritably. The cats sat on the edge of the counter and pretended disinterest, but, when she set the pee on the corner of the bookshelf and took out a can of cat food, they crowded over immediately, trying to read the label to see if it was one of the flavors they might deign to eat.

"Actually, I had the dream this morning. Just a little while ago. What's happening with you? It was a wonderful dream."

Sarah opened the can, divided it into two bowls, and put one down in front of each cat. The black cat sniffed at his bowl condescendingly. Then he casually crossed the counter to where the little ginger-colored cat was eating hers and knocked her aside. She jumped fearfully to the floor and cowered under the table.

"I'm fine," Sarah said. "What's so wonderful about swallowing a penny, and why are you calling me at this hour?" She went over and peeped inside the test tube and saw a misty shape forming at the bottom.

"Why, to tell you my dream and to let you know I was thinking of you. Ella is sick."

"What's wrong with Ella?"

"Something with her gallbladder."

"Is it serious?"

"I hope so. I hope the old crone dies an excruciating death."

"Robin, for God's sakes."

"Oh, don't worry, she's tougher than a rubber pork chop. She's going to live at least another two or three thousand years. A little thing like a gallbladder won't be what does her in, believe me."

"I have to go," Sarah said. "I need to get ready for work."

"But my dream! Isn't it wonderful?" Robin laughed happily.

"Are you taking your medication?"

"Of course I am. I'm fine. You're going to be fine too. You'll see."

"Good-bye, Robin. I've got to go." She hung up the phone.

In the bottom of the test tube was, of course, the doughnut shape the instructions directed you to look for. She had briefly the sensation of falling, of falling through dark space with not a handle or doorknob to grab onto.

She made Milo promise not to tell anyone for a while. She wanted to wait a couple of months to make sure everything was going all right, to give herself a chance to adjust to the idea.

She was unremittingly queasy, and had trouble keeping anything but saltines and ginger ale down. Milo, who had never seemed happier, now strolled through their little apartment whistling and humming and looking about him as if what he saw was much more than their ceilings, which needed repainting, and their beat-up furniture and floors. He was constantly debating with himself whether the crib would be better here, or the changing table there, and he ate as he went, leaving behind him carefree crumbs and cans of beer, cupcake wrappers and trails of popcorn. He began to take on a prosperous little paunch.

"I can't stand this," she said. "What's the matter with you?"

He looked at her good-humoredly. "Whaddaya mean?"

"I mean all this disruption, all this reaarranging of my furniture, all this debris, all these little snacks that you don't clean up. You have to stop it. You're getting fat, and you're driving me crazy."

"This is all hormones, Sarah. Hormones and imagination. Why don't you just cool out?"

She realized with a sinking heart that he was going to be absolutely no use as a father, feckless and irresponsible, that the apartment was always going to be a shambles, and that, in any case, it was absurd, wasn't it, this custom of having two people promise to spend their whole lives together?

Furthermore, part of her found it impossible to believe she was actually pregnant. It nagged at her that there was not, after all, one real shred of proof, other than the doughnut-shaped ring in the bottom of the test tube and the fact that at inconvenient hours of the day—it might be right after breakfast or in the middle of a summation—she would be possessed with a ravenous appetite for some sickening thing like a fried fish sandwich. This was not, she was sure, her own appetite, but, on the other hand, it was certainly almost impossible to believe that a tiny fetus, no bigger than a dime, could so profoundly desire a fried fish sandwich.

She did not find the doctor convincing either. He beamed a light up inside her and poked around while he held a spirited Talmudic discussion with Milo on baseball and somebody-or-other's RBIs.

"You see it?" she asked nervously.

He looked up at her as if surprised to find her there. Then he smiled. "Everything looks fine." He put one hand up inside her as far as he could get it and then, with the other hand, pressed down on her abdomen so that she felt all her inner workings push up against her heart and stars filled the examining room. "Fine," he said again. "Everything appears normal."

That night in bed, she turned to Milo and said, "You know, he never actually came out and said I was pregnant."

"What? Who never came out and said you were pregnant?"

"The doctor."

He looked at her in disbelief.

"I mean he said I was fine and everything, but he never said anything about pregnant."

"Whaddaya think, Sarah, you think he had his hand all the way up there because he was looking for his car keys?"

"They always do that, Milo. They always stick their hand up there like that. It doesn't mean anything in itself."

"You're a real stitch, Sarah." Milo laughed. He kissed her and turned out the light.

A damp, licorice-colored cloud of gloom and pessimism began to follow her about wherever she went. She lived in constant terror of accidentally exposing herself to toxic substances, of breathing or eating something with an unsympathetic nature, she worried about aerosol spray cans and fresh paint, she worried about bug sprays and the carbon monoxide emitted from the city buses that accelerated off of every corner. She feared hidden MSG in Chinese take-out food, the caffeine in chocolate bars, potatoes with black spots. She not only feared the invisible treacheries of the immediate environment, that, for instance, she might go to somebody's house for dinner and fail to be informed that just that afternoon they had cleaned their oven but also feared her devious unconscious self, which might get up in the middle of the night, sleepwalking, and drink a beer or eat a nitrate-loaded hot dog.

She was pretty sure that all of her worrying had already permanently damaged the baby's personality and it was going to begin its life a morose and blighted human being.

"Don't be ridiculous," Milo said. "The baby doesn't feel you worrying."

"You don't think I'm dumping a lot of adrenaline and other poisons into its system?" she asked plaintively.

"The baby is protected. The doctor has told you at least a million times. The placenta screens most of the bad stuff out. You have to stop worrying so much for my sake. You're driving me crazy."

It appeared to her, however, that the more she worried, the happier he got.

When she could no longer close her jeans and had to put a rubber band through the buttonhole and around the button to keep them up, it was late spring. It was hard to believe they had come around once more to where you could take off your jacket and tie it around your waist and have cherry blossoms drop out of the cherry trees onto your head like pink silk parachutes.

One evening she had been standing in the middle of the kitchen simply staring out the window when Milo came in from his run. He pulled off his sweatband and dropped it on the table. Whistling, he rummaged around in the cupboard till he found a box of pretzels, then he yanked open the refrigerator and pulled out a beer. He sat down at the kitchen table and worked off his running shoes.

"Are you just going to leave those there?" she asked ominously.

"Leave what where?"

"Those," she said, pointing at his shoes.

He looked under the table and stared at the shoes. Then he looked back at her. "Of course not." He began to munch happily on his pretzels and regaled her with stories about his afternoon on intake. He had a new client, an elderly lady, who told him at great length how she wanted him to do something about her landlord, who was sending ultrasonic radio waves through the ceiling into her rent-controlled apartment in an attempt to take over her mind and get her to move out. Milo, who could be very good with old ladies, told her there was nothing he could do for her legally, but, in cases like this, he often suggested wrapping aluminum foil around the TV antennas so as to safely collect and discharge all the radio waves in the apartment. He sent her off, he claimed, madly in love with him.

Sarah, dwelling gloomily on this story, reached into the box and took out a pretzel.

"Listen," Milo said, "it's time to call some select people and tell them the news."

"Uh-uh."

"Oh, come on, Sarah. What is your problem here?"

"No way."

Milo looked at her speculatively. "I bought you a little present." He got up and went out into the other room and came back with a flat little paper bag, which he handed to her. Inside was one of those photographic books depicting and describing in awestruck, breathless captions the development of a fetus. She looked down at it in horror.

He took it out of her hand and leafed through it till he got to the page that showed the baby at five months. "Look," he said proudly. Curled up in the photo was a tiny creature with limbs no thicker than dandelion stems and with skin of such translucent paper fineness that all its major blood vessels clearly showed through. Never had she seen anything more unprotected looking. A wave of queasiness rose up into her throat. She bent down and picked up Milo's running shoes from under the table and carried them off to his closet. On her way back, she stopped in the bathroom and threw up her pretzel.

When she returned to the kitchen, Milo, on the phone with his mother, was eating an ice cream sandwich and describing how it felt to him when the doctor put the little amplifier to Sarah's belly and the baby's heartbeat came tumbling and thumping into the examining room. After his parents, he called her parents, then his sister, his best friend, who now lived in Texas, the two guys he ran with on weekends, and, last, but not least, Fred. He handed her the phone each time, and she bore everybody's congratulations with what she considered to be miraculous fortitude. At the sound of her own mother's joy, she almost wept, but then caught herself, remembering how many times, and in how many ways, this selfsame mother had told her that becoming a parent was the same thing as throwing open your doors and inviting all the world's floods and tornadoes and plagues of sorrow to come in and stand by the fireplace to warm their bottoms.

When Milo was done calling everybody, in a great gesture of goodwill, he pushed the phone over to her and suggested she call her crazy friend, Robin, and tell her the news.

"I think I'll wait on that one," Sarah said politely.

Milo shrugged and rose and headed for the shower.

"You cannot seriously be intending to leave all this junk just sitting on the table?"

Milo turned around and looked at the table in surprise. There was his sweatband, the beer bottle, the empty box of pretzels, and the ice cream sandwich wrapper. He sighed. He very deliberately put the sweatband back on his head and rinsed out the bottle at the sink and stuck it on the windowsill with the other empties. He tossed the ice cream sandwich wrapper in the garbage, then he picked up the pretzel box and turned it upside down and shook it over Sarah's head so that all the salt and crumbs came raining down around her.

"I can't believe this is happening to me!" she screamed.

"Wouldya lighten up already?" he said, giving the box a final shake.

Late in the evening on Wednesday, Fred stopped in after teaching his class at the university. Sarah opened the door, and he stood there grinning. He was neatly dressed for Fred, in clean sneakers and blue jeans and a white T-shirt with the words EAT BEANS, NOT ANIMALS on the front and a silk-screened cow grazing placidly beneath a tree. "Oh, God, I'm so excited," he told her, and he tried to lift her shirt to get a look at her stomach.

"What are you doing?" she yelled and slapped at his hands. At this moment, Milo appeared in the hallway.

Fred rushed over to him and kissed him on both cheeks. "What a regular miracle," he said delightedly.

Milo blushed modestly, Sarah noted, as if some great feat of strength or intelligence had been involved.

"I have an idea for an experiment," Fred told them excitedly. "Just an informal little thing—between friends." He put his hand proprietarily on Sarah's gently bulging stomach. Sarah jerked away.

"You must be out of your mind," Sarah said.

"Come on in and have a beer," Milo said and led the way into the kitchen.

The two men went into the kitchen and started opening the refrigerator and the cupboards and unloading snacks and beverages. Sarah stood in the doorway. "I just cleaned up in here," she said threateningly.

"Hormones." Milo smiled. "Pay no attention to her."

When they had enough stuff to last them several nights, they sat down.

"Sarah, please let me see it. C'mon," Fred pleaded.

She came over to him reluctantly. She was wearing a large white T-shirt of Milo's. Her brother lifted it up with the most reverential of hands and, bringing his mouth right up to the front of her swelling belly, he said, "Hello, in there. This is your uncle Fred. Soon we will meet. I have great stuff to show you." He stroked her stomach lightly. "It's a boy," he said.

"Oh, c'mon," Sarah said.

"How do you know?" Milo asked.

"See the way it sticks out in the front and comes to a point like that? Means it's a boy."

Sarah rolled her eyes.

Milo laughed. "A boy," he said happily. He crumpled up an empty bag of potato chips and lobbed it at the garbage can. The bag landed on the floor, several inches shy of its target.

"Do you know what he does?" Sarah said in a low, ominous voice. "He parks his gum on the back of kitchen chairs. He takes out the milk, and then he never bothers to put it back. He eats potato chips in bed."

"These allegations are outrageous," Milo said.

Fred let the T-shirt fall back down over her distended stomach. He leaned back and took a sip of beer. "How do you think you'd feel if Milo woke up one morning and he'd suddenly been transformed into someone very neat?"

"Great. I'd feel great."

Fred raised his eyebrows and crunched thoughtfully on a carrot.

"So what's the experiment?" Milo asked, putting his feet up on the table.

"Get your feet off the table!" Sarah screamed.

Milo sighed and took his feet down. "She thinks a little germ or something is going to ride in here on my foot, then jump down on the table and wait around to crawl into her soup so it can make the baby go blind."

Fred considered, smearing a bagel with cream cheese. "And have you given any thought to how it would be for you if she suddenly stopped worrying about everything?"

Milo ignored him. "The baby's going to be fine!" he yelled at Sarah. "Tell her, Fred. Tell her the baby's going to be fine."

Her brother smiled. "You wanna hear about my idea?"

"Forget it, Fred. You think I'd let a madman like you experiment on my baby?"

"Don't you wonder what it must be like in there?" Fred said, pointing at her belly.

She wondered, but she certainly wasn't about to let Fred know this.

"Whether he's picking up in any way on the events out here? Whether he's going to *remember* anything about his first nine months?"

Sarah eyed him nervously. "Don't be an idiot. Of course it's not going to remember anything. What's there to remember?"

"Oh, c'mon, Sarah," Milo said. "Let's just see what he has in mind. Aren't you curious?"

"No."

Fred leaned over and picked up his knapsack. He had a large smudge of cream cheese next to the corner of his mouth, and his hair stuck out happily, as it always did when he was about to embark on a new experiment. "Look, I brought all my equipment with me."

"You can't imagine I'm going to let you hook me up to a lot of electrodes and timers and things?"

Fred undid the straps of his knapsack and pulled out a battered old harmonica and smiled at her.

She looked at this uncomprehendingly.

"Now, here's what we do. We choose a song and we sing it. Then, every night at the same time, you sing it again, even if I'm not here to supervise."

"Whaddya mean?" Milo asked, puzzled. "What kind of song?"

"Well, hmmmm . . . a song like . . . How about 'Eensie Weensie Spider'?" He leaned forward, played an introductory note on the harmonica, then began to sing.

> Eensie weensie spider
> Went up the water spout.
> Down came the rain
> And washed the spider out.

Milo cleared his throat and leaned forward to join him.

> Up came the sun
> And dried up all the rain.
> Then eensie weensie spider
> Went up the spout again.

The men sat back and looked at Sarah expectantly. "Well," her brother said, "did you feel anything?"

"Just the usual," she said impatiently. "It twirled around a few times, and now it's got the hiccups."

"Very interesting," her brother said. "Now, the vital thing is to remember this. You sing the song every night at the same hour until the baby is born. Then—after the baby is born, for the first six months, no one, absolutely no one, is to sing 'Eensie Weensie Spider' in his presence. When six months is up, and the baby is old enough to make some deliberate and interpretable responses, I will come over and we'll sing the song together and I'll make written observations. OK?"

"Sure." Milo smiled.

At this moment the phone rang.

Fred looked around guiltily. "If that's Tony, tell him I'm not here. I'm on my way."

"Who's Tony?" Milo asked.

"A new friend?" Sarah asked pointedly, relieved to have the attention diverted from herself.

Fred perhaps did not hear them. He hastily shoved his harmonica back in his knapsack, did up the straps, and, as Sarah picked up the phone, whispered to her, "Don't worry about a thing. The baby is going to be fine." Then he was through the door.

Sarah said hello into the phone, curious to hear the voice of this new mystery person. It was, however, Robin.

"Why didn't you tell me you were pregnant?"

"How did you find out?"

"I used to be your best friend."

Now Sarah went over to the window and looked out into the upper branches of the city tangle of backyard trees. Through the veil of green she saw, across the way, a little girl practicing the piano in her living room. Sarah could not hear what she was playing, but at this moment the girl stopped, adjusted the barrette which held her bangs off her face, and began to twirl around on the piano stool.

"I'm sorry," Sarah said. "I seem to be having some trouble coming to terms with the reality of this thing. But I should have told you."

"It's a girl," Robin said.

Someone must have yelled at the little piano player to get back to business, for she sat up now guiltily, looked behind her, then returned her hands to the keys. Sarah wanted to believe in it, that the day would come when she would yell tenderly at her own small piano player, but she could not take herself so far, fearing she might call down the wrath of some jealous god or other. "How's Ella?" she asked.

"She's in the hospital."

"Gallbladder?"

"No. Bad deeds. All her bad deeds from this life and all her past lives, come back to haunt her. May she die an excruciating death."

"Robin," she chided.

"Don't worry, she's having a wonderful time. Two private duty nurses have already quit. She accused the first one of being a man wearing a dress who snuck into her bed every night. The second she accused of stealing her teeth. She's much crazier than I am."

"Is that possible?"

"I'm perfectly sane at the moment, and, when the baby is born, I'll come in for a visit."

"I'll call you."

"Sarah, I had a dream. She's going to be a movie star, and get married four times."

"I've gotta go."

"She's going to be fine. Stop worrying."

"OK. Sure."

She had planned to work right up until the birth of the baby, but, increasingly, she found that those she had always defended with such goodwill and competence, the muggers and the turnstile hoppers, the prostitutes and car thieves, refused to take her seriously. When they saw who had been assigned to protect their inalienable rights, depending on their temperaments and the nature of their crimes, they either made lewd jokes or looked around in despair. At the end of July she requested an early leave of absence, and this was granted to her. She packed up the contents of her desk and the philodendron that hung in the window and went home and began to clean the apartment with a vengeance. She went through every closet and kitchen cabinet, dusting, throwing away, reorganizing. She washed all the curtains and blankets and rugs and took all the books off the bookshelves and put them back in alphabetical order.

"You think the baby is going to care whether the books are in alphabetical order?" Milo asked bewilderedly.

She wasn't about to answer questions like this and just ignored him.

Summer took over in its thuglike way. She could not believe how uncomfortable she was, that nature could have deliberately designed such a torment, that the torment would ever end. After a while, she could neither stand nor sit, nor lie down in any one position for more than a few minutes at a time, and, by the end of a day of relentless cleaning, she felt like a tugboat with half an engine, huge and lost, steaming with pitiful, dreamlike slowness down an utterly unfamiliar jungle river.

When she could do no more, she would lower herself onto the bed with a groan. She did not care whether she ate or not, but Milo, who was more interested in food than ever, would bring her some supper on a plate, and she would half sit up and try to eat it, while he lifted her T-shirt and sang "Eensie Weensie Spider" into her belly button, as if her belly button was, somehow, a telephone from here to there.

Towards the end of her pregnancy, the baby seemed to grow very restless whenever it heard this song. No sooner would the spider be ascending his spout than the great dome of her stomach would begin to heave and shift from side to side. Sometimes a small fistlike, or perhaps footlike, knob would appear against the surface of her skin and then disappear.

"It knows I'm here," Milo would whisper, awestruck. "It's trying to talk to me."

"Yes, and it says, 'My God, is that hippopotamus my father?'"

Milo, who was now, in this stage of her pregnancy, unbearably high-spirited, would pat his little paunch affectionately and continue to eat whatever he was eating. Crumbs dropped like snow, all over the bed.

On the night of their fourth childbirth class, the childbirth instructor pulled down a movie screen, turned out the lights, and showed them a short film of a woman screaming and panting and sweating and writhing and eventually producing a small, cheesy-looking thing that everyone proclaimed was a baby. Sarah was horrified beyond speech.

When the lights were turned back on, she saw that Milo and several other men (no women, she noted) were weeping tenderly.

When he reached over and squeezed her hand, she did not return the gesture, but sat staring at him in stony silence. He squeezed it again, and she withdrew it and rested it where her lap once used to be.

Later that evening when they were home and he leaned over and began to sing, nothing happened. The baby did not move. Her stomach stayed still and round and firm as a cantaloupe.

"Sing it again," she ordered.

He did. Still nothing happened. "It's sleeping," he said and ran his hand lightly over her stomach. She pushed it away.

"Something's wrong," she said flatly.

"Stop worrying, there's not a thing to worry about. It's just getting very crowded in there. The doctor told you not to expect much movement towards the end."

"I'm not due for another three weeks."

"I *know* when you're due. Why don't you get some sleep now while you can? I'll turn out the light. OK?"

She did not answer, but turned slowly over onto her side and closed her eyes.

The baby, she knew, had given it up. Unable to forgive her for her cowardice and revulsion, her sadness and anxiety and utter failure to do anything to change the cruel nature of the world, it had disconnected the lifeline and floated back into the void.

Sarah lay in the dark and wept bitterly.

After a while the cats jumped up on the bed and circled around her warily, sniffing. She expected them to try to crowd themselves onto her pillow, as they always did, but tonight they sat down in watchful positions at the foot of the bed and waited. At around eleven Milo came in and lay down next to her, and, unable to deal with giving him the news, she pretended she was asleep. In a few minutes, he was snoring gently.

At around midnight, a great thunderstorm came crashing out of the east. First the wind came whistling shrilly down the alleyways and rolled all the garbage cans out into the street, then the thunder came booming and clapping over the roofs. She was surprised at how the cats stayed in their positions at the foot of the bed. For a second or two at a time as the lightning flashed and illuminated the whole room, she would see them staring up at her watchfully. Then everything would be plunged back into darkness. Milo slept innocently through the whole storm, never stirring.

At around one, however, when the downpour had almost stopped, Milo sighed and woke up. He got out of bed and tiptoed into the kitchen and opened the refrigerator and took something out. She heaved herself over on her back and lay there in despair and tried to tell from the sounds he was making what he was eating.

When he got back in bed with a little grunt of satisfaction, she could smell clearly what it was. She was surprised to find herself filled with indignation.

"Why are you getting up in the middle of the night to eat peanut butter? Don't you know that the middle of the night is the worst time to eat anything? That the calories go straight to your fat cells when you eat in the middle of the night?"

For a moment he lay in the dark surprised and startled by this ambush. "I wasn't eating peanut butter," he said to her at last rather huffily.

She struggled to turn towards him, then gave it up. She felt herself utterly abandoned, sent out in a colander to paddle helplessly upon a wildly tossing sea.

"I smell peanut butter," she said, at last, to the ceiling.

He sighed.

"How will I ever trust you again?" she whispered. "How will I be able to live with you and not be full of doubt?"

He sighed again. "Sarah, doubt—especially lately—is your middle name. Doubt seems to be what keeps your hair on and your pants up. But the truth of the matter is that getting up in the middle of the night and eating a spoonful of peanut butter is not a crime or a calamity and is not going to cause the world to come to a screeching halt."

Sarah rose and took her pillow and her blanket and waddled out to the sofa, and, as soon as she lay down, the baby gave her one great savage kick in the ribs and her water broke. When she sat up more water came gushing out.

"Milo!" she yelled.

He was either fast asleep or ignoring her, but the two cats jumped up on the sofa, sniffing with great feline proprietariness at the wet spot that was spreading around her. She tried to throw them off onto the floor, but they just jumped right back up.

"Milo!" she screamed. "The baby!"

A moment later, Milo was standing there in his underwear staring wildly around the living room as if he expected to see the baby come crawling towards him. "What's going on?" he demanded.

When she explained what had happened, Milo, who usually traveled so light, went dashing all around the apartment gathering together a strange assortment of items he apparently thought they were going to need at the hospital, including three pillows from the sofa, a Parcheesi set, and a flashlight. Sarah, watching him, was surprised to hear herself laugh. She felt, at last, a little door blow open inside herself, and the air of a calm and moonlit night seemed to fill the room.

PART II

Towards the end of the labor she had a strange experience. She had been hating Milo and had yelled at him to take his hands off her, for he, wanting desperately to be of some use, had been rubbing her back. She saw his face up close and all distorted as if she were seeing it reflected in a hubcap or the bottom of a silvery bowl, and it was full of compassion and a terrible relief that it was she and not himself who was suffering this thing. Then his face disappeared, and there was just the silvery bowl, which seemed to be full of light and to lift up like a little flying saucer and float errantly about the room until it came to rest in her own hands, upon which the doctor told her that here was the baby's head and to push as hard as she could and she felt as if she were experiencing lift-off, being pressed back against the bed, unable to move, only able to stare out at the earth disappearing beneath her. Milo was yelling at her from very far away, and she forgot to look in the mirror they had placed at the bottom of the bed. A few minutes later they put the baby in her arms.

The baby was wet and slimy and very red in the face. When she looked over at Milo, however, she saw that he was holding his breath and peering at it closely as if it were glass or air or beauty itself, making a brief personal appearance before it vanished back to wherever it had come from. When she reached out to squeeze Milo's hand, she saw that he did not even seem to realize she was there.

After the nurse had wrapped the baby in a blue paper blanket and carried it off for a cleanup, Milo sat down on the high, narrow bed and rested his forehead on Sarah's shoulder. He whispered something into her hospital gown.

"What? I can't hear you."

He lifted his head and gave her a sheepish, anxious glance and looked away. "Do you think it'll be all right?"

"Why, what do you mean?" she said.

"I mean, what if they mix the babies up? I mean, we don't know anything about that nurse. She could drop it. She could stick it in her handbag and take it out of the hospital and sell it."

Sarah peered at him closely. It occurred to her that he wasn't even sure what sex the baby was.

"You're imagining things," she said gently. "The baby's perfectly safe." But he didn't seem to hear. He passed his hand over his face and groaned as a person does when he is just realizing the magnitude of trouble he is in.

The baby was a boy, and he was named Jake, after her grandfather. They brought him home from the hospital in the amberous light of a September morning. Sarah put him in the bassinet and then put the bassinet near the kitchen window so he could watch the tops of the trees in the tiny city gardens just beginning to turn gold and red.

"But we don't have any window guards yet," Milo said anxiously.

Sarah blinked and looked down at the baby, who was in a stuporous sleep, still journeying in from wherever it was he had come from. He was only two days old and could neither lift his head nor roll over.

She looked at Milo. "You think he's going to crawl over to the window and manage to hoist himself up and fall out?"

To Sarah's delight, he blushed. She went over to him and tried to hug him, but he pushed her off, annoyed. "Of course not. What I mean is, this is the kind of thing we're going to have to be careful about now. You, especially, will have to think defensively, as you will be doing the bulk of the child care. And we'll have to see about getting those guards put in soon."

"Defensively?"

"You know what I mean."

She had arranged to take six months maternity leave from her job, and, now, to her surprise, she realized she did not miss it at all. The baby was a perfectly ordinary baby, with a round, good-humored face like the moon, and Sarah found she could not imagine a set of features more utterly suited to her taste.

The cats seemed unimpressed with him, but, as the days grew cooler and he still couldn't move around much, they made the best of the situation by sneaking into the bassinet with him and trying to make themselves cozy. At first Sarah shooed them out halfheartedly, but after a while she found herself giving in. The sight of them all together, sleeping so peacefully, seemed to confirm her unexpected discovery of a vast and oncoming harmony. Having a sense, however, that Milo would not approve of the arrangement, she would dump the cats out on the bed before he came home in the evening, and they would stare at her for a moment derisively, then curl up on the pillows.

Each night when Milo came home from work, he would begin to order her about anxiously, fussing around the apartment and rearranging all her arrangements. He would insist on bathing Jake himself. She saw quite clearly that he did not trust her, though every night after dinner, as he filled the little plastic tub and then lowered the baby into it, he would break out into a cold sweat.

Sarah would watch them with secret pleasure while she did the dishes.

The baby would coo and gurgle at Milo reassuringly and grab at the washcloth and suck on it.

"Hey! Don't do that!" Milo would yell in a panic, grabbing the washcloth back. "That's polio water!"

The baby would look up at him seriously and study Milo's face as if it were a map of the rapidly expanding universe with an explanation written in code that only babies can read, of where we are all headed.

Sarah, moved to rapture by the way the lamplight shone upon the baby and the two inches of water and Milo's face, fierce with concentration as he tried not to drown his only son, would turn away and try to sober herself up by sweeping the floor or scrubbing at the old stains on the kitchen counter, but it did no good whatsoever.

She spent most of the winter in the house, because Milo would yell at her whenever she tried to take the baby out. He was sure they were going to get picked up by a passing tornado, or clonked on the head by the falling debris from some satellite decomposing in outer space. If neither of those things happened, then they were certain to freeze to death.

"What's the matter with you?" he would say in exasperation if he caught her trying to put on the baby's snowsuit. "Didn't you hear the weather report? Don't you realize he's just a tiny baby and his thermostat doesn't work like ours? You can't go dragging him around in weather like this."

"This is all hormones," she would tell him, smiling happily. "You're imagining things." But he paid no attention, and it did not, in any case, matter much to her. Being in or out, living in a bear cave or a tepee, it was all the same to her as long as she had Jake with her.

Every Friday night Fred came over with his harmonica and had them sing different songs to the baby. They never, of course, sang "Eensie Weensie Spider." They sang "Give My Regards to Broadway," "Oklahoma," "How Much Is That Puppy in the Window?" "Good King Wenceslas," and a medley of Mick Jagger songs. When the singing was over, Fred would make copious notes.

The baby clearly adored his uncle, for every Friday night, when Fred came into view, he would stiffen and turn red and, giving a loud shout of glee, try to vault himself out of Sarah's arms into the air.

He seemed, too, to love the whole singing ritual, the mysterious circle of attention, the way they placed him on the sofa surrounded by pillows, turned the evening lamps down low, then burst into song. In the first months, he always lay quietly, listening and watching their faces. As time went on, he would coo and gurgle and string long chains of vowel sounds together.

Sometimes Sarah and Milo looked over Fred's shoulder at his notes.

"J. alert and calm. Stuck F.I.E. Smiled at refrain. Arched back invitingly."

"What's F.I.E.?" Milo asked nervously, as if this were the baby's first report card.

"Finger in eye," Fred explained and, lowering his head towards the baby, who was reaching for him, blew into his ear and nuzzled his neck till he squealed with delight.

Milo, Sarah saw, watched this with some jealousy. He kept quiet until Fred left, but then would often remark on how peaked her brother was looking, or how thin. Sarah would merely nod judiciously and kiss him.

When Christmas was over and the baby, who had been residing with them for four months, could roll himself over on his back, grab his feet, and solemnly shove a couple of toes in his mouth, Milo came home a little early one night.

"Where's Jake?" he asked.

Sarah was scrubbing a potato at the sink. Without thinking, she told him he was taking a little evening nap. Milo stole quietly into the bedroom to gaze at him adoringly and discovered the orange cat curled up tightly against the baby's sleeping back. The other one was down by his feet.

Milo threw a terrible tantrum. He threatened to take the cats to the ASPCA. He threatened to take them up to the roof and throw them off. How could she have permitted such a thing? How could she be so careless? Didn't she realize they could sit on his face and suffocate him? Didn't she keep an eye on him when he was sleeping?

She told him solemnly that they had never done anything like this before. She didn't know what had gotten into them. She promised it would never happen again, and she scolded the cats roundly. They pretended to shame and remorse and went and hid under the bed.

That night Milo woke her at around three, shaking her arm.

"What?" She sighed.

"Put your hand here. I think my heart is skipping a beat. Do you feel it?"

She put her hand there and felt nothing but a nice steady thumping. "You're imagining things," she said.

"Am I? But something feels fluttery in there. I've never felt this before."

"Go back to sleep. It'll feel better in the morning." She slid back into her sweet, relaxed slumber, but at breakfast he was pale and haggard. When she questioned him, he said he hadn't slept a wink.

After this, he woke her every night and placed her hand on his heart nervously. She could not convince him that nothing was wrong and finally suggested he go see a doctor. At last, he steeled himself for the worst and went off like a condemned man. He returned home that evening with the news that he needed to lose some weight.

The very next day he embarked upon a strict low-fat, high-fiber diet. She, who was breast-feeding, and the baby, who was growing at a wild and unbelievable clip, continued to gorge themselves without conscience, while Milo downed three chocolate-flavored chalk shakes a day and, in the evening, consumed a meal consisting of a tiny potato, a tiny portion of chicken or fish, and a half a cup of string beans or spinach. His clothes rapidly began to hang loosely about him, and, within a few weeks, he was thinner than she had ever seen him.

Soon after this, he began to clean up after himself and, sometimes, even after her. No longer did his socks dangle out of his drawers. No more did he leave coffee cups under the sofa, where they could grow algae. If she left a book open on the sofa while she went to change the baby's diaper, he would put a bookmark in it and tidily stow it away in her nightstand.

She saw that Milo had been taken hostage, that he loved this baby more than he had ever loved anything or anyone before, that he had no idea how he would survive if anything ever happened to him.

In spite of the fact that, for her, loving Jake was like discovering that gravity no longer had any authority over her, that she could cover any distance and leap over all obstacles with only the slightest and most delightful of efforts, she was seized with jealousy and wondered how long, if ever, it would take him to come back to her.

One evening she suggested they try to get a sitter for Friday night and go out to a movie together. She knew of a teenager down the block who liked babies. He looked at her thunderstruck, as if she had suggested they all get into a car and drive themselves straight off a cliff.

Sarah said no more, but, on Friday night when he arrived home from work, she was at the kitchen table with Bernadette O'Day, the redheaded teenager who lived three houses down the street. Jake was sitting on Bernadette's lap, gazing up at her. Bernadette had silver braces on her upper and lower front teeth, which sparkled and shone whenever she opened her mouth. From her left ear dangled three earrings, one a gold hoop, one made of feathers, and one of blue enamel in the shape of a star. Her other ear was unadorned, but around her neck was a silver chain with a whistle and several keys hanging from it. Jake, overcome, stared at her in openmouthed admiration. She had been telling Sarah about her three boyfriends and how they had all accidentally met in the lobby of a movie theater last night. When Milo came in, however, much to Sarah's disappointment, she circumspectly closed her mouth. Jake immediately reached up and tried to pry her lips open so he could see her braces again.

Sarah looked up at Milo defiantly.

"No," he said.

"Come on," she said cajolingly. "Let's give it a try. We'll just go to dinner, and then we'll come right back."

Milo grilled Bernadette mercilessly, as if he were a combination of Landlord-Tenant Court and the Spanish Inquisition. Have you ever taken care of such a small baby before? What are your feelings about very small babies? What would you do if the baby choked? What would you do if you ran out of diapers? Supposing you had the baby all undressed on the changing table and you noticed smoke coming out of the kitchen?

Bernadette, Sarah saw with great relief, seemed not the least bit put out by these questions. In fact, she seemed delighted to have such an occasion to rise to. Her sister had a little boy, and she had been taking care of him since he was no bigger than a toenail, not to mention all the other families she often sat for. Once her nephew turned blue and his eyes bugged way out, so she did the "Heimler" maneuver, and this entire pair of little white ankle socks shot out of his mouth. She knew how to make diapers out of dish towels in an emergency. As for fire, fire she didn't mess around with. She'd wrap the baby up and get out. She loved babies, particularly the very small ones that smelled of milk and spit-up. She couldn't wait to have one herself, but first she intended to finish high school and college and probably medical school.

Milo looked at Sarah and he looked at Bernadette and he looked at the baby. Sarah knew he was beaten.

"Nothing will happen," Sarah said.

"All right," he said grimly and stood up. "We'll go to dinner. I will write down the number of the restaurant and the pediatrician. Over here, next to the phone, are any other emergency numbers you might need."

Sarah felt sorry for him, but how pleased she was with herself, her personal powers of persuasion, her timing, her unshakable sense of good fortune. She guided him, pale and silent, out the door and held his hand all the way down the stairs.

They walked down the avenue into the wind and headed towards the Mexican restaurant wordlessly. A cold, spitting sleet blew into their faces, and the sidewalks were slippery. As they stepped off the curb to cross the street, she suddenly heard, from Milo's immediate vicinity, a loud crunch, and he slipped from her grasp and crumpled, cursing, to the ground.

"Good God, Milo, get up. What's wrong?" she demanded.

"What's wrong? What's wrong? What do you think is wrong? I've fallen and broken my ankle. I told you something like this would happen."

She was furious. What was he anyway? Just a husband. Some person her brother had introduced her to, a guy who had moved in with her and walked around in his underwear and acted like he knew her from the beginning of time.

He sat there on the curb, his foot in the street, and moaned triumphantly. She helped him up as kindly as she could, and he leaned on her as they hobbled back down the street. When she got them into the apartment, she settled him on the sofa and took off his shoe and sock. The ankle was swelling nicely.

"Can you move it?"

He groaned but wiggled it obediently. "I think maybe it's just twisted," he said.

She sent Bernadette home, which caused the baby to howl with fury, but Milo threw him in the air like a little pancake, then caught him safe in his arms, till, at last, he gave in and squealed with the pleasure of flying and falling and being safe as houses. The cats, who did not like games in which large objects went hurtling and chortling through the air overhead, went and hid under the sofa until better times should come again, and Sarah went to get some ice to put on Milo's ankle.

On the first Friday night in March, Fred came sauntering in the door with his harmonica. The baby was teething and had been irritable all day. The moment, however, that Fred came in the room, he ceased his complaining and rushed over to him and grabbed onto his pants leg. It was true, Sarah thought, that Fred did look a little under the weather tonight. There was a tightness around his mouth, and a darkness under his eyes, that she had never seen before, but he brought with him a damp and spicy smell of mud, as if he had walked through the park, and he scooped the baby up and they inhaled each other happily.

Milo, deeply immersed in the paper and an article about how the scientists were predicting that the end of the world was going to arrive much more quickly than previously thought, paid no attention to any of them.

"Well," Fred said, "are you guys ready? The baby is six months old."

Sarah froze in alarm. "No," she said and quickly counted up. It was true.

"Time for 'Eensie Weensie Spider.'"

Milo looked up.

"This is ridiculous," Sarah said. "Of course, he's not going to remember anything from back then. It's just silly, and, in any case, I don't think tonight is such a good idea. I mean, the baby's been teething and he's in a terrible mood."

"Whaddaya mean?" Fred asked. "He's happy as a pig in mud. Look at him." Jake giggled and hiccuped and rubbed his own tiny pink, drooled-up face against Fred's large, rough, unshaven jaw.

"Yeah, come on, Sarah. Let's do it," Milo said. He was looking at her from across the water, keeping his eye on her from a little wind-tossed boat. It was difficult to read what he was after.

She took the baby over to the sofa reluctantly and settled him amongst the pillows. The baby appeared very calm and expectant, eager to receive whatever it was they wanted to give him. He lay there smiling, looking around at their faces.

Fred played a few warm-up notes, then began to sing. Milo joined him.

> Eensie weensie spider
> Went up the water spout.

The smile left the baby's face.

> Down came the rain
> And washed the spider out.

He stuck his fist in his mouth and gnawed on it furiously.

> Up came the sun
> And dried up all the rain.
> Then eensie weensie spider
> Went up the spout again.

This last bit was almost completely drowned out by the baby's loud screams. He kicked his feet, craned his neck, then flipped his whole body over and wailed furiously, burying his face in the sofa.

"My God," Fred said, "he's never done this before. This is amazing. He seems to be associating this song with something. But what? What could it be? I wasn't expecting this."

Now Milo stood up from the sofa and pointed an accusing finger at Sarah. "This is all your fault."

Sarah stared at him. "What do you mean?"

"All that demented worrying you did when you were pregnant. Look what you've done to him."

She glared at him furiously. "But you always said I was being ridiculous, that the baby was completely protected."

"I said it because I wanted you to stop worrying, because you were being an idiot. But think of all the adrenaline and other toxins you probably dumped into his bloodstream. You think that made no difference?"

"He's teething!" Sarah yelled. "He's just not in the mood for this, I tell you." She picked the baby up and held him to her breast. He nuzzled and wept and gnawed her collarbone. "You're both idiots. You're a pair of idiots. Why don't you go up together and hold hands and jump off the roof? I'm going to nurse the baby and put him to bed. Good night." She lowered Jake onto her hip and stalked off into the bedroom, slamming the door.

When Milo apologized to her a few days later, she pretended she had no idea what he was talking about, merely smiled and continued shoveling peaches into the baby's mouth.

One Saturday morning, not long afterwards, Jake woke very early and it became absolutely clear to Sarah that he was not going to go back to sleep, that he knew something was going on out there and he wanted to go out and see what it was. She dressed them both as quietly as she could, but before she could hustle them out the door something in Milo's dreams alerted him and he came lumbering into the living room in his underwear. He stared at them, horrified. Where were they going, he wanted to know. The baby eyed him fondly. "Agua," he said.

"My God, Sarah, did you hear that? That's Spanish for water."

Sarah looked at him hopefully. "We're going for a walk in the Botanical Gardens. Why don't you come with us?"

Perhaps he saw that it was useless, that the game was up, that it was, after all, spring and he wasn't going to be able to keep them in the apartment anymore. In any case, to her surprise, he agreed. "But you're not going to leave all those dishes in the sink are you?" he asked disapprovingly. "You always yell at me when I do that."

She laughed. "I'll wash them while you get dressed."

"All right, wait for me," he said anxiously, as if he feared they might go out ahead of him and get themselves picked up by a passing hurricane.

So they stepped out into the early sunlight as a family. The air was warm and still and fragrant with mud and the scent of snowdrops and crocuses, which advanced in small battalions across the front yards. The squirrels raced each other up and down the fences and clowned around, and the baby, in the stroller, was beside himself. He hooted and burbled and kept opening his blue eyes wide and raising his eyebrows and generally seemed not to be able to believe his good fortune. There wasn't a hurricane in sight.

When they turned through the gates of the Botanical Gardens, the bright street and early morning traffic disappeared abruptly, and they stood at the silent beginning of two long avenues of blossoming trees. Being crab apples and cherries, these trees did not stand straight but leaned and arched and whispered in each other's ears, and those who walked through were clothed first in light and then shadow and then light again.

As they stood there silently, perhaps trying to decide which avenue to choose, the baby began to wiggle and yelp and then growl.

Milo was kneeling in front of him instantly. "What is it?" he yelled into the little face, as if he imagined that if he spoke loudly enough the baby would leave off his foolishness and admit to understanding English. The baby, of course, began to yell louder.

"Let's go this way," Sarah said, pointing down the avenue of trees where there was no one to be seen. Down at the end of the other one was a figure clothed in gray, staring up into the branches of a white-blooming pear tree (man or woman, it was impossible to tell).

As they headed forward into the trees, Jake began to scream even louder.

"But, my God, Sarah, what's wrong with him?" Milo demanded.

Sarah shrugged her shoulders. "Who knows? He gets into these things. You want to know my theory? My theory is, he gets tired of being a baby. He senses all the powers to come and is furious at not being there yet."

"Well, isn't there anything we can do?"

She sighed and stopped the stroller and looked at the baby thoughtfully. She kneeled in front him and felt around inside his clothing. Not finding him wet, she lifted him out of the carriage in a tender swoop and held him high over her head. "What is it, Dewdrop?" she demanded. Milo looked at them jealously. "Are you hungry?" she asked. She sat down on a bench and lifted her blouse so he could suckle. He pushed her away with his fist, disgusted at her stupidity, and set up a tentative wailing and lamenting.

Milo grabbed him up anxiously. "Come," he said, "we'll sit in the sun and watch for squirrels." He sat Jake upright in the stroller and turned him towards a pink-blooming crab apple tree. There wasn't a squirrel in sight, and Sarah was sure that, in a moment, Jake would work himself up into hysterics. To her utter surprise, he stopped crying and began to giggle and flirt happily with something over Milo's shoulder. What could it be? She turned to look, and there, coming towards them, was a man in a dark gray suit carrying a gold-knobbed cane. Sarah looked at him curiously, and, for the space of a second, she thought he was young—this because of the suppleness and the upright aspect of his figure. And she thought, too, there was something familiar about him. Then she looked at him again and saw that he was actually quite old, with a yellowed linen handkerchief peeking out of his pocket, and that she did not know him at all. The baby gurgled at him invitingly.

"What a very attractive child," the gentleman said.

To Sarah's surprise, when she looked over at Milo, she saw he was pale and sweating. Whatever could be wrong with him now?

"I don't suppose you'd be interested in selling him?" the gentleman asked with a smile.

Clearly this was just a joke. However, when Sarah looked over at Milo again, he seemed to be teetering, maybe about to faint. Had he eaten something that disagreed with him?

"Sviff," the baby said.

"Actually," Milo breathed, "he's a holy terror. Last night he screamed for four hours straight, and he spits up in your hair whenever you burp him."

The gentleman listened to Milo with a little smile on his lips. It was true that for an old man he looked exceedingly cunning and strong. He leaned towards the baby. "I don't suppose you'd be interested in coming along with me?"

"Urbli," the baby said.

The gentleman held out his cane, and the baby leaned forward to reach for his reflection in the gold knob. At this moment, to Sarah's utter bemusement, she happened to see Milo surreptitiously reach up behind the baby and pinch him in a tender spot in back of his ear. The baby instantly straightened and began to scream. The gentleman frowned. He looked at Sarah suspiciously, since she was giggling.

"Gas," Milo said and lifted Jake out of the stroller and patted him on the back.

Suddenly Sarah saw what it was that Milo was thinking and she couldn't believe it. Her own dear husband, a man with absolutely no imagination whatsoever, a man who had always believed that the world operated upon the most orderly and predictable of principles, maybe not all discovered yet, but certainly available to be discovered and quantified, this same man was imagining that here was Death himself, come by to make a play for his baby.

She stared at Milo wonderingly. Marriage, she thought, was just a little boat made out of a twig and a leaf and some chewing gum. She felt sorry for him in his suffering, but, even as she stood there pitying him, an odd look of triumph suffused his face. When she turned to see what it was he was looking at, she was strangely unsettled to see nothing. The old man had vanished.

She went to put her arms around Milo. Whether she did this as an attempt to comfort him or because she missed him terribly, she wasn't sure. In any case, he did not pay much attention. He stood vigilantly watching the empty avenue. After a moment he gently shrugged her off.

"What we oughta do, is get a sitter and go out to a movie," she said loudly.

Milo said nothing for a moment, then he seemed to realize she was waiting for some sort of reply. "There's nothing playing that you'd want to see," he said quickly. "Believe me. I looked in the paper this morning. It's just stuff for people who are brain dead and some old Garbo movies we've already seen." He looked up into the blue sky, then put the baby back in the stroller and carefully opened the stroller shield and adjusted it over his head as if he was expecting hail.

One evening in early summer, the doorbell rang and there, at last, was Robin. She wore an old pink peasant blouse with mirrors sewn all over it. She looked sleepy and worn, as if she had just arrived from another planet. She had flown in expressly to see the baby, she said. She was staying with her father. She would only stay a few minutes. She had a present. Her rough, dark hair was loose as always, and Sarah was deeply moved to see how gray it had gone. Milo, she knew, would have a fit. And, indeed, as soon as she brought Robin into the living room, where he was lying on the sofa, he jumped up and dragged Sarah into the bedroom.

"I don't want her in the house!" he hissed furiously.

"She's my oldest friend."

"She's a schizophrenic. This is misplaced loyalty, to expose your child to her. Whoever she is now, she is not who she was then."

"But, Milo, you could say that about anybody you know for any length of time. Friendship begins in one place and then goes other places you have no control over. Do you abandon a friend just because she hasn't turned out happy or rich or sane or politically correct or whatever? Don't you think there's an obligation that goes along with friendship to see things through? Robin needs me. She needs to see my baby."

"Oh, Sarah, what a lot of hooey. How can you be friends with someone who thinks the doorknobs are talking to her? Supposing she does something violent or takes all her clothes off in the middle of the living room and does one of those rain dances?"

Sarah shrugged. She was sure Jake would be enchanted if it started raining in the middle of the living room. "Don't worry," she told him. "Everything will be fine."

For a few minutes after Sarah brought the baby out, Robin focused all her attention on him. She held him awkwardly in front of her and sniffed at him. Milo hovered ferociously in the background, but Robin acted exactly as if he wasn't there, which was what she always did.

"May this baby be able to see all the way down to the end of the river and back again without getting lost," she pronounced solemnly and brought out her gift, which was a shiny rattle, handmade from a gourd. It had a face painted on it with blue eyes and red whiskers, and Jake instantly tried to put the whole thing in his mouth. "It will protect him from the demons," Robin said and then, abruptly, seemed to lose all interest in him and handed him back to Sarah.

Milo relaxed and went back to lying on the sofa and watching TV, and Sarah and Robin sat in the kitchen. Sarah nursed the baby, and Robin went through a peculiar cycle over and over again of slouching down and then suddenly straightening her back hard up against the kitchen chair. She spoke in the familiar slurred and deadened voice which Sarah knew she would never grow used to. "I'm doing all right," she said. "Me and Ella, we do our thing. I have a couple of friends. I've taken a part-time job at the library. So I'm all right. I take my medication and I don't get those wild highs anymore. It's just that I always feel this underlying feeling of sadness. Do you know what I mean?"

Sarah looked away from her guiltily, down at the baby, who had fallen asleep, his mouth against her breast, snorting. Then she looked back at Robin and found her jerking herself upright again. "Is something wrong with your back?"

Robin stared at her in surprise. "Do you hear her, too?"

"Who?" Sarah asked uneasily.

"My mother. She keeps telling me not to slouch. Did you hear that?"

After a while Sarah got up and put the baby in the crib. A few minutes after she returned to the kitchen, Robin said she needed to go to the bathroom. She was gone a very long time. After twenty minutes Sarah went in search of her and found the bathroom empty. The baby's crib was empty, too. She raced silently through the apartment. Milo was asleep on the sofa, and Robin had disappeared, taking her coat and her backpack.

Sarah saw what a mistake she had made. All the blood seemed to rush up into her face and her head. She breathed shallowly and rapidly, and her hands went numb. She stood there in the hallway, shaking them furiously, trying to bring them back to life.

She wanted to go to Milo and bury her face in his chest and tell him how sorry she was, how right he had been, how she saw now what a delusion she had been laboring under, how much she loved him, and that it was the very end of the world. But she knew it was useless, he would never forgive her, never look upon her with trust or tenderness again.

Without waking him, she threw on her coat and ran down the stairs to the street. She was surprised to find that it had started to rain and that the streets were nearly empty and shone in the lamplight.

She raced towards the subway, thinking Robin must have gone that way and maybe she could head her off. She stopped once in a little all-night grocery store because the light which streamed steadily out of its windows and doors onto the pavement seemed so certain and mindful of the night, but the young Arab man inside, behind the rows of gum and chocolate bars, had seen nothing of a tall and dark-haired madwoman rushing by with a baby in a blanket.

By the time she reached the subway station, she was certain she would find Robin and the baby there, waiting on the platform for the next train. Where else could she go on a night like this, but back to her father's house? But when she got down the steps, the station was empty. The man inside the token booth said the last train had been over half an hour ago, and he hadn't seen any dark-haired ladies carrying any babies.

Her heart failed her. The world was so big, and there were so many things that could go wrong that she hadn't believed in, hurricanes and madness, lead poisoning and gas leaks, heart attacks and kidnappings. She understood now that she would never find Jake all by herself. She would have to go home and wake Milo and call the police. She climbed back up the stairs into the rainy night. The smell of wet street and the first roses unfolding somewhere nearby filled her with nostalgia, and she saw plainly how you only had to go as far as from here to the next instant for everything to reverse itself completely. She walked fast, her eyes blinking against the rain, searching the avenue and side streets fiercely. As she passed by the schoolyard not far from their apartment building, she saw now a dark, slouched figure standing by the swings and one swing flying high, high up into the rain.

She raced through the gate and past the empty sandbox and the monkey bars, which shone wet and silvery in the rain. When she had nearly reached the swings she stopped, for Robin was singing "Eensie Weensie Spider," and the baby was laughing uproariously. Both of them seemed completely indifferent to the fact that they were soaking wet. In fact, the baby, at this moment, turned his luminous little pink face up to the dark sky and opened his mouth and drank. Then he spotted Sarah and pointed at her solemnly, and Robin turned around and saw her, too.

Sarah went over and stopped the swing and pulled Jake out. She pressed her face against his, and he opened his mouth again, this time to suck on her cheek. She saw that, for some reason, he was going to forgive her for everything.

Robin stood there watching them, her arms hanging emptily at her sides. "Ella died," she said.

Sarah looked up at her in surprise. "Why didn't you tell me? When did this happen?"

"Three weeks ago. She left me everything, the old witch. There's a lot of money."

"What will you do? Will you move back here now?"

"No, I don't think so. She left me the house. I'm going to stay there, I think. People know me. They've gotten used to me."

Sarah was filled with remorse and was filled, again, with intimations of all the things that were to come for her and her child, but now Jake pulled her glasses off and gurgled. Sarah gently tugged them out of his hand. Unable to look at Robin, she said, "I sometimes wonder if he thinks he's pulling part of my face off when he does that."

"I always thought a baby would be nice to have," Robin said sadly.

"Oh, sweetheart," Sarah said, "oh, Robin, you'll be all right." She tried to hug her with Jake between them, wiggling and wiggling, struggling to get his hands free so he could hold them out into the rain. "I'll call you."

Robin nodded and, bending her head against the rain, turned and trudged up the hill towards the subway.

Milo did not hear her when she slipped in the door quietly with the baby. He was sitting on the sofa weeping. It was an arresting sight. She saw that he knew something awful had happened.

She entered the living room slowly, and he stopped in the middle of a sob and regarded her as if she were a ghost. She went over to him and put the baby in his lap and knelt submissively in front of him. If he wanted to strike her head off, she would regard this as just.

For a while there was only the baby going "Ah di, ah di, ah di." Then she felt Milo's hand on her shoulder, and she looked up.

"What are you doing here?" he asked in wonder.

She looked at him uncertainly. "I'm here to apologize. To tell you I see how careless I've been with our lives." She said this as obediently as she could, though even as she said it she felt, to her horror, something rebellious rise up in her, some foolish and hormonal misunderstanding, some belief in the essentially bountiful ordering of events in the universe.

But he did not seem to be paying much attention anyway. He grabbed her by the shoulders. "I thought this was it for sure. When I woke up and found you were gone, and understood that you'd decided to run off with Robin and the baby, I saw how selfish I'd been, worrying so much, how I must have been driving you crazy."

"But, Milo, I didn't—" She stopped.

He kissed her face. "We'll get a sitter Friday night. That teenager with the braces. If she can't do it, we'll ask Fred. We'll go to the movies. OK?"

"Sure. OK." She contemplated him and saw that what he suffered, he suffered, in part, so that she could be free, for once in her life, to make her way with a light heart, to know happiness when it came. She saw, too, that it wasn't going to last forever and that she ought to be grateful while she could. She leaned forward to give him a return kiss but found that he had forgotten all about her.

He was gazing at the baby adoringly. Now he lifted him up into the air as if he were a diamond or pearl which needed, for more accurate appraising, better light. The baby looked at him and smiled. Then he burped and, still smiling, not seeming to notice what he was doing at all, spit up onto Milo's pants.

"Hello, Vomithead," Milo whispered.

Sarah wanted very much to laugh, but made no sound. She knew perfectly well that it was wise to whisper, that one did not want to draw the attention of any jealous gods.

8

AT THE SIGN OF THE NAKED WAITER

AFTER SARAH HAD TUGGED and pulled her brother's dog from out of the backseat of the car, he had taken one indifferent look around at the purple and crimson hollyhocks, the swallows' nest over the front door, the trees and the long downhill sweep of grass to the pond, and he had crawled under the rhododendron bush.

He was a medium-sized brown dog, whose face, up until Friday, had always borne an expression somewhere between high self-satisfaction and sheepish apology—as if he had just eaten one of your shoes. Fred had thought him gifted and brilliant and, for some reason, believed he was bilingual, so he often spoke in French when the dog was around. Jake, who was now nearly three, had picked up numerous interesting expressions in this way, and as soon as he saw the dog he would shriek in delight, *"Allez oop! Fermez la bouche!"* and the dog would jump up and lick him all over the face, which almost always carried on it some delicious remainders of peanut butter and jelly or SpaghettiOs or whatever his last meal had been. Then they would embrace like lovers who had been separated for a hundred years by a combination of their own foolishness and the evil enchantments of jealous bystanders and roll about clutching each other tightly under the tables and chairs.

However, Fred had died on Friday. He had been dying for over a year. In the end pneumonia carried him off suddenly, and Sarah, not expecting it, was way up in the country in this rented house with her husband and child. Milo had suggested that he stay with Jake while she went down to the funeral by herself. It made no sense to put a three-year-old through such an ordeal, he said. Sarah was furious, knowing it was really for himself that he made this suggestion. He hated death and wanted nothing to do with it in any of its forms.

"But, for God's sakes, what about Fred?" she said. They had been eating dinner out back at the picnic table under the apple tree.

"What do you mean? What about him?"

"Don't you think he'd want us all to be there?"

"I think that the man, being dead, will be about as interested in our whereabouts as a doorknob."

"But he was my brother and you were good friends and this is death. This is no joke. Here it is. Don't you want to pay some attention or express some grief?"

He shrugged. "Of course, I do." With deliberate and surely foolhardy defiance, he shook pepper all up and down his ear of corn and then took a bite.

"I'd like Jake to have the chance to say good-bye to his uncle."

Milo sighed restively and took another bite. "Children do

not say good-bye at funerals. At funerals they are filled with nameless horror and boredom and they fall off their chairs and pick their noses and electrify the old ladies with their hideous behavior."

"I'll have to take the car. How will you manage all by yourself? You've never been alone with him for more than six hours."

"Just make sure you're back by Sunday night. I'll be fine."

A year and a half earlier, when Sarah found out her brother was dying, she got right in the car and drove over to his apartment and kept her finger on the buzzer until he came to the door. He had tied his dark and wiry hair back in a pony-tail, but several pieces of it had escaped and stuck up absurdly over his ears. It was the beginning of winter, but he wore beach sandals and, over his gray sweatpants, a short-sleeved, flowered shirt with scarlet parrots flying against a turquoise sky. He looked as tall and as deathless, as addlebrained and disastrously handsome as ever. His dog barked and yipped and danced a frenzied dog jig around her boots, but she did not bend to kiss him hello, just glared furiously and disbeliev-ingly into her brother's eyes.

"Ah ..." He smiled at her and ushered her in.

His apartment always took her breath away. He was con-sidered—as she knew from his own description and from vari-ous other sources as well—an astrophysicist of exceeding promise and imagination, but he had never been able to keep his mind on mere outer space, and his apartment was a terri-ble mess of not only telescopes and star charts but also test tubes and zoology books and petri dishes of mold and terrari-ums croaking with frogs. This evening, it was obvious, he was working on another of his contraptions, for on the worktable were strewn about the insides of several old alarm clocks, while in their midst there arose a strangely turreted and ticking mechanical device.

"It's a radio," he said modestly.

"Fred, for God's sakes . . . " She grabbed him by the shoulder and pinched him. "It isn't true is it? It's our mother exaggerating things, right?"

"Whaddaya mean?" he said as he tinkered with his machine. "It's a radio, though rather a remarkable one, if I say so myself. What does our mother have to do with it?"

"Fred, stop playing with that stupid thing and look at me."

He looked up at her for a minute sharply. "What are *you* so angry about?"

She blushed miserably. "I'm sorry," she whispered. "I'm sorry. But talk to me. Tell me what happened."

For just a minute he allowed his voice to rise. "Why? Why do you want to know what happened? Do you think there's a moral to this story? Do you wish maybe there was somebody to blame?"

"I wasn't thinking of that," she protested.

All the anger went out of him. "No, of course, you weren't. I can see that. It's what *I* want sometimes. But I've mostly gotten over that now."

She waited for him to say something else, but she saw he wasn't thinking of her.

She stepped towards him and put her arms around him and tried to squeeze it out of him, his terror and his regret at leaving everything, particularly her, behind. He put his arms around her lightly and rested his chin on her head. She felt him looking out past a great and open distance. "It has always seemed to me that it is all illusion, this notion that each of us is a singular, discrete kind of thing. Really we are nothing that stays the same from moment to moment, just a chain of events with a memory attached and it seems pretty ridiculous when you look at it that way to worry about the beginning or the ending of the matter. For a short time we carry these bodies around, then we split apart and scatter, and all our bits and pieces attach to other bits and pieces and re-form to make new things. I'm not afraid. Not really. The universe is so full of pattern and design. I have no worries about being ended or lost."

"But Fred . . . ," she said plaintively. One more time he was going to swivel and feint, break a dozen hearts, and vanish utterly from the scene of his crimes.

"What?"

What was it she wanted him to say? She saw that she was completely selfish. That she wasn't worried about him at all but wanted *him* to comfort *her*. How empty the place would seem without him. If he had been annoying and elusive, he had never stopped throwing open windows and doors and asking busybody questions and shining illuminating beams of light into everybody's eyes. She pressed her head against him miserably and wept.

"Oh come on, Sarah, come on. What are you carrying on about? I have at least one or two good years left. I have several very interesting projects I hope to get done. There's lots of things I want to show Jake, and we'll have lots of time to talk. I promise."

At this moment his radio began to make screeching and whooshing sounds. He disentangled himself from her arms gently and went over to it and began to make adjustments. "Sunspots," he explained happily.

But, in the end, somehow it had never come, this promised talk—though she had seen him often, though he was always dropping by with little presents for Jake and staying for dinner and hanging around to watch baseball games with Milo.

In the last months, she had hours of sitting by him in the hospital, and she watched him endeavor to meet what was coming with an open and curious mind, while he lost his hair and his unfailing appetite, while he bled and he dwindled and struggled to breathe. And she kept thinking there would be more time, time enough to undertake to say all the things they had forgotten to say, or never been able to say, or been too embarrassed to say, or been too stupid to say, and then there was no more time. And though she was glad for him, that the end, when it came, came to him swiftly and gently, she couldn't help feeling completely cheated.

She drove down alone Saturday morning and spent the afternoon helping her mother sort through Fred's old things. She spent the whole of the hot, still summer's night in Fred's old bedroom waiting for something. There was a mosquito who toured the room with a ceaseless, infuriating drone, and the moon came in the window at around four and alighted first on his old terrarium and then on a pair of his old basketball sneakers. She considered each of these visitations hopefully but, in the end, knew they didn't add up to a hill of beans.

She certainly did not expect him at the funeral. A person's funeral is the place they are most expected to be missing from. But if Fred was not there, everyone else certainly was, and afterwards, back at her parents' house, among the ham sandwiches and potato salad and carrot cake, all of these relations and neighbors, students and old teachers, friends and lovers, variously wept and told jokes, read aloud from his many notebooks, remembered his theories, and competed with each other to recall the most outrageous of his experiments. There were a few, too, who stared brokenheartedly about the room as if there wasn't a familiar object or face left in the world to look at.

She knew it was ridiculous to expect that he would come and stand opaquely among them, steadied now by the journey out, well again at last, and filled with compassion and amusement at their pitiable state of aliveness. Nor, certainly, was it reasonable to hope that he might thread his way through the crowd to where she stood, picking miserably at a little plate of chicken salad, and, one last time, inclining his large, unruly head towards her, one last time, turning the full and electric force of his attention upon her, tell her where he was going and why she was still here and what it was she was expected to get done.

She stared down at the paper plate in her hand, and, when she looked up, there was Robin.

"Why, here you are!" Robin exclaimed. "I've been looking for you for half an hour, but I had to keep stopping to listen to all these people who needed to talk about Fred and how they never knew anybody like him. Did you know Fiona was here? Remember old Fiona? You wouldn't recognize her. I heard her asking for you. I have to leave in ten minutes. My father is going to pick me up. He doesn't like the idea of me wandering around loose in the old neighborhood. I have to fly back in the morning because that's as long as he'll put up with me."

Sarah embraced her, hoping it would make her shut up, hoping maybe the two of them would be magically picked up and transported back to the days when they were so close you couldn't slip a blade of grass between them, and Fred sprawled on the front steps reading the encyclopedia, and every summer afternoon lasted at least a month.

Sarah knew it was useless. Robin's body felt stiff and embarrassed in her arms. She stepped back and looked at her again. They spoke on the phone regularly, and Robin had come out once or twice in the last year or so. Each time,

Robin looked more weathered and round-shouldered than she had before, as if she was continually being beaten down by some force that was determined to flatten her to the ground.

"Listen, I'll be here tonight. You want to go out and have dinner? How about it?" Robin asked.

"I can't," Sarah lied. "I have to drive back up to the country tonight."

Robin sighed. "You never told me Fred was gay."

Sarah shrugged her shoulders. "I don't know if he was gay. I think he just didn't make the same distinctions most other people make."

"I should have married him. All this would never have happened."

"What are you talking about?" Sarah said sharply. "He never asked you to marry him."

Robin sniffed and touched the untidy bun of dark hair that she had pinned up at the back of her neck. "First of all, how do you know that? Second of all, people don't always know enough to ask for what it is they want." Now she looked around the crowded room and sighed. "It was fairly incredible, wasn't it, the way Fred looked into your eyes and found whatever it was about you that might be interesting? All these people who are sure they were his true soul mates."

"Yes," Sarah said bitterly, "and all he really cared about was his dog and his frogs and his experiments."

"You're just mad at him because he died," Robin said. "You're just waiting around here for his spirit to show up, right? So you can yell at him to stop annoying you."

"I don't think Fred believed you could come back like that. He didn't believe in spirits. He believed in quarks and neutrinos and that when you died you got broken in a million pieces and scattered all over the place." Saying this, she shivered, having an odd sense of something watching her. Looking around hopefully, she found no shadow of Fred, but Fiona watching them from nearby, just like in the old days.

"Fiona," Sarah said shyly and stepped forward, holding out her hand.

Fiona came up to her and, ignoring her hand, kissed her. "I'm so sorry," she said.

Though she still wasn't pretty, she had turned into a tall and graceful woman. She had a wide-seeing and sad—though not melancholy—gaze, and, at the center of that gaze, Sarah saw Fred, and saw how generous it was of Fiona to be offering sympathies. "I'm sorry also," Sarah said, and they were both silent a moment, understanding each other. "What are you doing these days?" Sarah asked.

"Math." Fiona laughed. "For a big think tank upstate. And you?"

"I'm in the law business. Criminal defense." Sarah decided not to ask her if she was married, or had any children, but to leave it as it was, and, at this moment, anyway, Robin jealously intervened.

"I'm a madwoman," she said, "living off the estate of another old madwoman, now dead."

"What else?" Fiona said and laughed again. "It's good to see you, too." She looked at Robin and then did not seem to know what else to say. "Well, I'd better go, as I have an appointment at three. Perhaps we will all meet again in some happier circumstance." And she nodded and disappeared into the crowd.

Robin instantly seemed to forget her and squinted up into the air. "When are you going to come out and visit me?"

"Soon," Sarah said. "Soon."

"That's what you always say."

"I will."

"I want you to do me a favor."

"Yes?"

"If you see Fred, send him my love, and tell him . . . tell him, 'maybe next time.' OK?"

"Sure," Sarah said. "Certainly." As she watched Robin go, she thought again of all the lost summer afternoons and wondered if they, too, scattered in a million broken pieces and went wandering through space.

Later in the day she called Milo and told him that her parents were beside themselves with grief and they needed her to help clean up. She would have to stay another night.

He was ominously silent, though in the background she could hear Jake. Maybe he was tearing the kitchen apart. There were pots being banged about, a crash as of dishes falling on the floor, and then a noise like the pantry being unloaded and all the cans rolling into the sink.

"Let me talk to Jake," she said.

"I know why you're hanging around there. You think I don't know why. But he's gone, Sarah. The end."

"What are you talking about? Let me speak to Jake."

"Listen, buddy, this morning I only had to spend an hour looking for the kid's blankie until I found it in the flour canister, where he must have put it after he had hysteria about wanting to make pancakes for breakfast. Then he insisted that he had to take all those wood chips that are scattered around in front of the house down to the pond and wash them off because they were dirty and then bring them all back and arrange them according to some incomprehensible plan. Then at lunchtime he became completely unhinged because we didn't have any bagels. After lunch he bashed one of the cats over the head with a badminton racket, and, when I yelled at him, he went and lay down in the dirt in the driveway and cried for you for most of the afternoon. I have only just recently got him into a reasonably calm frame of mind and if you think I'm going to put him on the phone just so he can find out you're not going to be back tonight after all, you are even farther beyond the pale than I imagined."

"I'll be back tomorrow. My parents are in terrible shape."

"Baloney. He's going to be extremely upset when he finds out, Sarah."

Surely it was himself who was upset, surely it was himself who was scared out of his wits, but since he hadn't a clue to what was going on, she hadn't an ounce of sympathy for him. "Try to get him to take a nap. He's much easier to handle if he's had a nap," she advised him.

"He won't nap. He says he's not going to sleep till you get back. Apparently he met somebody in a dream he wasn't too thrilled with, but he refuses to talk about it."

"I'll be back tomorrow as soon as I can."

She spent the second night in Fred's apartment, looking through all his notebooks and debris, his telescopes and rock samples and mold studies. Just before the disease had taken him for its final ride, he had become convinced that his radio was picking up a communication from some planet out by the Big Dipper. Because of the tremendous improbability of such a thing happening by chance, he thought it likely that whoever they were had chosen him for this message on purpose. Most of his colleagues did not appear to believe him, but she saw, bitterly, that his conviction solaced him in a way that nothing or no one else could have done. What the message was trying to tell him, he didn't have a clue, and, though he hoped to have the means and the time to decipher it before he died, she could tell that he didn't really care if he failed. It was the fact of the message itself, its success in traveling so far from one point of light to another, over so much black space and time, that brought for him such unexpected encouragement.

She twirled all the little knobs and dials on his outer space radio until she got, above the static, an intermittent buzzing and clicking. Then, she climbed into his bed wearing a pair of his blue cotton summer shorts and one of his old red T-shirts that said THINK SOLAR on the front, and she waited. But, though she lay awake all the darkest part of the night, listening alertly, nothing much happened. At around five or six she must have fallen asleep, for when the phone rang with a shrill sound of protest later in the morning, she was not, for a few moments, sure where she was. Then she rose and, very cautiously, answered it. It was Bill Farnsworth, with whom Fred had shared an office at the university and who had agreed to take Newton, the dog, when Fred died. He was calling to say that he had just received a phone call offering him a study grant in Chile at the big observatory there and he had phoned her parents to see if they were interested in the dog and they had said to ask her first. The dog, he should warn her, had not eaten since Fred died and was perhaps determined to follow Fred out to wherever he had gone.

It was thus that she arrived back in the country with Newton asleep on the floor of the car.

As she parked alongside the old barn, Milo appeared, pushing Jake's little red plastic shopping cart. It was filled with a great pile of the wormy green apples that fell so abundantly from the old apple tree in the back of the house. He straightened up but made no move to approach her as she got out of the car. The house stood looking down on a small valley with a pond at the bottom. A great swath of green lawn had been cleared all around the house and a path had been mowed through the high grass down to the pond, but otherwise a dark and piny green forest encircled them. The next house was at least a half mile down the road. She drew near Milo and saw that he looked red faced and half asleep, like a man who has been forced to follow an exhausted and maniacal three-year-old around in the sun for three days.

"He hasn't napped since you left," Milo said in ominous tones as she drew near.

She kissed him coolly. "You should have come with me."

"Sure, I bet it would have been really soporific all that wailing and lamenting and rattling of coffin lids."

She waited for him to say something more, to comfort her or express some grief, to send some message of fellowship across the little spit of lawn. "It wasn't like that at all," she said at last.

Now here came Jake, unsteadily rounding the side of the house, carrying in his arms another load of wormy green apples. He wore a white T-shirt and a pair of green overalls, and his hair, which was fair like hers and curly like Milo's, caught the sun like a dandelion gone to seed. He was frowning and talking to himself, but when he saw who had arrived he dropped all the apples with a cry of relief and astonishment and lunged towards her.

"Hello, baby! Hello, Dewdrop." She crouched down so she could catch him in her arms. "You see," she said into his hair. "I told you I would be back very soon." She felt his mouth slide open on her shoulder, and then she felt his little pearly teeth dig into her flesh and start to clamp shut.

"Hey!" she yelled, caught by surprise. "No biting."

He started backwards, and she saw first fear and then confusion pass quickly across his round, flushed face like little clouds. "No, no," he said, meeting her gaze guiltily. "I was just licking your shirt." She saw now that he was very tired. His whole body was set stiffly against the weariness, which threatened to overcome him at any moment.

"I missed you very much," she said. "It seemed like such a long time. It made me mad, too. But look what I brought back with me." Now she went over to the car and opened the back door.

"Nuden," Jake said wonderingly and wriggled out of her arms. He peered in at him excitedly. "*Comment ça va?*" he demanded.

The dog didn't move. Milo stood there staring at Sarah in angry astonishment.

"You cannot be serious?" he said.

"He hasn't eaten since Friday," Sarah said.

"What happened to that guy Farnsworth, the one who worked with Fred in the observatory? Wasn't he supposed to take him? I thought it was all arranged."

"It was. But then he got offered this big research grant thing to go to Chile and he'd have to put the dog in quarantine for six months, so we decided I'd better take him instead."

"Couldn't you have found somebody else?"

"I didn't try."

"You should have called me, Sarah. What about the cats, for God's sakes? This is a very big commitment here."

"My brother just died," she snapped. "If you have no heart, at least have some manners."

"What do manners have to do with this? We have a tiny little apartment, a not quite three-year-old, and two deranged cats. What, in God's name, are we going to do with a dog?"

Jake had crawled into the car with Newton. He lay down on the seat with him, and Newton licked his face briefly and then laid his head, as if it were terribly heavy, down on Jake's chest.

Sarah and Milo bent down to look in at them.

"Nuden is so tired," Jake said sotto voce.

"Newton is so sad," Sarah told him.

Jake stayed where he was, but his fair eyebrows pinched together in consternation. "Why Nuden is sad?"

"You know why, honey. Because Uncle Fred died."

"But Uncle Fred will be back soon to take care of him?"

"You remember what I said, don't you, about how when you die you go back to nature and you become part of the trees and the sky and the birds and the earth?"

"Uncle Fred is kaput," Milo said.

Sarah closed her eyes. What she had never been able to understand was, why Milo? Was it a thing that had been handed down from the stars? Or was it just a mere chain of befuddlements and accidents? Had her brother not introduced them and had they not started going out and then broken up and then bumped fatally into each other at the dry cleaner's a year later, would she have missed him altogether? Or would she inevitably and after all have met him somewhere else, at some Lawyer's Guild dinner, perhaps, or found herself thrown into his arms by the errant braking of a subway train? She had loved several men who, it seemed to her, she recognized from previous lives, whose hearts and minds seemed to meet hers in ancient kinship. But the longer she knew Milo the more it seemed she had just met him yesterday.

She opened her eyes and thought she saw a hummingbird flash through the snapdragons. "I can't believe you said that. Even if it were true—and I don't believe it for a second—it just isn't something you say to a small child."

"What's pakut?" Jake asked.

"It means no more, all gone," Milo said, undeterred. He nodded at Sarah. "A small child deserves the facts as much as anybody else."

"These are not facts. You know I don't believe such a

thing to be a fact," she said. She heard her voice rise angrily and tried to control it.

He smiled. "I'm speaking what somewhere in your heart you know quite well but are afraid to own up to, Sarah."

"You? You're going to tell me feelings *I* don't own up to? That's a laugh, buddy."

"I know why you brought this dog back with you. You think I don't know? You're letting yourself imagine that Fred is in there. That he's going to make some final appearance in the shape of a dog."

"Fred loved this dog."

"If he did, it was probably the only thing he did love," Milo muttered.

"What? What do you mean by that?" Sarah asked angrily.

"I mean Fred was a very interesting and curious and intelligent man, and there was something about his attention that was very flattering, but he was about as capable of sustaining relationships as a fruit fly."

"So you think he deserved what he got?"

"Don't be ridiculous."

"Sure you do. You'd like to think that having sacrificed all your freedom and curiosity to a domestic arrangement such as ours, you're going to live forever."

Sarah could see from the color of Milo's face, from the way his jaw worked and the way his blue eyes had turned dark against the light and elastic summer afternoon, that he was thinking of all it had cost him to be here in this place being somebody's husband and somebody else's father, and she regretted having opened her mouth.

"All right, look," she said quickly, "I'm sorry I brought the dog back without consulting you first, but you like dogs and here he is, and he's going to die of a broken heart if we don't find some way to get him to eat."

"Oh, stop worrying about the goddamn dog. The dog will eat. It is the nature of dogs to eat. Worry about the welfare of your child. Look at him. Look at what you've done."

Jake's face was turned towards them. "Is his heart broke? Is it really broke?" He sobbed.

"You think I did that?" Sarah snapped.

"I'm going to take a nap. I'm exhausted. I've been dealing with this for three days. It's your turn now."

He slammed the screen door of their borrowed house behind him and disappeared into its cool and shadowy interior.

She leaned into the car and gently pulled Jake out, and, as he turned his face up towards her, the skin of his face seemed so delicate and poppylike, so warm and pink and radiant, she stared at him in astonishment. Where could he possibly have come from? He looked at her beseechingly, as if she held all the cards of the world in her hands.

"What's with these apples?" she asked to distract him. "What were you and Daddy doing?"

"Nuden!" he yelled. "I want Nuden."

She sighed and put Jake down and reached into the car for the dog. She pulled and yanked and tugged at him till she had him out on the ground. He gazed around at the summer afternoon, at the raspberries and the swallows, the hollyhocks and the long grass possibly full of rabbits and other things to delight a dog, and he gave a little moan and then crawled under the rhododendron bush at the side of the house.

"Come," she whispered to Jake, "help me bring this stuff into the house, and then we'll give Newton some food and water."

Jake looked at her hopefully and followed her into the house. It was a mess—toys and clothing lying everywhere, and in the wide, light kitchen there were dishes in the sink and all over the counter. There was flour on the floor, and remainders of their last meal still sat on the table.

"What did you have for lunch, Boo-Boo?"

He looked at her from the corner of his eye, suspecting a trap. "I had hangabar, corn, and I spit out a pea."

"Sounds pretty good." She put her bags down and washed her hands. "Come here, Little Peach, and let me wash your face and hands."

"No."

"Come on, sweetie."

"*No.*"

"Whaddaya mean, no? You're all yucky."

"I don't want to discuss it."

She laughed and grabbed him and hauled him over to the sink. "You look like an old potato."

"No, I don't," he wailed. "I look like a boy. I'm a boy."

"You look like an old potato to me," she said as she wiped him up with a wet paper towel.

"No, no! Look, I'm a boy! I got hands!" He waved them desperately around in the air.

"That proves nothing," she said and grabbed his hands and stuck them under the faucet. "You're a potato."

"Look! I have a mouth," he sobbed. "I'm a boy. I can talk."

"Quiet down out there!" Milo yelled from the bedroom. Sarah ignored him. She leaned forward and peered closely at Jake. "Well, my goodness, now that you're all cleaned up I can see that you're right. You *are* a boy!" She kissed him on the head. He was breathing heavily, eyeing her with terrible mistrust.

She got them each a drink of apple juice, then she took out one of the cans of dog food she had bought and opened it and scooped it into a bowl. "Now, you carry this out to Newton very carefully and I'll bring the water."

Jake carried the bowl with a deep frown of concentration and set it in front of the rhododendron bush. Sarah put her bowl of water down, and they peered in at the dog. He rested his chin upon his paws and did not look at them.

"Come on," she said. "Let's leave him alone and give him a little time to get used to the place. You and me will go throw some seed out for the birds and lie on the chaise lounge and see what we see."

"No nap."

"Certainly not," she said, throwing her hands up in mock horror. "We'll just sit and talk and observe. But make sure you bring your blankie so we can be really comfortable."

She threw a handful of mixed birdseed out in a wide arc, and then she turned the lounge chair away from the house so that it faced down the hill towards the pond and the bird-seed. She set the chair so that it half reclined and climbed in. Jake climbed in next to her and settled his head in the crook of her arm.

"Now, we have to be really quiet," she said, "so we can see what we can see."

Behind them the house slept wrathfully. The house and this wide sweep of lawn were perched on the rim of a small valley that had been cleared out of the middle of the forest. On the other side of the valley, the grass had been allowed to grow wild, and from out of these wild grasses blew occasionally, if the breeze was right, a deeply rich and spicy scent. In the bottom of the valley lay the green pond, and from this pond could be heard a ponderously slow conversation between two frogs. "Baduum," said one frog, and then a minute or two later the other answered, "Guumpa." The first one perhaps thought it over and then fell asleep and then woke up and answered, "Baduum." "Guumpa," said the second several minutes later. They pondered the question, whatever it was, slowly but relentlessly, while from all around them arose a great, thoughtlessly industrious chorus of afternoon insects. The woods themselves, green and full of blue and watching shadows, were perfectly silent.

"Now get yourself very comfortable," she whispered.

"No nap," Jake repeated firmly but wadded up his little scrap of flannel blanket and stuck it between his ear and her shoulder.

"Did you have a dream last night?"

He stuck his finger in his nose and explored the inside with his eyes closed. A minuscule, spring green bug landed on his smooth, bare forearm.

"Look," she said softly.

He opened his eyes and stared where she pointed at the tiny insect.

"He looks like a helicopter," Jake whispered happily.

"Yes," Sarah said. "Let's blow him gently, gently, back into the grass where he belongs."

Together they blew as softly as they could until the insect appeared to blink and then, quite suddenly, seemed to vanish.

Jake said, "A dream is a big hole going in the nighttime and you jump in it and then you jump back."

"Right," Sarah said. "Did you jump in the other night and see somebody you didn't like?"

Evasively, he pulled his little blanket out and opened it up and spread it over his eyes. "Daddy is mad," he said.

"Oh yes? Why is Daddy mad?"

"'Cause I won't go to sleep."

She took the blanket off his face and smiled at him. "I don't think so. I think he's mad because Uncle Fred died."

"He's mad at Uncle Fred?" Jake asked doubtfully.

"No. He's sad and that makes him feel angry. He doesn't like to feel sad."

"Me too."

"Shh, listen! A cardinal. Do you hear him?"

She could hear him clearly, a bright red note *tsking* towards them through the trees. "Do you see him? I can't see him."

Jake pointed up into the sycamore overhead, and there he was, eyeing first them and then the birdseed.

"Now we have to make him feel perfectly safe so that he'll come down and eat the birdseed."

"How do we make him feel safe?"

"By being very still and quiet so he'll know that we won't try to startle him or hurt him."

Jake settled back into the crook of her arm, his eyes on the bird.

Over and over again, the bird *tsked* the same note, hopping each time he sang. "Here I come," he seemed to be saying. "Here I come. I'm working up my nerve. I'll be down in a minute." Or perhaps he was saying, "Cats? Cats? Are there any cats?" Or perhaps he was talking to some mate nearby that Sarah could not see, "Wish me luck, wish me luck. I may get killed, so wish me luck."

Sarah sighed and thought with no small resentment of her own mate, snoozing peacefully inside in the upstairs bedroom. Except for that brief period after Jake was born, he had always been unwilling to contemplate any danger or discomfort. When had he ever gone out and braved the jungle for her? Why, he couldn't even bring himself to go to a funeral.

When you thought about it, what, after all, was this big insistence that the soul must find a second self and, finding it, must bind it fast to make it endure a lifetime of union? If two people of the usual sort, distinctly separate and highly incomplete, were given, for the space of a season, the chance to come together and make the rapture of a whole, to find in that wholeness the eyes and ears to glimpse the fearfully wide and dancing secret of all that cartwheels through the heavens, then let those two count themselves lucky, let them be modest and sensible and not try to make the thing last a lifetime. People were never made to get along for any length of time. In the wink of an eye they started getting on each other's nerves and demonstrating themselves to be completely incapable of reason. Even your own children, the ones who fit with perfect weight in the crook of your arm and touched your face wonderingly as they sucked upon your breast, even they soon became vigorous and wily opponents, lying down in the middle of the sidewalk when your arms were full of bags of groceries and refusing to get up unless you agreed to go all the way back and buy an orange plastic water gun.

The cardinal dropped down now and began, with terrific enjoyment and anxiety, to crack open just his favorites, the sunflower seeds.

"Look," she said to Jake. But he was asleep.

The frogs, she noted, had fallen silent for a time, and even the insects, here in the hot, still middle of the afternoon, were droning more slowly. But, wait—there—wasn't that him again, a tiny, iridescent hummingbird spinning through the crimson hollyhocks? Her heart beat with excitement. How she wished her brother were here to see it, or even, she thought generously, Milo. Still, what was the use of such a wish? Though you might attempt to become one with another by the bumblingly childish stratagem of asking them to look at something beautiful with you, it never worked. If beauty might possibly be a reason for hanging on, still you hung on by yourself. And, in a minute, when the tiny bird had zoomed on, she, too, was asleep.

* * *

When she awoke, sometime later, it was to the sound of a low growl and then a hiss. She sat up quickly and turned around and found their little ginger-colored cat, backing slowly out of the rhododendron bush.

"It's all right," Sarah whispered to her, but the cat only hissed again and turned and ran as if the hounds of hell were after her. Newton gave no sign of having noticed her.

Jake sat up sleepily and looked around. "I seed him in my dream again," he said.

Sarah bent over him quickly and touched his ear where it was all pink from having been slept on. "Who?" she asked.

"Uncle Fred."

Sarah started. "Did you?" she said, then quickly pressed her cheek against the loose, silky hair at the top of his head. "How did he look? Did he scare you?"

"No," said Jake. "Not this time. This time he came to see me all lighted up."

"Why, what do you mean, Sweet Pea?"

"He was all full of little lights in his hair and his fingers and his buttons, and he asked me to blow him up to the sky. I thinked he was too heby for me to blow him, but he tole me he was light as a nothing and I blew him up, up, up until he was gone in with the Pan Star."

She frowned. "The Pan Star? What do you mean?"

"I mean the Pan Star, you silly."

Was she silly? She supposed she was. "But what else? Didn't he say anything else? Did he want you to tell me something?"

"No, no, no!" he said impatiently. "He tole me about Nuden, something not to forget. But I forget." He scrambled up off the chaise lounge and headed for the house. "I see if Daddy is mad anymore." He slammed the screen door.

She went to check on Newton. He was awake, but there

was hardly any light in his eyes. He avoided her gaze. "How about a hamburger?" she suggested. "A nice raw hamburger?"

She went into the kitchen and put some raw hamburger in a bowl and brought it out to him. He didn't even lift his nose to smell it. She sighed and went over to the grill and filled it with charcoal and sprinkled it with lighter fluid. Inside the house there was a great uproar of a man pretending to be a lion and chasing a small boy around the bedroom and then catching him and tossing him in the air. Out here, in the pause between late afternoon and evening, it was still quiet. She was standing under the apple tree. The sun was sinking quickly, and the air, caught in the low, long shafts that shot down and out of the upper branches of the trees, was turned to an astonishing pure clearness. It seemed to her that, in such a light, it would be the simplest matter to read the heart of another. How could there be any obscurity here? But though a small green apple fell with a soft *thunk* to the grass and rolled a little way down the slope of the hill, no one appeared with any messages, obscure or otherwise. She went into the kitchen and, cleaning and tidying as she went, gathered things she would need to make dinner— hamburger and hot dogs, rolls, and a tablecloth. She made a salad and put on a pot of water to boil for the corn, and then she went back outside to set the table.

She had laid the plates and the forks when she heard the screen door open behind her. There was Jake coming towards her with a peculiar slow and deliberate gait. His blankie was draped tastefully over his head.

"See my lovely wedding?" he asked.

"Oh yes, dear heart, I see. You look beautiful. Who are you marrying?"

"Daddy," he said happily. "He's not mad at me now 'cause I took a nap."

"That's very good news. Would you go tell him we'll be eating dinner in about twenty minutes? And would you tell him please to change your pants because I see you're all wet in the back?"

"OK." He turned and again marched solemnly off at the head of a long and invisible wedding procession.

In a few minutes she heard him come shrieking happily through the kitchen, and behind him she heard the low rumble of Milo's voice. Jake came tumbling through the door, but Milo peered out and then decided to stay in the kitchen. She could see him take out a box of pretzels and sit down at the kitchen table with a newspaper.

Jake stood in the grass before her, completely naked. He was turning and turning, his arms up over his head, drenching himself in the green and gold air. His little behind flashed white as eggshell, while the rest of him was a light nut brown. Here he was, her fragrant and smooth nearly three-year-old, impossible to imagine that one day he would grow up to be a big, smelly, disappointing man. Now he stopped turning and fell dizzily to the ground. He lay on his back and stared up through the branches of the apple tree into the sky, sighing with pleasure. When the world stopped spinning at last, he sat up and looked around him thoughtfully. "Let's pretend this is a restaurant." He raised his arms over his head and gestured across the air around him. "I'm the waiter."

She smiled down at him from where she sat at the picnic table. "But you have no clothes on."

He rose up from the grass and approached her formally. "What do you like to eat?"

"Haven't you got a menu? I need to see the menu before I decide."

"Well . . . ," he said and frowned, "yes, I got menus." He turned around and went into the house, banging the screen door. When he emerged again he was carrying an abridged edition of *Webster's Third*. "Here I am giving you a menu."

"Hmm," she said, taking the book and leafing through it. "So what do you have that's good?"

He rapped on the menu indignantly. "We got everything."

"Everything?"

"We have bread and podadoes and samwishes and cheese."

The sky, where it met the trees, at the edge farthest from the sun, was turning from green to a deep, iridescent blue. Sarah could see Milo lift his head from his newspaper from time to time to watch what they were up to, but she knew there was no way for her to get to him without a space suit and oxygen and several light-years of travel, and certainly he would never come out here on his own.

"How about fish cakes? You got fish cakes?"

"No. I don't like those."

"Oh. I see. Well, bring me a sandwich and some potatoes."

"OK. I will go cook it."

When he went back into the house, she got up and turned over the hamburgers and hot dogs. She took one of the hot dogs on the end of a long fork and carried it over to Newton and laid it down in front of him along with the dog food and the raw hamburger. "Newton, Newton," she said cajolingly, but his eyes stayed closed.

She went back over to the picnic table and sat down and heard Milo ask Jake what was going on. In the stillness his voice seemed to come from right by her side, and, a moment later, when the frogs began their argument again, she jumped, for they seemed to be speaking from right at her feet.

"Baduum."

"Guumpa."

"This is my restaurant," Jake was telling Milo. "Mommy is out there in one part and you're in the inside part and now I'm gonna give you a menu."

"You got pigs' knuckles?" she heard Milo ask.

It was difficult to understand how her brother could be nowhere when she was sitting here under this tree in the falling green and gold light of apples, with a little rabbit browsing fearlessly down below by the pond and the frogs taking up their eternal commentary in the same place where they left off.

"OK. Here's your pig uncles. Now I gotta go outside."

In a moment, the waiter appeared in the doorway. Caught in the last low light of the sun, he seemed, as he stood there gazing around, to be made of gold and to have just returned from some entirely unknown and distant country. He wore his nakedness with the disregard and utter unconcern of a blue jay, and she saw that he was losing his rounded, buttery soft-ness and straightening and lengthening out into some entirely new version of himself. She saw that she was going to forget, that she was going to be unable to remember each moment. That it might be as her brother had said, that we were, each of us, no one thing but a billion different events strung out over time.

He trotted over to her, holding a load of invisible foods in his hands. "Here it is," he said excitedly. "Your samwish and your podadoes."

"Waiter! Waiter!" came a peremptory voice from the other dining room. "Come here, please."

Jake looked at her and sighed. "I gotta go." She knew that if she tried to take him in her arms and kiss him all over the face it would be useless. He would wiggle and protest and stick his elbow in her eye, so she said nothing and just watched him go.

When he got inside, she heard Milo say to him in a low voice, "Here, I want you to take this to the old lady out there with my compliments and ask her if she would mind if I joined her for dinner."

"Oh-oh!" Jake exclaimed. "Can I have a piece, too?"

"Sure, this is for you. This is your tip."

A minute later Jake appeared, chomping away mightily. "Here. Dumblemint gum." He held out a stick of gum. "The other customer sent it with his compulents and wants to come out and eat."

"OK," she said. She pushed her hair back from her face and sat up stiffly.

Jake led him out the door and over the grass by the hand and sat him down across the table from Sarah. "This is Daddy," he said to her.

"I recognize him," she said.

"And who's this lovely lady?" Milo asked.

"That's Mommy."

"Indeed?" He leaned forward and squinted at her doubtfully.

"You're a slob," Sarah said. "I couldn't believe the state of the kitchen."

"You knew I was a slob when you married me, Sarah. That's partly why you married me. So I would express for you all your pent-up yearnings for anarchy and chaos and you wouldn't have to take any of the heat."

Two apples fell out of the tree and rolled softly across the grass. The sun had set, and the air was languid and light and green and sweet. An insect, who sounded like he was playing a pair of castanets, began to tune up in the high grass beyond the tree.

"Hey, look, Jake. A couple more apples. You better get them for your collection," Milo said.

"What are you doing with all those apples?" Sarah asked.

"Collecting them," Milo said, as Jake went after the two that had just fallen. "Collecting them, and then we were going to throw them over the roof."

"So guess what he dreamt?" Sarah said challengingly. "He dreamt that Fred came to him all lit up and he had a message for him about the dog, and then he asked him to blow him up to the stars. What do you think of that?"

"Oh, for God's sakes, Sarah. Nothing. I don't think anything of it. I wish you wouldn't let your imagination run around wild like this. It's not good for the kid."

The kid came toddling towards them, dropping apples as he came. He plunked the ones he had been able to hold on to down on the table.

"But that's why you married me, Milo—so I could express for you all your own outrageous fears and fantasies and you could go on appearing to live an interior life of unremitting safety and boredom."

"Don't be ridiculous. I married you for your legs. Everybody knows that."

Jake looked from one to the other of them and then crawled under the table and examined Sarah's legs curiously.

"What was the message Fred gave him about the dog?" Milo asked.

"He doesn't remember."

"Yes. I do," Jake said indignantly from under the table.

"Do you?" she said. "Do you? Come here, sweetheart." She put her arms around him as gently as she could and pulled him out. "Tell me."

Jake squinted up towards the slowly falling evening. "He said, 'Le chien aime les omelettes.'"

Sarah was staring at him in amazement.

"Oh come on, Sarah, don't be a jerk. That's just one of those little French things he remembers Fred saying."

"But how could I have forgotten?" Sarah said, hitting herself on the head. "Of course the dog loves omelets. Don't you remember? Fred used to always give him one on his birthday and holidays." She was already out of her seat and headed towards the kitchen. "Listen, you take care of that stuff on the grill. It's just about ready, I think. I'll be back in a few minutes."

When she came back out she had a large cheese omelet attractively arranged on a plate with a sprig of parsley. Milo and Jake were eating hot dogs and throwing apples over the roof.

"Here," she said to Jake. "It's your restaurant. You give it to him."

She helped him carry it over. "Now," she said. "When you give it to him say, *'Bon Anniversaire.'* That means happy birthday, in French."

"Bone onna stair," Jake said carefully and laid the omelet in front of the dog.

At first the dog did nothing, merely lay there, sleeping or pretending to sleep. Then a little breeze blew in from out of nowhere and wafted the smell of the omelet to his nose. He opened first one eye and then the other. Jake pushed the dish a little closer, and the dog lifted his nose and sniffed.

"Here," said Sarah. She reached in and broke off a piece and held it out. The dog, without getting up, licked it once, then grabbed it in his mouth and swallowed it hungrily. Then he stood up over the plate and, in two or three huge gulps, swallowed the rest down. Jake, naked and gleaming in the falling twilight, crawled into the rhododendron bush with him and fed him the raw hamburger and then the hot dog and then the dog food.

Jake stuck his head out of the rhododendron bush and said to Sarah and Milo proudly that this was his restaurant, it was always open, and they could come any time.

Sarah said to him, "Come out now. See if Newton will follow you."

Jake crawled out, yelling, "Come on, Nuden! Come out and give me a kiss."

Newton followed him out and knocked him down and stood on his chest and licked his face, while Jake choked with laughter and pulled on his ears.

Milo, who couldn't bear to miss out on any melee involving children and dogs, pretended indifference. "You see, I told you the dog would eat eventually." He finished his hot dog and then got up and went and lay down on the grass, so that, in an instant, they were all over him, licking and wrestling, yelling and barking.

Sarah went into the house and got the corn and the salad and brought them out and ate dinner while the stars came slowly wheeling into the sky. When it was almost dark, Milo brought out pants and a shirt for Jake and a couple of flashlights, and then he and Jake and the dog set off for the pond to look for frogs. She watched them until they disappeared into the darkness and all that could be seen of them, at last, were the little beams of their flashlights bobbing unsteadily along the edge of the water.

Her brother, she thought, was pretty nearby, maybe up in the apple tree. She waited quietly, trying to think what to say. After a while, she remembered Robin's message. "Robin sends her regards," she whispered. "She says to tell you, 'maybe next time.' Fiona says hello, too, I think."

Naturally, there was no answer.

She sat in the darkness on the bench, hugging her knees. It was getting chilly.

In a little while she saw the beams of the flashlights coming unsteadily up the path through the long grass, then they stopped. "Look," she heard Milo say. "Look up at the sky. See," he said. "There it is—the Big Dipper."

"You mean the Pan Star," Jake corrected him.

"Sure," Milo said. "The Pan Star. Let's go in and make a fire." Then they went right by her in the darkness, perhaps not even realizing she was there. They went in the house, and, at the instant the door closed behind them, all sense of safety deserted her. She was afraid even to get up from the bench and cross the short space between here and the back door. She sat very still and very cautiously looked up at the sky. The stars, which had come in slowly at first, one at a time, familiar and lovely, had now, in the darkness, filled the sky with such an infinity of distant burning fires, had pushed the boundaries of the world so far out beyond any human reckoning she was filled with shame at what a fool she had been.

"Gone," she said, trying it out loud. "Kaput."

She heard Jake yelling that he was not going to take a bath, and now the dog, who had gone inside with them, came and stood at the door and barked importantly.

She rose, and—hoping that, taken together, the barking and yelling, the deep and resonant voice of her husband, the mess and the firelight would all have managed in her absence to make the inside of the house bigger than the outside—she bounded across the dark space as fast as she could, swung the screen door open, and jumped in. The door, with a little slam, shut behind her.